Also by Prentice and Weil

Black Arts
(The Books of Pandemonium: Book 1)

THE BOOKS OF PANDEMONIUM: BOOK 2

DEVIL'S BLOOD

ANDREW PRENTICE AND JONATHAN WEIL

David Fickling Books

31 Beaumont Street
Oxford OX1 2NP, UK

Devil's Blood
is a
DAVID FICKLING BOOK

First published in Great Britain in 2016 by
David Fickling Books,
31 Beaumont Street,
Oxford, OX1 2NP

978-1-910200-57-5

1 3 5 7 9 10 8 6 4 2

Papers used by David Fickling Books are from well-managed forests and
other responsible sources.

DAVID FICKLING BOOKS Reg. No. 8340307

A CIP catalogue record for this book is available from the British Library.

Printed and bound in Great Britain by Clays Ltd, St Ives plc.

To Freya
and to Sarah, again.

As a new heaven is begun ... the Eternal Hell revives.

William Blake, *The Marriage of Heaven and Hell*

He thought about himself, and the whole Earth
Of Man the wonderful and of the Stars
And how the deuce they ever could have birth;
And then he thought of Earthquakes, and of Wars
How many miles the Moon might have in girth
Of Air-balloons, and of the many bars
To perfect knowledge of the boundless Skies;
And then he thought of Donna Julia's eyes.

Lord Byron, *Don Juan*

We stepped out gaily on a carpet of flowers, little imagining the abyss beneath.

Louis Philippe, comte de Ségur

Prologue

This is the place that we call Hell.

The bridge curves away forever in both directions, over a sea of flat white light. A million ruined towers rise above it; a million crumbling arches hold it up. There is nothing else but the bridge. No day or night. Nothing to mark seasons, no change in the wind or the light. The wind shrieks through the towers; the bridge groans.

One day – though you could say hour, month or century for all the difference it makes in this place – the bridge will fall.

The creatures in the towers were once all-powerful. Prophets and pleasure-seekers, with suns for playthings; kings of light; warriors, clashing in the empty dark between stars.

The suns are all snuffed out. The stars have ceased to shine. The kings have lost their thrones. In this colossal ruin, nothing remains of what they were, or what they had.

Nothing but the memory – and their names.

Flies whisper hate. Always buzzing.

There is still one way out of Hell.

'*Sargastes . . .*'

A dry, dusty voice, coming from very far away.

'Atherouor aoio. Maialario aoria iaio.'

The light was changing.

'Aieu, u eiou. *Sargastes.*'

Sargastes heard his name, and saw the light pucker. A point where the light was no longer flat. A point where it had depth.

Now it was a trough; now it was a whirlpool.

Sargastes heard a dry buzzing all around him. Jealous – angry. Forbidding him to go. It was the voice of a king, and once Sargastes might have obeyed.

But not now.

The call was growing stronger, pulling, dragging him down; no resisting it, but Sargastes didn't want to resist – this was it, the way out. He had nothing but his name *and it had been called* – down becoming up, sea becoming sky, up, up and up towards that fixed, final point.

'AEOIO. AOIO. SARGASTES.'

'ZakatakakakaWOURAGH!' roared Sargastes, racing up through a tunnel of light.

The bridge was far behind. Ahead, beyond, was life. For an instant, Sargastes was looking out on the whole glorious mess of it – spinning with stars, foaming with light and activity; what a riot, what a revel after the dreary place he'd quit – and then the tunnel closed in again, dragging, sucking him down, to *this*.

A star set within a circle, marked in charcoal and blood on a hard earth floor. The spellseller standing with arms raised, watching as the star filled up with flat white light. In the centre of the star, a carved red bead – Sargastes' new home.

Escape in return for service: this was the bargain. Some devils might buzz and rail and plot to overturn it, but Sargastes was not one of these. He was bound into the bead, never to escape. He did not resist. All that was asked of him was to follow his lust.

Sargastes came to the city of Alexandria on a slow, sticky afternoon during the donkey days of summer – a time for sweating in the shade and dreaming of the cool season – but there was no cooling the satyr, now that his power was loose. Within the quarter hour, everyone in the spellseller's family was roaring drunk. By sundown, there was not a man, woman or child south of the Soma who had not been dragged into the revels. They flowed through the cramped streets of the Egyptian quarter like wildfire, then on into the rich district near the Moon Gate. The City Watch were called in, and were themselves overcome. They threw down their weapons and danced while the city burned. The revels lasted for three days and three nights. And for a trembling moment, in the joy of Sargastes' becoming, it seemed as if the great port of Alexandria might fall.

Word of Sargastes' power spread quickly.

The red bead was sold, after a furious auction, for the princely sum of eighteen golden *octadrachm*. The buyer was a rich Phoenician merchant. That very same day he rowed his prize away from Alexandria, in a galley specially commissioned for the task. No wine, dice, music or dancing were allowed on board; but Sargastes was there, and the voyage was a wild one.

In his new home in Sidon he was placed at the heart of the merchant's pleasure palace, buried beneath the hearth-stone. This was the task for which he had been summoned – and as devils do, he embraced it. He put down roots. The pleasure palace, which became known as the Rose, was soon famous all over the world for the beauty of its dancers, for the heady sweetness of its wines, and the unrelenting ferocity of its parties.

The Rose roared away for seven generations until – Sargastes long forgotten – the hearthstone was dug up and thrown out on to the midden-heap. Sargastes' red bead went with it.

Within a week the dancers went lame, and the wine turned sour. All the roses died.

Amongst the trash, the bead caught the eye of a street scamp. He wore it threaded on a string as a lucky charm for one blinding, ecstatic year, before falling, drunk, from the roof of the Temple of Ba'al Zephon to his death.

Sargastes quickly found a new partner, and for the next thousand years this was how it went. Sargastes stayed a week, or a decade – time had little meaning compared to the consuming joy of the revels – reeling from one wastrel's hand to another, among the dirty, bustling ports of the Eastern Mediterranean. Sargastes' lust never lacked for a vent, for such places are always well supplied with drinkers and gamblers, revellers and rogues.

None of them recognized the treasure they had.

The slowest stretch was a fifty-year spell buried in thick mud at the bottom of Heraklion harbour. Luckily for Sargastes a greedy grouper, and a well-cast net, resulted in the bead ending up in a bowl of fish soup served to the Archbishop of Crete.

The authority of the diocese never recovered.

It was a Norman knight who changed Sargastes' path for ever. He carried the red bead north as a gift for his wife – away from the warm sea and the sweet wines of the east, to the bitter beer and frozen mists of England.

Sadly, the wife was never to receive her present. On the

very morning that the knight's boat came winging up the Thames, she died of the plague. The red bead disappeared sometime during the knight's wild grief, falling between the floorboards of a London tavern.

And there it sat, forgotten. A year later, the tavern burned down, but they soon built another over it, which burned down in turn. This became a habit. On that same spot over the next five hundred years nine taverns – which soon began to take the name of the Phoenix – burned to the ground. Sargastes had always felt that a party didn't really get started until the roof was on fire.

The tavern keepers didn't mind. By the time the revels got too hot, they'd always sold enough stingo and stout to retire rich and happy. Another tavern always rose from the ashes like fireweed.

Nor did Sargastes miss the warm southern seaports. Northern revels burn twice as bright, when the cold rain falls and the nights draw in.

London was a fine old place to settle down.

Chapter 1

One brisk September morning in 1592, a boy sat on a roof eating an apple for breakfast. A copper key hung around his neck. His hand was stained rusty red, the same colour as the apple he was eating.

The stain was an accident. The key was a gift.

The apple tasted delicious.

High above, a great flock of kites swooped circles in the sky, watching for scavenge. The smoke from twenty thousand chimneys rose up in thin etched lines around them. From up here, the spires and crooked rooftops down below looked no bigger than toys – a small, busy heap between the green of the Thames valley and the silty brown of the estuary.

Occasionally one of the birds would plummet, diving for butcher's offal or a bloating dead dog.

Down in the streets, the top-heavy buildings blocked out the sky. The air was thick with drovers' curses and smells both abominable and mouth-watering. The smells came from food stalls, tanners' vats, boozing kens and slaughterhouses; from churches, palaces and hovels – and ripest of all, from the mud. London mud was rich and thick and black as ink, and in this wet autumn it coated everything: prince and pauper, merchant and thief; crackpots, magicians, beasts, actors, and a few brave and fuddled foreigners wondering how they ever ended up in this damp and vicious riot.

London was the greatest city in Christendom, or a murderous dungheap, or almost anything in between. It all depended on where you were standing, and what you chose to see. But it was always alive.

Just how alive was a secret known to a very, very few. Mostly you had to look underground, digging down through layers of destruction and fire and cannibal growth. Down into the city's lost past, sifting through the rubble and trash.

It was there that you'd find most of them. How deep depended on how long they'd been here – and some of them had been here a very long time. Brought here in their thousands, over a hundred generations – captured in amulets, magic rings, cunning charms; bound into statues and palaces and temple altars. Their original masters had turned to dust, but the devils of London continued to work their magic. Magic upon magic, rising up, until you could not tell one twisting spell from another.

Some were half remembered in legends and curses and tall, dark tales. Black Dog of Newgate; King Lud; Old Thames the River Father. But for each of these there were hundreds more that had long been forgotten. Most hoped to stay that way.

Of all the Londoners alive today, very few knew the truth about devils. And only one, out of all the city's teeming populace, knew how to find them.

'Ack Ack! Swinepork stinkard you be—'

'What?'

From up on his rooftop, Jack heard a thud below.

'Uncrouch, filthnest lokmok.'

'H-hold there. Hold! Imp!'

'Up-up, nitwit Kit. Up-OUT!'

A screech of scraping chair legs, and a smack.

'Hellspawn scullion!' Kit bellowed. Charging footsteps shook the house. They stopped short with a thwack, and a tinkle of breaking glass.

'*Ack!* Clumsing dolt-head! *Out*, before all shinies be shattered!' The thwacks sounded thick and fast.

Jack took another bite of his apple, still gazing out at the city. On a morning like this it was a sight to tingle the humours – the dawn coming up through a skein of blue smoke; a thicket of steeples; the merry brown river; the half-ruined tower of St Paul's. You could almost believe it was a peaceful place, sitting up here.

Jack swallowed, forcing down the bittersweet fruit. Looking out at the city of devils, knowing what lay in wait for him, tied his stomach in knots.

Later today, he'd be in amongst it.

Another crash from downstairs. Jack scowled. Kit and the imp: like the stain on his hand, they'd come to him by accident, and just like the stain, he often had cause to regret them. A scurvy scheming intelligencer for a friend, and a sprite of Satan for a servant. No wonder they were always making trouble.

Down on the street, the front door burst open and Kit stumbled out.

'Jack! Yes you, you abominable pigeon: don't pretend I'm not here, I can *see* you!'

Kit stood in the road, craning his neck. A drawn sword trailed from his right hand.

'How's the morn, Kit?' said Jack.

'I'll tell you how it is. Your servant has crossed me for the last time. No more. No more, I say.' Kit took a savage cut at thin air, then stopped as he remembered something. 'Oh, and I need to borrow . . . or rather, I have borrowed . . . you know. The four shillings we talked about. Brings our reckoning up to . . . let's see . . .' Kit sheathed his sword, fished out a leather-bound book from the breast of his doublet, and riffled through the pages. 'Here we are. Sixteen shillings, thruppence ha'penny.'

'*Sixteen*, Kit?'

Kit drew himself up straight. 'You take that tone with me? Me, who has saved your sorry life three times? Aye, sixteen shillings, thruppence ha'penny. Scant good it did me, neither. Those dice-men don't play straight.'

'Dice-men?' said Jack. 'That four shillings – that was for the Plan. That was . . .' He was suddenly so angry he could hardly speak. 'I'm going into town today, for *your scheming Plan* Kit, and all you had to do was spend *my money* on a band of *musicians* . . . and you've lost it at dice . . . ?'

'Don't splutter, Jack, it's ungentle. The money is gone. We still want musicians. Now be a good boy and lend me another four shillings. If you can manage that, *perhaps* I will condescend to repay you when *my* Plan bears fruit and we're all as rich as Zacatecas.'

Jack shook his head. 'That four was our last. Lud's blood, Kit . . . There ain't. No. Money.'

Jack spat the words out, bitter as rue. Kit's Plan: aye, but Jack was the one putting his head in the cauldron. Today. He couldn't believe it had come so quickly.

He felt a tingle – not quite heat – in his stained right hand.

'Well?' Kit was still waiting.

'Stew yourself, Kit,' said Jack. 'You want money, go peddle your arse for shoe leather.'

Kit made a face at him, thrust his debt ledger back into his doublet, and walked off down the road.

From the house below came a tuneless humming and a brisk, triumphant sweeping sound.

The Raven alehouse had been Beth Sharkwell's idea to begin with. In the spring, when she and Jack had cheated a devil and mudlarked his gold – a wild, impossible weight of gold – the first thing she'd done was purse her lips and come out with one of her grandpa's Thieving Laws: 'Hope for the best, allow for the worst.' The first thing to make sure of was a bolthole, somewhere small and cheap and murky.

The Raven was murky enough, Jack reflected, as he lowered himself in through the attic window. Hunkered down at the north edge of the old Convent Garden, the only reason it hadn't fallen down yet was that there was so little of it to fall: just the one room downstairs, a cellar beneath, and the attic above. Now that the worst had duly come about, and their gold was stolen, and Beth's bolthole was all they had left, it looked murkier still. Sour beer, sour prospects: customers few and dwindling; the last remnant of their fortune staked on a Plan that was apt to get Jack into exactly the sort of trouble he'd sworn to avoid for the rest of his days.

Jack slid down to the floor of the attic. A stale, harsh smell hung in the air – the tobacco that Beth had been smoking the past week in order to perfect the disguise she'd been working up. The tobacco smell reminded Jack of his ma, who was dead, and of Harry the horse-cope, who'd shared a pipe with Jack on the way to the gallows, and who was also dead. He decided to leave the window open.

They couldn't go on as they were. Jack had told himself that many times in the days leading up to this particular day. And Beth liked the Plan. There was the nub of it: Beth liked the Plan very well indeed.

Downstairs, the imp had finished its sweeping. Jack watched as the broom floated across the room to nestle up against a small rag on the front windowsill. The broom went still; the rag stirred into life.

Every other devil on Earth was stuck with whatever home it had been bound to. The imp was the only one that could be whatever it liked. It was a wondrous magical ability that puzzled the greatest wizards in Christendom.

The imp mostly used it to clean things.

The floor of the boozing ken – or the Saloon Royale, as the imp insisted on calling it – was scraped clean of any trace of dust. The furniture was arranged in rigid ranks against the walls – the long table, the four broke-backed chairs, and Kit's favourite, a low horse-hair couch. A square of embroidery hung on the wall over Kit's sleeping spot, stitched with big red letters. It hadn't been there yesterday. Jack squinted at the writing, mouthing out the words:

EVERY COUCH, WHEREON HE LIETH, IS UNCLEAN: AND EVERY THING, WHEREON HE SITTETH, SHALL BE UNCLEAN.

'Imp? You been needling Kit?'

The imp was enjoying itself, deep into its role as a polishing rag, only just visible as a circular blur over the pewter mugs and spoons laid out on the table.

'Imp . . .' said Jack.

'Needling, tsa!' The rag stopped mid swish, flapped over to the embroidery and did a few twirls around it. 'Last night I was needle, see? Threading Levitick from the Big Book! What entklessent book that is.'

'More Leviticus,' said Jack.

'Tcha! Lokmok mislikes it, ekt?'

'Aye, I think he does . . .'

Jack still wasn't sure about having Bible verses around the tavern. The drinkers of St Giles parish were not clean men, and nor were they reading men; and even if they had been, Bible verses were not likely to spark their humour.

The imp went back to its polishing. Jack didn't see how the spoons could be any shinier than they already were.

'You nearly finished, Imp?' he said.

'Shiny shiny shiny *shiny* . . .'

'Cos I'm ready to go.'

'Sheeny gleany glintick-gleam . . .'

Jack reached into his sleeve for his roll of tools. There was no point reasoning with the imp when it was cleaning. It needed a direct command, or nothing.

Leaning over to spread out the roll on the table, Jack felt the key around his neck swing out on its string. The key that King Lud had given him. A devil's gift – a pointless, tarnished thing that didn't open any doors that Jack knew of – and yet he couldn't bring himself to throw it away.

He reached into the special padded pocket he'd added alongside the loops for his gilks and picks. Inside was a giant dead beetle, as big as the apple Jack had eaten for breakfast, with long feathery feelers and jaws fit to bite off thumbs. Before it became the imp's favourite body, it had been part of the magician Dr Dee's rare insect collection. The Goliath beetle, Dee called it.

'Come here, Imp. Time to hop over.'

The rag whisked past his ear and landed on the table, quivering with anticipation. Jack laid the Goliath beetle down on top of it. The rag stopped quivering, went limp. The Goliath beetle stirred, spread its wings and buzzed up into the air to land on Jack's shoulder.

'No more time for glintick?'

'Later, Imp.' Jack forced some cheer into his voice. 'Tell

you what: things go right today, I'll buy another spoon. A silver one.'

For a moment the imp was struck dumb.

'Eckt . . . *silver* . . . shiny?' it managed, finally.

'Real silver, aye.'

The imp chattered with delight. 'Joy of krettenheft, boy-master! All to go rightly-sprightly, shuklet will see to it, tcha!'

'Let's hope so,' said Jack.

'And so, first we visit with lovey-dove, nei?' said the imp.

'She ain't—' Jack shook his head. 'Never mind.'

'Bethany Lovely-face Shark-tongue—'

'Aye, her,' said Jack. Beth Sharkwell – the real reason he couldn't stop what was happening today. She was already out there, in the thick of it, starting the Plan. By most reckonings, she was risking more today than him.

'And thence to Smithfield devil-roost,' said the imp.

'Aye.' Jack felt a flutter of panic. It was happening; it was really beginning. 'You stay quiet now, Imp. Don't want me taken up for witchcraft again, alongside everything else . . .'

The imp burrowed down inside his doublet. Jack tucked his tools up his sleeve. He couldn't be any more ready than this.

Jack opened his front door and set off down Broad St Giles – heading east, into the City of London, to steal away a devil.

Chapter 2

Smithfield market was where London's meat came to die, and at ten in the morning it was a river of glaring bullocks, a spillage of sheep like apples from a tub, a rout of panicked swine.

Harry Slubber's Meat Parade sagged across the whole north face of the market, a canker of horrible old sheds held together with grime and ropeways and peeling paint. The Slubber had bought up the site a dozen years ago, when the old Phoenix tavern burned down. Less than half was slaughter sheds; the rest housed the Slubber's various entertainments – wine shops, stew booths, dicing kens, puppet shows, cockpits and skittle alleys, all thronging with custom.

Out of all the milling livestock, the ones headed for the Slubber's pens moved with a particular purpose, their drovers goading them along, anxious to get their business done and settle down to the pleasures of the Parade.

And out of these, one ragged little herd was moving quicker than all the rest.

There was something wrong about this herd, over and above the haste. They were an odd, mismatched medley – a dozen breeds from a dozen different counties, with an enormous shaggy ox-like creature borne along in the middle.

The only thing more ragged than the cattle was their drover – a stunted creature riding on the back of the ox (a disreputable, undroverlike thing to do), dressed neck to knee in raw sheepskin, puffing on a pipe and lashing the cattle on with a nine-foot leather whip. A filthy vagabond, even by Smithfield standards.

Any honest man looking on would know what to think: *cattle thief.* Just the kind of degenerate shabaroon that Harry Slubber's slaughtermen welcomed with open arms. They always got good prices from thieves.

'Pace it, gutch-eye.' Beth Sharkwell whacked the ox's behind with the butt of her whip and cursed it for an idle pissabed scoundrel. The ox wasn't really idle, just old, but Beth didn't care.

Beth was angry.

She could remember times in the past when she hadn't been angry. Whole days, sometimes. The last was the day before Harry Slubber burned down the Crooked Walnut

26

tavern, where Beth's grandpa had held court as the scaliest villain south of the river.

The Slubber had timed his attack well. Beth had been quilting her gold at the Walnut until it could be moved to her new bolthole. Harry Slubber fired the tavern on the first of June – less than a month after old Sharkwell was killed by a devil, and only a day before the gold was due to be shifted. Slubber murdered Mr Smiles, Beth's most loyal follower, that same night. The message was clear: goodbye Sharkwell, from henceforth Southwark has a new king.

Most of the Sharkwell Family had accepted it. They worked for Harry Slubber now. Word had gone out soon after: Beth Sharkwell was to be scragged on sight, with a handsome purse for her killer. She'd fled the city, leaving behind everything she knew. Worse – leaving behind her gold, and Jack's and Kit's too, that they'd trusted her to keep safe.

She knew that riding right up to her enemy's back door, doing her utmost to attract attention, might look rash to some. Law Eleven, by the Sharkwell Code: Never stick your neck in the noose.

Law Eight, on the other hand: Never suffer an insult without vengeance. And Law Eighty-eight, one of her grandpa's favourites: If you're angry, it's probably because you need to kill someone.

Beth was angry. She wasn't going to kill anyone, not today – but vengeance?

Harry Slubber had taken her place, and her people, and her treasure.

Vengeance was long overdue.

'Out o' my road, shite shepherd!' She coughed, long and hard, and spat something brown and solid at the swineherd who'd crossed her path. The harsh pipe smoke had turned her voice to a villainous rasp. It was the best way to mask a girl's speech. One false squeak here, and she was finished. Stories were told about the Slubber's swine sheds – how his enemies had a way of disappearing, no corpses found.

Beth tried to imagine being cut up, sold and eaten after she was dead. Worse for the ones doing the eating, she decided. Though anyone used to eating the Slubber's meats wouldn't know the difference.

The truth was, Harry Slubber had never been a very good slaughterman, nor even a very good villain. The Parade was the source of his fortune and all his power. It was always full, even though the wine was sour, the beer was stale, the trugs were poxed and the games were rigged. Even though everyone knew the Slubber was a gull-plucking knave.

People said there was a charm, a sort of lucky spirit haunting the sheds; that all the Slubber's infernal good luck over the years was paid for in blood.

According to Jack, they were only half wrong. According to Jack, there was a devil buried somewhere inside. Beth would have laughed at such talk once, but now she knew better.

Devils were real.

Up ahead, she could hear the bellows of dying cattle. She was drawing close.

The Slubber always kept his slaughter sheds well guarded. Four long sheds arranged square fashion, facing inwards onto a central yard, with a single entrance blocked by a heavy wooden gate and two heavy-set men.

Beth's leading bullocks lowed as they approached, scenting the fresh blood. The two slaughtermen ambled over, toting bull hammers: these could be the same ones who'd killed Mr Smiles, back in June. Beth felt a fresh jet of rage, and forced it under control.

It was time to play the lay.

Beth gave a hacking cough, waved at the slaughtermen, slid off the ox's back and began jostling her way through the herd towards the entrance. Squeezing through the sweaty cattle, she started to grin. It was big, this Plan of Kit's.

Vengeance on the Slubber would be sweet; but after and beyond that, if Kit knew what he was talking about . . .

Let the rufflers and the whiddlers cut each other's throats over gutter pickings south of the river: henceforth the Sharkwell Family was on a higher lay altogether.

As for today, as for now – she was Beth Sharkwell, and she still had enough game in her to cozen a poxy meat thief.

*

Jack's face was buried in sweaty ox. The rank, homely smell of it filled his nostrils, along with a sticky, winding strand of belly hair. He wanted to twist and turn to get it out, but he was trussed too tight for that.

Not for the first time he wished they'd tied him to the ox's belly face down.

'Time is ripe, boymaster?' whispered the imp. 'Time to make oxenprance?' It was clinging to a clag of hair beside Jack's head. Jack could hear its wing cases whirring with excitement.

'Not yet, Imp,' he murmured. 'Wait till we're in, then make 'em prance all you like.'

The ox was breathing hard. With each inward heave, Jack's face was pressed harder into its belly. The twine bit into his shoulders, back, knees and ankles.

They'd stopped moving. He trusted Beth to get them in all right. It was the next part that had him worried.

He could hear Beth chewing up the Slubber's men. She cursed hard, working in the anger that was part of the lay, but also came naturally to her these days.

She hadn't stopped being angry since the fire. She'd turned up at the Raven three days later, in a high fury. It wasn't her fault, what had happened, and Jack didn't blame her for the loss of his fortune; but he knew he could never tell her that. Her pride wouldn't stand for it.

Jack knew what would make things right between them: vengeance on the Slubber, and a big pile of riches to replace what was lost. That was why he'd agreed to this, tamping down all his fear until it was small, tight-packed, tucked away out of sight . . .

Trouble was, fear had a way of getting loose.

'*Dead*, is what you'll be,' came Beth's voice. 'I *know* Harry Slubber. Aye, well, soon as I speak to him you're dead meat, both of you. Keep your god-damned . . . no, give it here, grouthead.'

A chink of coins, and the perfect rasping snarl from Beth. 'Six, you said – *six*, can't you figure? What's your name? Tell me your name, dung, so's I can tell Harry who to scrag slower.'

'Tsa!' said the imp approvingly, stirring beside Jack's ear.

'She's good at threats,' whispered Jack. 'Always was.'

Jack heard an angry mumble from the slaughtermen. No more coins. A final curse from Beth and the ox shifted its hindquarters, thrusting its hair deeper into Jack's nostrils, and began to move forward.

Ten slow paces. They stopped again. Jack heard the creak of the gate swinging open. None but the Slubber's trusted slaughtermen were allowed beyond here.

The red stain on Jack's hand was itching now – his index finger most of all. A little twinge went through his right eyeball, and one of the tiny muscles in his eyelid began to twitch.

This was what usually happened when Jack was around devils. An itch, a tingle of heat; sometimes, around the big ones, it could be painful. This one today, though – this one shouldn't be bad, Jack thought. A ticklish sort of devil. Not one of your flaming tormentors. And it was good he was feeling it all the way out here – a lively one meant finding it would be easier – though as to what came after . . .

Jack didn't know about that. He'd never done it before. To dig up a devil, to hold it in his hand – he didn't know about that at all. He tried to picture the Beth's smile, if all went well. He tried to picture the Raven tavern thronged with laughing, free-spending topers.

He flexed his itching finger. Beth had got them in. Now it was his turn. His Nipper's Claw – a two-inch sliver of metal, attached to his fingertip – bit into his palm, cold and razor sharp.

'Now, Imp!' he whispered.

The imp buzzed from its hiding place. Mouthing a prayer, Jack bent his elbow till the Claw touched the twine at his shoulders.

Above him, the ox gave an indignant bellow.

He sliced. The twine unravelled, plunging him into knee-deep mud. Jack rolled aside, and pushed up into a crouch. He wiped the filth from his eyes just in time to see the imp spread its jaws wide and bite a bullock on the nose.

The bullock squealed; the imp moved on; the forest of

legs around Jack twitched and stirred as the panic spread. He jumped to his feet, ducking low to remain hidden. A bullock bellowed close by, and all of a sudden the entire herd was churning for the gate. Their panic left him exposed, but no one would be looking – not with a stampede to contend with.

A few quick steps and he was up against the slaughter-shed's wall, sliding to the door, peeping in.

No one about. Jack ducked inside and turned to admire the mayhem.

The imp had done well: every plunging beast in the yard desperate to escape; every slaughterman and meat porter striving to stop them.

All well there, then.

Jack took a deep breath, dreading what came next. It was dark inside the devil's shed, with a thick ripe smell that caught in Jack's throat.

He shut his left eye.

Devil-sight.

He'd been fighting it for months. He'd got so good at blocking it, for a moment he thought it wouldn't come at all. It was almost a relief to think so – and then, all at once, it was upon him.

Devil-sight. The world was misty and red and slow as treacle. In the shed the carcasses hung in silence, hardly there at all. All of it water: all of it surface.

Jack was fishing for what lay beneath.

His right hand throbbed, stronger than he'd been expecting. He bit his lip against the pain, raised his arm, holding it out straight from the shoulder, and turned in a slow circle.

Round – round – slowly, dowsing for it . . .

The throbbing in his hand quickened, suddenly hot, then died back.

Hot again.

Back again.

Hot. So hot he had to force his hand to hold steady.

There.

It was buried in the far corner of the shed. Now that Jack knew where to look, all the surface stuff vanished – the walls, the packed earth of the floor – and he could see it.

The devil showed dimly, a glimmer like a distant lantern at twilight.

Jack blinked hard, shook his head, and the surface world was back.

He groped forward. The pain in his hand got worse with every step. His head bumped against a carcass dangling from the ceiling. Flinching to the side, he hit hard against another.

His hand was stinging, worse than wasps. He hadn't thought it would be this bad.

He checked again with the devil-sight.

It was right beneath him. The devil was bound inside something small, buried about ten inches under the dirt floor. He could see a deep amber glow pulsing up through the earth. It was – asleep? Dreaming? Doing whatever devils did, when they weren't driving people mad or killing them.

His hand was trembling hard, and his head felt light, swimming, as if he had a fever – the Shaking Sickness . . .

Just do it, Jack told himself, and be done. He grabbed the trowel stuck in his belt and attacked the earthen floor. He worked fast – if he didn't, he was apt to turn and run. His stained hand felt huge, like a big fat wineskin full of pain. Much worse now – worse than he'd ever felt it. *Alkahest* was what Dr Dee called the stuff in the stain. *Alkahest* – a sizzling sort of word – and Jack could feel it now, sizzling like oil, frying his skin, broiling his bones. The trowel bit into the earth. Jack started counting to himself. Five . . . ten . . . time was slowing with the pain. Eleven . . . he'd bear the pain till twenty, and then . . . twelve, thirteen . . .

He couldn't leave empty-handed. Imagine Beth's face. He tried to imagine it, but the pain drove out thought, and now he really couldn't bear any more . . .

The trowel grated against something hard.

The amber glow of the devil blinked out.

The pain was gone.

Jack rocked back on his heels. This wasn't supposed to happen.

He scrabbled in the hole he'd made and felt stone. He waggled, found an edge and levered up. There was a hollow space beneath. He reached inside and pulled out a small package wrapped in old, half-rotten cloth. Pulling away the cloth, he saw a small, dark bead with something carved into it – hard to see what, in the dim light of the shed.

Still no devil-glim; still no pain. It didn't make sense. Jack shook the bead, then rapped it against the floor. Nothing happened.

'Come on come on,' he muttered. 'Where are you?'

He tossed the bead from his left hand to his right. Nothing: not the slightest prickle. He squeezed it hard in his fist.

'Come on, you—'

All the breath whooshed out of Jack. The pain roared back, mangling, crushing everything. Something gripped his hand, pulling him down. He saw a wizened face, convulsed with awful rage. He saw a sea of flat white light.

The devil grinned.

Jack fell into the light.

Chapter 3

Hauling her mud-draggled burden, Beth squelched through the gateway at the top of Charterhouse Lane, staggered out of the road and sank to the ground against the gatehouse wall. A drove of swine were milling about, waiting to go down to Smithfield and suffer the change into hams and chops and blood pudding. One of them nosed at Jack, grunting and twinkling its inquisitive piggy eyes.

The imp buzzed in its face. It ran away squealing.

Cradled in her lap, Jack's head lolled, dead-weight heavy. Spit trickled out the corner of his mouth, and there was a bluish tinge to his lips that made Beth want to sob. The only part of him that seemed alive was his right hand, clenched into a hard fist. From his eyes, glassy and heavy lidded, not so much as a flicker. The imp flew in tight circles, buzzing in shrill despair.

Sightless eyes, slow shallow breathing – the closest Beth had seen to it was when one of her grandpa's men had been kicked in the head by an iron-shod horse. She remembered the man being brought into the Crooked Walnut, laid out on the big trestle table. He'd died within the hour.

'Hold on, Jack. Bide a while, will you?'

Beth couldn't keep the tremor from her voice, nor from her limbs, which were jellified with exhaustion. She'd dragged him this far – not too hard to get clear of the Meat Parade, with chaos all about – but she couldn't drag him any further.

She knew what she had to do.

'Imp,' she snapped.

The imp kept buzzing in senseless circles. It hadn't spoken a straight word since it came to tell her Jack was lost, devil-hexed, dead to this world.

Beth snatched it out of the air.

'Imp,' she said, making herself speak clear and cold. 'You obey me now, if you want your precious master back. Hear me?'

She felt it scrabble against the inside of her fist, then go still.

'Good,' she said. 'There's one man in London can help Jack. You're going to fetch him.'

*

Dr Dee came in person, black-robed, white-faced, mounted on a chestnut horse big enough for two.

By the time he arrived the blue tinge had spread as far as Jack's ears. Beth was chafing his cheeks to keep him warm – though his skin under her hands was still icy cold. She'd started singing to him. People turned to look as they passed. A part of Beth knew this was reckless, to be marked so close to Smithfield; another didn't care. She kept singing.

Dee reined up in a spatter of mud and leaped from the saddle like a much younger man. He didn't greet Beth, gave no sign he knew her even. All he did was nod down at Jack's body and say, 'Up.' Beth obeyed, taking one arm while the doctor took the other, hauling Jack up and over the horse's back.

She had only seen the Queen's magician once before, when she'd come to his house with her grandpa on purpose to cozen him. It was an unpromising start – and this was an even less promising way to go on.

She knew Jack had helped Dr Dee, when the red-handed preachers were baying for sorcerers' blood. Without Jack, the magician could have ended up hanged; at least that was what Kit always said.

She hoped Kit was right.

She hoped Dee remembered.

She hoped, hoped so hard she was biting her lips white, clenching cuts into her palms, that he'd be able to save Jack.

*

As befitted the Queen's own magician, Dr Dee had two houses. One was at Mortlake by the river – a rambling, comfortable old manor of a place where the doctor took his ease, watched the Thames flow and thought on deep matters. The other was much smaller, quite secret and situated on Milk Street, just south of Cheapside; right in the dirty heart of the city.

The Milk Street house was neither easy nor comfortable. It held a small library, which was also a fully equipped alchemical laboratory, and a wide array of devices for the detection of devilry. It was a place for taking the pulse of the city, and seeking remedies for its fevers.

A place for times of danger.

They entered by a back way that Beth hadn't known about before. Dee tied up his horse and then the two of them hauled Jack upstairs to the library. Beth watched as the doctor bent over the floor with a stick of chalk and began sketching out a big five-pointed star with furious energy.

'Well, this is a fine thing you've done,' he said. His voice was low, his face pale with fury. 'Stealing a devil . . . arrant, reckless . . . and why? Why do such a thing?'

He punctuated each word with a violent stroke of chalk.

'We thought we could use it,' said Beth. 'In the Raven.

Our place. We thought it would make people come and spend money.'

It sounded so feeble, said like that. She tried to remember the way Kit had told it – the magical success, the devil-fuelled riches. Taking Jack's curse and turning it into a blessing.

Aye, what a blessing. She wished Kit was here, so he could tell it. She could strangle him right after.

'So this was Jack's idea?' Dee had finished the star: now he was scratching crooked symbols at each of its points.

'No.'

'Confound it!' Dee rubbed something out with his sleeve, took a breath and started again.

Beth wasn't sure if Dee had heard her. He kept on muttering as he scrambled about on the floor.

'Is this why he disappeared, hm? Is this why he threw off my offers of honourable, *useful* service?'

'He didn't want to serve you,' said Beth in a small voice. This was true at least. 'He didn't want no more to do with it – devils, and magic and such.'

'Oho?' Dee moved about the star, adding a mark here, a number there. 'And yet now we find him struck down by a devil. Was it at your behest?'

His eyes sought out Beth's. They were merciless.

Usually Beth could stare down anyone she liked; but now she found she couldn't meet the doctor's gaze. Dee had

41

the truth of it. Jack had gone into this, against his fears, against his better judgement – because of her.

She looked down at Jack, lying cold and still on the floor. She tried to speak but couldn't.

With a snort of disgust Dee returned to his chalk, laying down a circle, spanning each of the star's five points in turn.

'Do you know what's wrong with him?' said Beth, once she'd got her voice in hand.

'No,' said Dee, with a fretful tug at his beard. 'No. I don't. I've never seen the like of this.'

Beth couldn't get the air to breathe. He didn't know. Dee, the great magician.

The prayer that had been rolling around her mind since she sent the imp to bring the doctor piped up loud and clear. *Let him come back, let the doctor save him, please, please, please . . .*

Dee knelt on the floor beside Jack. He picked up his right hand, and eased open the red-stained fingers. The imp hovered just above the doctor's shoulder, crooning softly.

Beth watched Jack's face, hoping for some movement, some response.

Something tumbled out of Jack's hand. Dee caught it as it rolled across the floor and held it up to the light.

He hissed.

It was a beautiful thing – a polished red bead no bigger

than a cherry stone, with an old man's laughing, sly face carved into it.

'What are you?' muttered Dee. 'What did you do?' He frowned.

'D'you—?'

'Quiet. I'm thinking.'

Dee shuffled across the floor on his knees and placed the little jewel in the centre of his star-within-a-circle.

'So . . .' He looked up at Beth and jerked his head towards the window. 'Fetch me the strongbox over there.'

Beth squeezed between a scarred worktable and a desk overflowing with dusty rolls of parchment. In her haste she brushed against a teetering pile of books, and sent it crashing to the ground.

'Careful!'

She bent down to lift the box and stopped dead.

The box was wooden, brass bound, with an emblem of a fly burned into the lid – the emblem of Nicholas Webb, the devil who walked like a man. She'd seen the same emblem on the boxes they'd raised from the Thames – small boxes, very heavy, filled with devil's gold.

'Haste, haste!' said Dee.

'But it's—'

'Zwounds! Do you question me? What is in that box may – *may*, I say – save this poor broken tool of yours. Now open it!'

Beth opened the box. Nothing happened. No swarm of hellflies came out to eat her up.

Inside was a leather bag and a roll of parchment.

'The bag, quick!' Dee produced a tiny pair of tongs from his robe, took the bag as Beth passed it over and tweezed out a grain of red powder. Here he was very careful. Beth watched his fingers trembling.

The imp hissed. 'Bindlick-meckt! *Alkahest!*'

'Hush, Imp,' muttered the doctor. Holding his breath, he leaned over the edge of his chalk circle, dropped the grain upon the little red bead and quickly drew back.

Nothing happened.

'Hmm,' said Dee. Bending over the stone with his tongs, he lifted up the grain of powder, replaced it in the bag and tied the drawstring tight shut. Then he picked up the bead and put it in his pocket.

He blinked, as if he wasn't sure what to do next.

'What?' said Beth.

'That was Alkahest,' said Dee. 'The same stuff that stained Jack's hand.'

'So?' Beth wanted to shake him. 'Why "Hmm"?'

Dee's eyes narrowed.

'Nothing happened. The effects of Alkahest upon a devil-bound object are usually . . . dramatic. If nothing happened . . .'

Dee cocked his head, considering the idea.

44

'The devil is gone. Jack is gone.'

'Gone *where*?' Beth struggled to keep from shrieking.

Dee shook his head and sniffed long and hard, wrinkling his nose. 'Only one thing for it,' he said. 'Fetch me the parchment from the box.'

He grabbed the roll of parchment out of her hands as soon as she presented it. Beth's heart thudded high in her throat. The doctor tugged at the parchment, hasty-fumbling. It whipped shut, coiling against his fingers.

'Confound it!'

'Here . . .' Beth took a corner and held it down. Dee took the loose end, pulled the parchment out to its full length – four foot if it was an inch – and rushed to weigh down the corners.

It took a moment for Beth to realize what she was looking at. Dense black lines, little rows of triangles like jagged teeth, tiny emblems and cramped black script . . .

And then the great hump-backed curve that was the Thames.

The Tower, standing tall in one corner.

St Paul's, with its ruined spire.

The Wall.

This was London. The jagged lines were rooftops. Beneath them, Beth could see each window, each cross-beam and threshold and door, picked out in devilish detail. Looking closer, looking at the tiny emblems, each with its line of twisting script, she saw what she was really looking at.

Devils. Hundreds of them – mapped out, drawn and named.

'Where, then?' snapped Dee. 'Where was it?'

Here was the Smithfield Market, thronged with live-stock. Here was Harry Slubber's Meat Parade, and here above it was a crafty, laughing old face, just like the one on the little red bead.

'Here,' said Beth.

Dee hunched over the map. Beth craned to look over his shoulder, to where one yellowed old fingernail was tracing a line of script she couldn't read.

'Sar – gastes,' Dee read.

'What?'

'The beast you were baiting. Sargastes the Satyr. Passing powerful, this one . . . Hmph. Mice won't do it.'

'Mice?'

'Won't do,' said Dee. 'The blood must fit the devil.'

The doctor sprang to his feet. 'You stay here. Touch nothing: you've learned that lesson by now, I hope.' He squinted down at her. 'You may hold Jack's hand – his *left* hand – and sing to him as you were doing when I found you.'

'Suchting remedials for master?' said the imp, buzzing up to Dee's eye level and glowing a hopeful shade of yellow.

'We shall see,' said Dee. 'Touch nothing.'

Beth did as she was told. In her hand, Jack's skin was cold and damp, like a drowned man pulled from the river.

Beth remembered how she'd played the Tartar with him – never given him a moment's rest since she'd lost their money, and her Family, and her place. Because she was angry.

He hadn't wanted this. He'd done it for her.

She kept hold of Jack's hand, not even stirring from her post when a crashing, swearing, squawking uproar erupted from the court below the window. She could hear Dee cursing – his voice cracked with worry – and then he was thundering back up the stairs. He hurried into the room carrying a large and furiously struggling cockerel by the legs. Then he grabbed Beth by the shoulder and marched her over to his chalk circle, scattering squawks and feathers.

'Now. You will assist me. It is quite safe, so long as you stay outside the circle.'

'I'm ready.'

'Hold this.' Dee handed her something heavy and cold. She looked down: she was holding a dagger, carved out of a single piece of midnight-black rock. The edge looked sharp enough to carve the wind.

'Spill its blood.'

'What?'

'The cockerel,' said Dee, speaking fast. 'Proud blood for

a strutting spirit – the blood must fit the devil, such is our law – now cut off its head, girl!'

Dee grabbed the now frantic cockerel by the head, still holding the legs in his other hand, and stretched it out in front of Beth, offering its neck to the blade.

Beth cut. Warm blood spurted on her hands. Dee swung the corpse in a broad arc, spattering blood across the circle and the five-pointed star set within in.

The air prickled. The smell of hot metal stung her nostrils. Beth remembered a locked room – that same smell – a bed full of flies and her grandpa's teeth buried in the headboard . . .

Devil magic.

Chapter 4

Cold.

Buzzing in his head.

Cold – getting worse.

The buzzing and the cold were close kin – brothers maybe. Or maybe the buzzing was the cold, and the cold was the buzzing.

Time ran different here. The buzzing might have been going on for years, or only a single breath.

But he wasn't breathing.

He tried to open his eyes. Did he have eyes, here?

He saw flat, white light. It was everywhere. Blank – smothering. Blindness made of light.

He knew it – the flat white light that magicians conjured up; the flat white light through which the devils came.

Only now, he was looking at it from the other side.

For a timeless, terrorstruck moment, Jack felt his mind skipping away like a stone skimmed across water.

And then the buzzing was back, and the light began to dim; and Jack was filled with a sudden, very strong sense of having been *seen*.

It started small – specks of blackness dancing on the light, like mayflies on a pond. Small; but the light was dimming, the specks were growing . . .

No: not growing.

Getting closer.

Coming on fast.

The light dimmed further. Specks became spots became clouds, great black thunderheads swarming together. They covered the light and now there was nothing but living darkness; the clouds were alive and they buzzed with insect voices and – *nowhere to run, no legs to run on here* – the buzzing filled his head and the shroud of chittering darkness swept over him.

A blizzard of madness. The swarm was upon him. He felt its ancient, ravenous hate. He felt a cold beyond cold, a cold that was death.

This was not the devil from the shed. This was something different, something worse, something vast.

Stringy centipedes bound his tongue; busy flies crawled down his throat; thin, icy feelers curled up his ears and nostrils.

The Swarm began to feed.

*

Dee raised his hands above his head, and spoke in a harsh new voice that Beth had not heard before.

'O EO. AEOIO.'

The strange syllables dropped from his mouth like stones. Beth saw sparks dancing in front of her eyes. She kept forgetting to breathe.

'AEO. LABAO. *Veni celeriter iubeo.*'

Outside the sun was shining; but inside the chalk circle the shadows gathered till they seemed almost solid. Beth couldn't look away. She felt the imp alight on her shoulder.

Jack lay pale and still on the floor. His face was shiny with sweat, but when Beth bent down to wipe it, it felt icy cold.

'*Veni celeriter iubeo.* I summon you, Sargastes, by the name you own.'

The hot metal reek was heavy in the air, stinging Beth's nostrils and making her eyes water; but still there was nothing to see. Nothing but shadows.

'Come on, come on . . .' she whispered.

'*Veni celeriter iubeo.* I, John Dee, summon you, spirit, by name. Come you, then, Sargastes. Come, and do my will!'

'*Hazz-tsat!*' the imp whispered.

The white light snapped from nowhere, stretched out

flat across the circle on the floor. It puckered and stretched – thrumming like a drumskin. Beth couldn't look at it: when she tried, her eyes skittered away.

The white light puckered again, like wind on water, and it wasn't flat now, it was *deep* – deeper than the sea, deeper than the ocean—

And then it was gone.

In its place was a naked old man, crouched on the floor in the centre of the circle.

A naked old *something*, anyway. A pair of goat horns sprouted from its forehead. Its chest and belly were matted with wiry grey hair. Its bottom half was as bare as the torso, and twice as hairy – like an animal's – and the knees were on back to front.

'Make up your minds, chumlings,' Sargastes said. One yellow eye flicked over at Beth, quick and crafty. 'In or out, eh? Here or there? Which is it to *be*?'

The devil's gaze switched to Jack's body, motionless on the floor.

'There he is!' The devil hopped high in the air, shaking his fists. 'Hahaha! Did him cold, didn't I?'

'Krrrt,' the imp muttered, close to Beth's ear. She felt its legs on her shoulder, then on her back. The imp was hiding. The imp was afraid of the satyr.

'You must restore him,' said Dee. 'Obey me now, or else by God I will send you back.'

The devil blinked his yellow cat's eyes, and stared at Beth, ignoring the doctor.

There were deep laugh-lines around those eyes, but the brow was taut and fresh. Impossible to judge his age: something troubling in that.

'Hmm, pretty girl,' he said. The voice was almost pleasant now – seasoned, rich. 'Perhaps you have a little drink for us?'

'No,' said Beth. She could smell a rank animal scent, like wet fur. 'Please,' she said. 'My friend. What've you done to him?'

'Dontcha know?' said the creature. He shrugged, and rolled his eyes. 'Pity about the drink.'

Sargastes stood up and stretched. His hairy legs bent backwards, then straightened. His shadow stretched out before him, cut off short at the chalk line.

'Well, *sirrah*, here you have me.' Turning to Dee, the devil gave a bow so slight, it was more insolent than staying upright. 'Ancient sprite of misrule. Revelling riotous nuisance. Some have called me Satyr.'

His arm reached out and brushed against the boundary, testing it. The fingers disappeared as soon as they crossed it. The devil flinched and drew back.

'*Tsssss!*' he said, shaking his fingers. 'And you, I see, are a wizard who knows his *mystery*.'

Beth shot a desperate look at the doctor. The cold was

coming off Jack in waves now. He couldn't last much longer: no one could, as cold as that.

Dee stared the satyr down. 'I do indeed. You should know better than to trifle with me. Tell me now: what have you done with the boy?'

The satyr burst out laughing. '*Zakatakawaka-ooooooo-OURGH!*' He grinned. His teeth were solid gold. 'You ask me that? You ask my help, after your little red-hand here done me out of my residence?'

On the floor, Jack stopped shivering. Beth squatted down and put her ear to his mouth. She couldn't hear breathing.

'Oho! He fades!' Sargastes gloated. 'That'll learn him to fox with me!'

Beth looked up at Dee. 'Quick,' she said. 'If there's anything, then do it quick! He's dying!'

'Let him,' said the satyr. 'Send me back *there*, would he? Spike me up with Alkahest? Cast me out like trash?'

'You misunderstand,' said Dee. He clenched his eyes shut. 'God's blood – you must listen, you must—'

'Naaaah. Must me no musts, wizard-man, you're short the wine and time for that. Your little red-hand did me out of my home. Now, 'less you can give it me back . . .'

'Do it!' said Beth. '*Do it!*'

'Yes,' said Dee. 'Yes, of course.' With a shaking hand, he reached into his pocket and brought out the little red bead.

The satyr licked his lips.

'Now,' said Dee. 'The boy.'

'Aye aye, wizard-man, I sees your price. Funny thing is, though, I tastes the want in here, I tastes it on you . . .' Sargastes frowned, and cocked his head to one side. 'But it's *her* I'd please the most, ain't it?'

The satyr stooped like a hawk, face barely a foot from Beth's, eyes spinning like yellow wheels. A forked tongue flickered out from between his golden teeth – slick and shining, and suddenly very sharp.

'Who's the red-hand, pretty?'

Beth glared back. 'His name's Jack. He's my friend, and I want him back, and if he dies . . .' Her throat closed up. She couldn't go on.

The devil put his tongue away, and chuckled.

'Dear me, you've a bad case of the sweethearts, ain't you? Better I hear his name from the one that loves him best: there's virtue in that. Love's a binder, stronger than all the rest. Need more than a pinch of it, for a task as tricky as this.'

'I don't care if it's tricky, just do it! Fetch him back! *Now!*'

The satyr winked at her, then whipped his head round to face Dee, eyes glowing like two pale lamps. 'Boy in the circle. Bead too, touching skin. Lips is good: moisten 'em with wine first, stronger the better. You stiff me on this bargain, I'll come back and haunt you something horrible, you hear me?'

'I will not *stiff* you, as you put it. Besides—'

Dee stopped, and cleared his throat.

The satyr was gone.

Everything happened very quickly after that.

Beth carried Jack inside the circle. His body was freezing cold and so light she could lift him easily. Dee snatched up a bottle full of clear liquid that stank stronger than ragwater – spirits of wine, the strongest liquor in London. He sloshed it over the satyr's bead and placed it carefully on Jack's lips.

'How long—?' said Beth – and stopped.

The bead began to twinkle. The face carved into it seemed to wink. Then it rolled from Jack's lips and skittered on the floor.

There was a flash of dazzling light.

And then Jack's mouth opened, and drew in a long, long breath.

Beth leaped forward. Dee's bony hand brought her up short, gripping tight on her shoulder.

'Let me go!' she said.

'Not yet,' said Dee. 'It isn't safe.'

'But he's moving!'

'Inside that circle is where the devils are. Do you trust the satyr?'

'You mean . . .'

'There could be anything in there. *He* could be anything.'

Jack was still sucking in air. It seemed impossible, but he was; and his face was working and flexing like a fish out of water.

'Come on, Jack.' Beth clenched her fists.

Finally the breath came to an end. Jack started to breathe out, and now a sound came – a horrible buzzing croak.

'Jack,' Beth said. 'Jack, please, please . . .'

Jack's eyelids snapped open. There was something crawling inside, where his eyes should be. Something black.

'Oh God,' said Dee.

Beth realized his hand was no longer holding her back. She sprang forward, into the circle.

The cold hit her like a punch, knocking all her breath out. Her arms and legs were seizing up with it. Her jaw locked rigid against her skull.

The thing that had been Jack sat up.

'Zzzzsnaaaaaaa!' The insect voice croaked again.

'NO!' said Beth, forcing the word out against the deadening cold. 'You're Jack. You're *Jack*!'

She reached out and took his hand – his right hand, his devil hand. As soon as she touched it, it went from cold to scalding hot. Jack doubled up on himself, so hard his head bounced off his knees. His hand wrenched out of her grip – and then Dee was pulling her back, dragging her out of the circle, holding her tight so she couldn't escape.

Jack choked. Dry heaves wracked his body. His mouth stretched wide – wider than Beth thought possible, so wide it looked as if his head must split in two – and then he vomited.

Out of his mouth poured a wriggling stream of blackness: flies, worms, grubs, beetles, creeping things with legs and teeth.

The creatures burst into flame as they poured against the invisible wall of the chalk circle. No ash fell. No trace was left at all.

None of them escaped.

Jack rolled onto his back. He raised his head – his eyes were bloodshot and filled with horror, but they were eyes again – and Beth sobbed, half relieved, half terrified still.

'Is it you?'

'Beth?' Jack croaked.

Beth ran inside the circle, and hugged him tight. Above their heads the imp whirled and spiralled, crowing with delight.

It was Jack. Just Jack, looking bleary. Just like in the old days when he'd first started working for the Sharkwell Family and she'd see him coming out in the morning from his sleeping nest in the warehouse, red-eyed and frowsty.

'Beth?' he said again. She hugged him tighter.

*

Beth helped Jack wash, gave him some hot water and wrapped him in a warm, soft blanket. The doctor paced about the room, gnawing at his lip. From time to time he stared at Jack, then looked quickly away.

'Stop that!' said Beth. 'Can't you see he's wrung out?'

Dee turned his glare on her, but the righteousness had gone out of it. This time it was Beth who stared him down.

The doctor was uncertain.

Could it be that he was afraid?

'You can keep that,' said Jack, pointing at the bead, still inside Dee's circle. 'I never want to see it. Nor any other.'

'Now you say so!' said Dee.

'Aye,' said Jack. 'I've had enough.' His hands clutched the cup of hot water. He hadn't stopped shivering since coming round. 'Where was I?'

Dee shook his head. 'I don't know.'

'What was it, came out of me?'

Again Dee shook his head.

'Don't think on it Jack,' said Beth. 'It's gone now.'

'It was like . . . a cloud.' Jack closed his eyes, remembering. 'No, not a cloud: it was alive. Lots of flies and things. Lots together.' Again he shook his head, his face twisting up. 'All different parts, but one . . . thing. A Swarm.'

Dee's face went pale.

'What?' said Jack. 'What was it? It was trying to come with me. It was trying to come *here* . . .'

'Hush,' said Beth. She didn't like the way Jack was looking at the doctor – hungry and feverish, glaring wild. 'Don't think on it. It's over. Finished. Time to go. Forget it.' Suddenly she couldn't stand to be in this room, with its reek of devils and liquor and vomit, for a moment longer.

'Perhaps that would be best,' said Dee. His fury was burnt out. Now he looked old and haggard, as if ten years had piled on his shoulders at a stroke.

'What was it?' said Jack.

Dee was silent.

'But you know, yes? You must know.' Jack heaved himself up and took a step towards Dee. 'Why won't you tell me?'

'I do *not* know,' said Dee. 'I do not know where you went, nor even when. Time runs differently for devils.'

'But the Swarm,' said Jack. 'It *hated* me. So much . . .'

Dee looked at Jack for a long time. 'I do not know,' he said at last, and his eyes flickered away.

Beth took Jack by the hand and pulled him to his feet. 'No more of this. We're going home. Goodbye, doctor.'

Dee didn't try to stop them. He hardly moved. As they went down the stairs he was staring at the smudged chalk on the floor, lost in thought.

They walked in silence.

Beth kept shooting Jack little glances, as if she couldn't

quite believe that he was there. Jack couldn't believe it himself. With every step they took, he expected to be falling again. Falling into the light, into the Beyond, into the place where the Swarm would find him, and feed . . .

He'd escaped it. He was alive. But he felt changed, somehow. Weak. Still icy cold.

'You had the right of it back there,' said Beth. 'No more devils. Never ever again.'

'Nix!' squawked the imp.

'Aye,' said Jack. 'No more devils at all. 'Cept you, Imp.'

No more devils: Jack should have known better than to make promises he couldn't keep. This was London. His hand began to prickle almost as soon as he'd spoken.

Strange. Maybe the prickle felt different – was there a cold, a numbness at his fingertips, mixed in with the usual Alkahest heat?

Jack glanced up and saw the gloomy walls of Newgate Prison looming ahead. Newgate meant Black Dog, the dungeon devil. Jack had met Black Dog up close and had feared it ever since.

As they passed through the gate he had the clear, unpleasant sensation of some great beast snuffling at him. The hairs rose on the back of his neck. Just as suddenly, whatever it was pulled away fast.

His hand stopped prickling. Jack shivered.

What had scared off Black Dog?

Jack stopped and looked about him, trying to reckon where the closest devil was buried.

A smell of sewage and rotting offal wafted up to greet them – the plaguey stench of the River Fleet.

'Holborn Bridge,' he muttered.

He turned left, Beth following.

They were in the middle of the bridge when he felt a faint itch. Jack stopped. Beth stopped too, with a questioning look.

Jack shook his head and concentrated, trying to feel if anything was different. Again his hand was throbbing. Was there a little sliver of cold mixed into the heat?

'Odd place to tarry, Jack,' said Beth.

Again Jack shook his head.

On a pillar rising from the bridge's parapet was a statue of a woman – ancient, lichen-crusted, smoothed down by years of London rain. It was hard to tell who she was, or why she'd been put there. Streaks of damp seeped down her cheeks like tears. Those who lived nearby called her St Bride, and came to have their marriages blessed there. No one knew why – except Jack.

This was one of the better ones, if any devil could be called better. Jack had spotted it with the Sight several months ago, so he knew that the devil itself was bound into a silver kissing cup – a beautiful ancient thing, hidden in a hollow inside the statue's pillar.

'Jack?'

He concentrated on his hand, feeling the faint itch running through his fingers. But it didn't tell him a thing. The itch seemed just as before, and the kissing-cup devil wasn't running from him as Black Dog had. He heard it whispering to itself.

It was an odd one. Whenever Jack passed it on his own, he felt a warmth about his heart. If there was a girl nearby, he'd find his eyes being drawn to her face. The girls were always pretty – at least, the devil made them seem so. Often as not, they'd stare back, too: sometimes blow him a kiss.

He'd never passed this way with Beth before.

'Jack?'

Beth grabbed his shoulder. The touch of her hand made his heart race and his whole body tingle, and he felt a strong urge to pull her to him and kiss her.

Jack fought it. He wrinkled his nose.

'D'you really mean it?' said Beth. 'About devils.'

'Aye,' said Jack, shaking himself. 'Be glad if I never saw one again.'

'Then throw away that key. The one Lud gave you. He's the biggest of them all, ain't he?'

'Biggest in London . . .'

'So throw it away. It's unlucky.'

Beth stared at him fiercely.

'A'right.' Jack reached into his shirt, and tugged the

string over his neck. He held up Lud's key. The tarnished copper was green and cankered with age.

A devil's gift. Jack remembered the night it was given – the mist upon the waters, the ancient forest where streets should be, the raven-headed King Devil croaking in the dark.

It didn't look like much, resting in his palm.

He raised his arm, fully intending to hurl the key into the stream; only at the last he hesitated.

'You sure?' he said.

'Knew it,' said Beth. Her anger flared quick. 'I *knew* it.'

'But, d'ye see – Lud's the King of London. And . . .'

'What?'

Something was coming. Jack didn't know how to tell her. And he was still fighting the urge to . . .

Kissherkissherkisshernow.

Jack blushed.

Kissherkissherkissher . . .

The devil's voice muttered away, soft and insistent.

'Are you going to throw it?' snapped Beth. 'Or are you going to stand there like a mooncalf Mes'potamian?'

He loved it when she scowled like that. Maybe he should kiss her and be damned. After what had happened today – he could have died! To die without kissing Beth seemed the worst sort of foolishness.

'What you grinning about, Jack?'

Kissherkissher . . .

'Enough. No more devils,' said Jack. He nodded. 'I swear it.'

He threw the key as hard as he could, out into the river. In the flow of turbulent filth, they didn't even see it splash.

Chapter 5

Back at the Raven, Beth chased off the topers and locked the doors.

'Bed,' she said.

Jack nodded. He could hardly credit he'd made it this far. It was as if throwing away the key had used up the last of his strength: the long walk down High Holborn had taken place in a daze, his feet floating along somewhere miles below, his vision clouding over, his right hand throbbing like a bad tooth. Still with that weird cold mixed in, too. When he looked at it, the numb place at his fingertip was marked by a tiny black spot.

He didn't want to think about it. Beth was right. He needed to rest.

Beth helped him up the stairs without another word. He slumped down onto the straw like an empty sack, and shut his eyes. Little snatches of what he'd been through kept floating up in his mind – flies, chittering madness and the cold hateful darkness crawling into him to feed. Prickly legs on his face, and a rustle of dry wings. It no longer felt unreal; it felt all too present: the sound was *here in the room with him*—

Jack shot upright, swiping at his face with both hands. Something whirred past his ear.

'Str'klext, boymaster!'

The imp. It was the imp. Not . . . whatever the other had been.

'S-sorry,' said Jack. His heart hammered in his chest, gradually slowing. 'Sorry, Imp, I thought you were . . .'

The imp was hovering in front of his face. Its beady eyes glowed, two points of gold in its strange little face.

'Thought how, master?'

'You know,' said Jack.

The two points of gold sharpened. At the same time, the rounded surface of the Goliath beetle shell lit up a pale, sickly yellow – the imp's colour for fear.

'I kennit nix,' said the imp – denying it, but all at once Jack knew it was lying. It *did* know. It knew something, at least, just as Dr Dee had known something, or guessed something . . .

'Tell me,' said Jack.

The yellow paled to grey.

'I command you to tell me,' said Jack. He could hear his

67

voice getting stronger. 'You know about . . . that. What came out of me. The Swarm.'

The imp made a small burbling sound.

'Tell me,' said Jack.

The same sound again. '*Blzlb'b*,' it sounded like, and this time Jack realized the imp was telling him something.

'What's . . . Bullzabub?' he said.

'*Blzlb'b*. Ist swarm-lord, master, Great Shuk of Shuks . . . but speak it not here, please not to think it, please not to name it once again!'

'It's a devil, then?' said Jack.

'Greatest of all,' the imp whispered. 'Lord of Legions. Lord of Swarms. Other shuks and shuklets come here to serve, like self to boymaster. *Blzlb'b* sayeth: nix to serve. Come to rule, or not at all. Come to eat up all.'

Eat up all – and again Jack felt it stir inside him, a swarm of cold hungry things under his skin, their mouths working. Flies, or – what was it, the plague Moses sent on the Egyptians? Locusts, aye: they'd covered the land and stripped it bare, come to eat up all.

'If that was a devil, then . . .' Jack tried to swallow, but his mouth was too dry. 'Say it was, then where I went – that place . . .'

'But nix to believe it, please not master.' The imp spoke shrill, insistent, as if it wanted to drown out Jack's thought. 'Better to think elsewise. Best to think on lovey-dove. Aye,

68

drive off badness: lovey-doveyness can do it! Bethshark did so for boymaster, when Swarm wast within.'

'She did what?'

The imp glowed pink, and shook its feelers. Before Jack could press it any further there was a tread on the stair and Beth appeared in the doorway.

'That's enough chatter,' she said. 'Jack, you look like death. You should sleep now. 'Cept . . . I made you something . . .'

She was holding a bowl of soup, Jack realized. A steaming bowl of watery soup, with a dubious smell to it. She placed it on the floor in front of him, and he saw large, soft chunks of carrot and a few stringy white strips that looked like bacon rind floating in it.

Jack couldn't help himself. Maybe it was the thought of the Queen of Thieves chopping carrots like a thrifty housemaid, or maybe it was just the release after all the fear and horror, but the laughter came out unstoppable, in great whooping gusts.

Beth went red, and looked down at the soup.

'Sorry, Beth,' said Jack, but then the look on her face set him off again.

'Huh,' she said. 'You don't sound sorry. Well if you don't want it I'll just have it myself.'

She reached down for the bowl, but Jack was too quick. Bad soup or no, it was steaming hot . . . and now that the gust of laughter had passed, quick as it came, he felt cold again. He snatched up the bowl and slurped at it, and he must have looked eager enough to satisfy Beth. She grunted and jerked her chin up before ducking under the curtain into her half of the attic.

By Beth Sharkwell's standards, that was as good as a kiss.

That night Jack had a hummer of a dream. He was swooping over London on powerful, black-feathered wings. He knew it was London, but it looked all wrong. For one, it had grown vast – even from up high there seemed no end to it. It had grown strange too: with his keen eyes he spied out a few familiar buildings in their rightful places, but next to them stood mud huts with branches for roofs and white marble palaces and giant towers built of glass.

Every street of this strange, jumbled-up London was empty. On the horizon, clouds like dark cliffs were boiling up.

In the thin places.

In the dark places.

The freedom of the city of Lud.

The voice was in the centre of his head, a dry raven's croak.

Jack's wingbeats crashed like thunder as he swooped and soared. From time to time he thought he felt someone gliding at his side, but whichever way he turned the sky was as empty as the streets. He flew on alone in the gathering storm.

Until all at once his black wings were gone. He was plummeting down like a stone.

London rose up to meet him.

Jack opened his eyes. Daylight seeped through the shutters. Rain pattered against the roof. His hand felt funny.

'You a'right, Jack?' Beth was leaning over him. She looked worried. 'You've rested up, anyhow. It's gone midday already.'

Still sleep-fogged, Jack realized his fingers were curled around something hard and ice-cold. He opened them up, and saw a key.

Lud's key.

Impossible. He blinked groggily, and moved his hand into the light.

Beth saw it then. Her face darkened.

There was no mistaking the key: ancient copper, lumped and greened over as if it had lain a long time underwater.

'What's that doing here?' said Beth. 'Palmed it, did you?'

'I didn't,' said Jack. 'I don't know how it's here. I threw it. You saw me do it . . .'

'Or I saw what you wanted,' said Beth. 'Od's Blood! No more devils, you said. You lied to me.'

'I *didn't*. I chucked it, I swear,' said Jack.

Beth's grey eyes narrowed as she watched his face.

'Give it me.'

Jack handed the key across gladly enough. Beth took it gingerly, as if picking up a scorpion.

'I'm making sure this time. Maybe your throwing arm's spavined, same as your wits.'

Jack was always amazed by how quickly Beth could change her appearance. She'd been using this face for months, so she'd got it down pat: with two smears of grease, a drab kerchief and a slump, she aged herself thirty years. Jack walked through Long Acre Field in the company of a worn out barrel-wench.

When they reached the river, Beth chucked the key far out into the silver-streaming current.

'I don't want it, hear me?' Jack shouted. 'I don't want any of it!'

'Who you shouting at?' said Beth, already walking away.

Jack didn't know the answer to that. He wasn't sure he wanted to.

Beth didn't say a word all the way back to the Raven. Jack had to hurry to keep up with her.

As they came up to the tavern, the door swung open, and at last Beth broke her silence.

'Oh bleeding baby Moses, will you look at that.'

Jack stared hard at the outlandish figure coming out

of the boozing ken, clutching a half-empty skin of wine.

Kit struck a pose, and twirled his mustachios. They were dyed deep purple. The rest of his costume was queer, even for him: flowing robes – purple, to match the mustachios – a tin crown and an immense embroidered codpiece jutting out between his legs.

'Halloo! Halloo!' cried Kit. 'Well met!'

Jack grunted a greeting.

'Been a-strolling by the river? How sweet.' Kit grinned. 'I'm not interrupting, am I?'

Beth snorted. 'What's your game today, Kit?'

'I have triumphed,' said Kit. 'I have triumphed so entirely, I would thank you never to doubt me again.'

'You're drunk,' said Beth.

'Part of my mystery, sour-tongue. And I'm just summoning my second wind.' Kit laughed, his eyes gleaming white and wild.

'Some triumph.' Beth narrowed her eyes. 'I should never have listened to you and your pox-pussed Plan. Do you know what happened to Jack?'

'My dear . . .'

'I'm not your dear. And your lay played out foul as muck. Jack nearly died. We're done.'

'Try telling that to Madame de Wilde and her fifty oh-so-friendly milkmaids. You'll see: things are falling out quite pretty.'

'*Pretty?*'

'And I know all about your little difficulties. Yes, I dropped in at Dee's. Very short, he was. I caught him at the door, he was leaving in a hurry, but I managed to get the bare bones of the affair . . .' Kit winked. 'Oh, and my thanks for not letting him know stealing that devil was my idea.'

Beth pursed her lips. 'You think I'd cry beef?'

'I know you'd never dream of breaking your precious Laws.' Kit sucked the last drops of wine from his moustache. 'And you must know there's no stopping this revel. The phoenix is out the cage. The bear is rampaging through the village. The lion—'

'Is going home,' said Beth, ducking under his arm and pushing open the tavern door. 'No more devil business. No more stratagems. No bacchanals, no— Oh.'

A large group of very drunk men stood by the beer trestle – half of them in mariners' costume, the other half in rouge and powder and assorted ladies' dresses. Several empty wineskins were scattered on the floor around them. In the corner, a band of musicians were setting up.

'See: our bacchanal is begun,' Kit said as he and Jack followed her inside. 'Lord Strange's Men, hope you don't mind.'

'Ballocks,' muttered Beth. '*Actors*. You need to send them away.'

'Why? They're paying for their drink. And I don't think

you understand.' Kit twirled a corner of his moustache. A spark of merry mayhem danced in his eyes. 'This revel will be for the ages. Can you smell that hog roasting?'

Jack sniffed. As usual, the boozing ken smelled of spilt beer and dirty rushes – but there above it, a faint smell of pork crackling. He remembered he hadn't had any breakfast. Or lunch.

'Prime Gloucestershire hog. A noble beast given a glorious end. They're turning the spit out back.'

Jack jumped at a hideous shrieking wail. One of the musicians was tuning his bagpipes.

'You just tell those caterwaulers to pack it up,' said Beth. 'They can take the hog with them.'

'Don't think so. Half of London is coming. Honestly, I don't know why I bother helping you two.' Kit winked. 'Gird your loins, innkeeps. Busy day ahead. Little surprise or two . . .'

'Wait,' said Jack. Something was up, he could smell it – but at that moment the door burst open behind them and in rolled a gaggle of giggling doxies with their hair down, pushing a grinning, bottle-toting, toothless, red-faced bawd in a wheelbarrow.

'Aha, Madame de Wilde!' cried Kit. 'Delighted to see you here. Welcome to the revels of the Raven!'

Beth drew breath to speak, but Jack caught her before she could.

'He's right,' he said. 'Look about you. No stopping this now.'

'But you need to rest,' said Beth. 'You need peace and quiet, not this . . .'

Jack wasn't so sure. He thought of going upstairs, and lying with his eyes closed while the events of yesterday came back to visit. He looked at the riot of players and trugs swarming about. Kit had achieved this much: there would be revels here tonight.

'No,' he said. He felt something stirring to life inside him, and now he was sure. He turned to Beth and grinned. 'This is right. Can't you feel it?'

She paused, frowned, and then nodded slowly. 'Aye,' she said. 'Aye, I think I can.'

Chapter 6

The Gloucester hog roasting out back was even nobler than Kit had promised. Two boys worked shifts to keep it turning over the fire, its sweet fat hissing and sizzling on the coals. Meaty fumes wafted out on the breeze and drew in passers-by like wasps to a honeypot.

Soon the tavern was packed. This was not usual. Maybe if Jack had stopped to think about it, he'd have wondered how Kit had managed such a triumph – but he didn't stop, or think. He didn't have time.

Jack and Beth served out their weak beer and foul-tasting ragwater as quick as they could pour. Their customers were overflowing the boozing ken and spilling outside.

Now and then a prickle ran across Jack's right hand like a needle-footed spider. There was no time to worry about it. The blackness he'd marked last night hadn't spread, and the twinges passed swift enough to be ignored. In fact, Jack was definitely starting to feel better. Even Beth was cheering up. After scarfing a platter of hogflesh she seemed to accept that there was no stopping what Kit had started – now the riot was begun.

Soon the band began to play in earnest. Their instruments were old and cracked, but they sounded sweet, laying down a tripping melody that made Jack's toes twitch in his shoes. The ale flowed in the sun; a few ragged couples began dancing in the lane, kicking up their heels in the mud. Jack didn't know whether to join in or to serve more beer. More and more people were arriving, sucked in from the Oxford Road by the hogsmoke and the leaping music.

The jugs of ale were emptying as quick as Jack could fill them, and the moneybag at his belt was getting heavy. Every twenty minutes he had to slip up to the attic to quilt away the cheat.

'Hoy there! Look at this!' Jack bumped into Beth on the stairs, and swung his bag of coins.

'Look at what?'

'Chink-chinky-chink,' said Jack, shaking the bag to make it jingle.

'You sound like Kit,' she said. 'You all right?'

A great cheer went up downstairs, followed by a roaring shout.

'Mine host! Mine host of the Raven, my little Hercules!

Show yourself, or my followers will tear this place asunder!'

Beth pursed her lips.

'Come on!' Jack laughed, tossing the money into the attic and taking her hand to lead her down the stairs. 'He was right, you know.'

'You sure you're well?' said Beth, peering at him.

'I'm grand,' said Jack, as they emerged from the stairway. Kit caught sight of them and leaped up onto a table, scattering mugs of beer.

'Well, Jack?' He bowed deep. 'Come, stand up with me.'

Jack glanced sidelong at Beth. He could tell she was struggling not to smile. 'Go on,' she said. 'I'll serve.'

The crowd opened up to let him pass, and again Jack felt a prickly thrill of pleasure run through him – everything falling just right, like magic – and then Kit was hauling him up onto the table and clapping him round the shoulders.

'Now: a toping song! Give us "Hold Thy Peace", you idle shabaroons. Wench!' He was addressing Beth, Jack realized – this was bold, even from Kit – 'Wench, hand me up a racing cup, filled with your godawfullest ragwater.'

Beth not only didn't stab Kit on the spot, she passed up the big two-handled cup after filling it to the brim.

'Hold Thy Peace, now,' said Kit, thrusting one handle of the cup at Jack, who grabbed hold of it, laughing.

Every drinker knew the song. And now Kit's voice rang

out – he had a clean, pure tenor, of which he was sinfully proud.

'*Hold thy peace, thou knave –*

I prithee hold thy piece . . .'

Kit thrust one hand between his legs, clutching his codpiece through the flapping purple robe. He raised his handle of the racing cup, pulling Jack's along with it – and the race began.

They drank together, cheek to cheek, Kit bending at the knees so his head was level with Jack's. Jack sputtered and gagged as the raw liquor burned down his throat. He hated ragwater. The actors joined in the song, in perfect harmony.

'*Hold thy peace, thou knave –*

Thou –

Knaaaaave!'

They drank on. Somehow Jack was keeping pace. He glanced desperately at Beth. She was singing too. Everyone in the tavern was. The song was galloping off like a runaway horse: the best Jack could do was cling on and hope for the best.

'*Hold thy peace thou knave –* bottoms up!'

Jack's belly was on fire. He'd never drunk like this before. Ragwater was running down his chin, and up his nose. His eyes were stinging. His hand prickled.

A mad notion entered his head: maybe he could win

this. He took a giant gulp, feeling the thrill as the crowd howled him on.

Kit must have noticed the fight in Jack's drinking, because he tilted the cup higher. A torrent of stinking rag-water raced down their throats. Jack couldn't stand it. He choked, gasped and pulled away.

With a bellow of triumph, Kit raised the cup high and began glugging the whole thing down himself. He tore off his codpiece and flung it across the taproom. An old man plucked it out of the air. A leering old man, with a taut-skinned forehead.

Jack blinked. His eyes were still streaming from the rag-water. When he'd blinked them clear, the old man was gone.

'*Hold thy peace, thou knave – thou – knaaaaave!*'

Kit dropped the empty cup and raised his arms above his head, accepting the crowd's adulation.

'Ah, hold your peace, you poor pitiful tippler you!' He crushed Jack in a hug and planted a smacking wet kiss on his nose.

'A jig now – a *victory* jig!' Kit shook his fist at the musicians. '"The Bear Dance", god damn your idle skins!'

The fiddler tapped his foot twice and flew off into the tune. Kit and Jack linked arms, leaped from the table and whirled off. As if by magic, a path cleared before them.

Jack didn't feel fuddle-headed. This was the finest sort of drunk he'd ever felt. He felt ready to fly.

Cheers and pounding feet. The whole room was stamping now. The fiddler and the drummer were deep in their music, the piper was screeching like a banshee – and suddenly, Jack was arm in arm with Beth.

At any other time, Jack would have paled at the bare thought of it. Now it felt like the most righteous thing in the world.

Beth's disguise had slipped. She looked like herself again – only better, because now she looked happy. Jack capered like a man possessed, whirled her near and far – let her arm slip, caught her hand at the last moment before she flew away, squeezed it as they turned.

To Jack's glowing delight, she squeezed back. They spun down the line together. Beth executed a triple twirl, her skirts whipping high.

Kit passed them, spinning a rouged and powdered boy. He winked.

'Wild time, eh, Jack?'

They danced on. The prickle in his hand was constant now, but Jack didn't mind it. All he could think of was the dance: the sweat rising and spinning off his hair; Beth's tight grip on his hand, and her lightness as she turned; the feeling that for just this moment, life was perfect.

At last Beth twisted to one side, guiding Jack into the small space behind the trestle table. They collapsed side by side, panting and grinning.

Beth's eyes were shining. She squeezed his hand. He hadn't realized she was still holding it. 'Drink?' she said.

Jack nodded.

Beth took up a cup from the table and filled it with wine. She looked at him over the top of it, and flared her eyes at him.

'Well, Jack?'

Jack felt the music surge inside him again like a tide – drumming louder and louder, shaking the floor.

He was supposed to say something. But what? Surely on such a night as this, the right words would come on their own.

'I—' said Jack.

Something pinched him hard on the arse.

'*Plaguey Christ* what was that?' Jack leaped to his feet, twisting round to see the imp, in its Goliath Beetle shell, crouched on the floor.

'You ain't supposed to be here!' Jack spluttered. 'Someone'll see you! And why – what you trying to do, make me bleed?'

The imp's shell glowed a faint sickly green.

Beth was scowling furiously. The drumming swelled still louder. The imp was saying something, but Jack couldn't hear it.

He bent down low.

'M-w . . . s-meckt cellar!'

'Did you say cellar?' Jack shook his head, trying to clear it.

The imp waggled furiously.

The floor shook once more, with a beat too loud for any drum Jack had ever heard of.

The cellar. The noise was coming from the cellar.

The cellar door was the sturdiest thing in the whole of the tavern – thick, ancient, cross-grained and studded with iron. Right now, reckoning by the racket that was coming through the oak, there were at least two dozen people dancing in there, along with a fiddler, a piper and a drummer.

Jack's right hand felt wasp-stung. It had been prickling all night – he wondered how he'd ignored it.

A puckish voice told him to keep on ignoring – to take Beth by the hand and lead her back into the dance.

'Whass 'bout, Imp?'

The imp flew over to land on the door handle, and waggled its feelers.

'Elsewhile shukness I kenning,' said the imp, its shell flashing with a confusion of colours. 'Mecktick waking.'

'What're you frothing?' said Jack. 'Speak plain, Imp.'

The imp drummed its legs against the door. 'Not possibling to speak plain,' it said. 'Nix plainness, nix of sense. All skrittert!'

'I'll give you sense,' said Beth. 'Night like this, when

we're short-handed, some sods thought they'd help themselves.'

'How'd they get in?' said Jack. 'You've got the key, right?'

Beth nodded – the cellar key was around her neck, like it always was.

'So what's that then?'

There was a key in the door. The wrong key. A key he'd seen before.

Copper, green with age.

'What . . . ?' said Jack.

'Why,' said Beth. 'Is that—?'

Jack nodded. 'Lud's key.'

'But I threw it in the river.'

'Right,' said Jack. 'And now it's back. Again. Believe me now?'

'I . . .' Beth looked lost. 'Aye, I reckon I do.'

Jack was trying to think. It was hard, what with the twitchy feeling in his toes telling him to dance, and the rising fear telling him to run.

Suddenly the sounds coming from behind the keyhole changed. The fiddle, pipe and drum were gone: in their place was a skirling, Moorish tune, and voices singing, shouting, chattering excitedly.

'*Ow!*' Jack doubled over as a bolt of pain shot through his hand.

'Od's blood, Jack, what was that?' said Beth.

Jack shook his hand. It felt jangled, half numb. It had never felt like this before. 'I don't know.'

'What's behind there?'

'Don't know.'

Jack crouched down and tried to see through the crack beneath the door. He couldn't make out what he was looking at. Dancing feet? The light kept on changing. Now it was flickering torchlight, now bright and steady like oil lamps, now silvery like the moon. The music was at it too: Jack couldn't tell from one moment to the next what instruments were playing, or what the tune might be.

'Ahem.'

The voice came from behind them, up the stairs.

'Might have known,' Beth muttered.

'What's, ah . . . what's afoot, then?' said Kit, swaying tipsily down the steps towards them.

'We don't know, Kit,' said Beth, perilous sweet. 'We don't know – but why am I thinking you're about to tell us, eh?'

Kit cleared his throat again. 'Well. Yes. There is something. Thought I'd wait till you'd enjoyed the result. Which is, I must say, impressive.'

He reached inside his purple doublet and pulled out his leather-bound ledger. He licked his finger and flicked through the pages.

'How much money have you taken tonight, Jack? More

than sixteen shillings, thruppence ha'penny, I'll warrant! Clears our little debt . . .'

An enormous thump sounded from behind the door, as if an axe had been buried in the cross-grained planks. Kit winced.

'What did you do?' said Jack.

'Only what we'd agreed.'

'Agreed?'

Kit nodded. 'I thought, Jack's had a shock, wits all astray, but why let that hold us back, hm? And Dee will never suspect, not after the *very convincing* way you told him you never wanted—'

'You stole it again,' said Beth. 'You stole the satyr off Dee.'

'. . . and buried it in the cellar here. Yes. Just as we'd planned.'

Beth strode up to Kit and slapped him in the face.

'What?' said Kit, with an injured look.

'Jack nearly died,' she said. 'It's not a game: he said he wanted rid of it.'

'Jack, you'll forgive me, won't you?' said Kit.

Jack didn't know. He was still too fuddled to feel angry, even. In his mind's eye he saw the leering old man. Horns sprouting from a taut-skinned forehead.

Beth spat on the ground at Kit's feet, spun round and returned to the door. 'Right, I'm getting this open, and then *you*, Kit, *you* are going into whatever mayhem's behind it and you're getting that devil-stone out of there, and taking it back to Dee.'

'I protest,' said Kit.

'Good for you.' Beth shook her head. 'We want rid of this, now.'

'I disagree,' said Kit. 'A false logic, Beth Sharkwell!'

'It's you was false,' said Beth. 'Now you play true, or else.'

She reached out and turned Lud's key in the lock.

There was a bone-shaking *chunk*. It filled the air all around them – as if the whole world was a huge rusty lock, turning all unwilling . . .

And the door whipped open. A wiry, grey-haired arm extended out of it, grabbed Beth by the shoulder, and pulled her in to a blast of noise and light.

It happened too fast. Jack didn't even have time to cry out.

One thing stood out clear: the figure in the doorway. A cackling old man with a woolly chest, and legs that bent backwards.

The satyr slammed the door shut.

Beth was gone.

The noise beyond the door shifted again. Jack hardly noticed.

The key was still there in the lock.

'Hmm,' said Kit. 'Something strange here.'

A tremor in his voice. His lips were pale.

'Strange?' said Jack. Beth was gone, and it was Kit's fault. '*Strange?*' he said, his voice coming out strangled. 'You did this, Kit! You lost her, you—' Words failed him. He grabbed hold of Kit and reached for the key.

'Stay, now I never said I'd go in,' said Kit.

'Ready, Imp?' said Jack. He felt the beetle land on his shoulder, its claws gripping tight.

'Come, Jack.' Kit was trying to shake him off. There was a time quite recently when he could have done it with ease; but Jack had grown over the past few months, and right now anger was making him as strong as he'd ever been. 'Jack! I never told her to—'

'Balkutt Yayn for lovey-dove!' cawed the imp, rearing up on Jack's shoulder.

'Wait!' said Kit.

Jack remembered where the satyr had taken him last time, and for a moment he hesitated. Then he thought of Beth, alone in that place. Alone with the Swarm. He turned the key in the lock.

Something went *chunk* inside his head, and then—

Time runs differently for devils.

For Sargastes the Satyr, words like yesterday, tomorrow, next year, were like the word *loud* to a deaf man, or *red* to the blind.

89

For Sargastes, there were only two times: now and then. *Now* was the nights when the revels screamed from the rooftops, the wine was drained to the lees, and the madness of the satyr reigned supreme. All these nights were now. All these nights were here.

These are the thin times, the thin places. On nights such as these, doors can open to strange ways.

All that's needed is the right kind of key.

Chapter 7

The air was winter cold. It smelled of flowers and rotting turnips.

Jack looked up.

It was night, and he was somewhere outdoors. Muddy cobbles stretched out in front of him. In the distance was a row of buildings over an arched colonnade. He was in a city. In a square, in a city. Everything was too big, and too straight: every building a palace, marble spires and columns marching off in all directions. People moved about here and there, wheeling barrows, setting up stalls. A marketplace? A marketplace built of marble.

Where was the cellar? Where was Beth?

Then two men stepped in front of him, blocking the view – one dressed head to foot in shimmering peacock blue, the other in black, with a face as white as a ghost's.

On both their heads were plumped up wigs of silvery grey curls.

Before Jack could move or speak, Peacock had him by the collar.

'*Voyons!* 'Ow did you come here?' A foreigner. French, by the sound of it.

'And whence did you come?' said Ghostface. His voice was English, Jack would have guessed – only he shouldn't have to guess, should he? There was something wrong with his accent. Like the place, like the clothes they both wore.

Jack began to point behind him, where the cellar door should have been. His hand was halfway up when a loud crash sounded.

'Unhand that boy!'

It was Kit. Roaring drunk, tugging at his sword hilt.

'Unhand him, I say, or . . .' Kit blinked hard, as he marked the change from cellar to marketplace – then he shook his head, finished drawing his sword and pointed it straight at Peacock.

Behind him, a flimsy door swung back and forth. Not the cellar door – a wooden shed, leaning up against the side of a building with lighted windows and sounds of music and wild revelry filtering out. Inside the shed, a bench with a hole in the seat. A privy stench wafted up from the darkness below.

Jack realized that the grip on his collar was gone. Peacock was two paces back, out of range of Kit's rapier; and somehow, he already had a sword out and ready.

'*En garde, cochon!*' Peacock whipped his sword back and forth. A flimsy-looking thing it was, with a gilded blade. Not a fighting sword at all.

Kit saw it, and giggled; but his eyes still followed the tip, deadly serious.

What was this place? Who were these people? How had Kit already managed to start a fight?

Kit feinted, slashing hard. The peacock turned the thrust aside neatly.

'Not bad, Mon*sewer*.' Kit nodded, as if the man had passed a test.

'Mock me, do you?' Peacock's red lips curled, a cupid's bow in his powdered face. He kissed the air, weaving his blade in lazy circles.

The two men circled each other, their points twitching a few inches apart. Jack spied a loose cobble, and bent down to pick it up. A cobble to Peacock's head would make it a short fight.

'I think not.' A sharp edge appeared at Jack's throat.

He looked up into Ghostface's smile.

The man kept his sword at Jack's throat. His face was dead white, like something carved out of bone. Tiny black patches were dotted over his skin – a heart at one cheekbone, a lily-flower at the wick of the mouth – like elegant flies on white sugar. His smell filled Jack's nostrils – an expensive stink like attar of roses.

Jack dropped the stone.

'Good boy,' said Ghostface. 'I think your friend is about to die.'

'No he ain't.'

Kit was good at fighting. He'd fought Nicholas Webb and his flying dagger without batting an eyelid. He was the best swordsman in London. Even when he was drunk.

There! Kit swiped low and hard, and the peacock didn't step back fast enough. The tip of Kit's sword slashed across his shin, drawing blood.

'So,' Kit laughed, springing back. 'Had enough?'

'*Pas du tout*,' said the peacock.

'It won't be long now, you know,' said Ghostface in Jack's ear. He could have been talking about the weather.

The peacock and Kit darted back and forth. Blades clashed in a quick flurry – then they were apart again, eyes narrowed, breathing hard. Jack followed every move. One step – two – the peacock moving dainty as a dancer, his point circling in the air, slow, slow . . .

One of his feet caught on a cobble, and he stumbled. For a moment, his guard dropped, his sword dragging on the ground as he tried to balance.

'Aha!' cried Kit, leaping into the attack.

'Sa-sa!' said the peacock. His sword flicked up, snake-fast. A spatter of loose mud flew straight into Kit's eyes.

The peacock stamped forward into a lunge, brushing Kit's sword aside. At the last, Kit swivelled and blocked the blow with his left hand. The blade sliced across his fingers.

Kit staggered away. He tried to wipe the mud from his eyes, but only washed them with blood. His hand was a mess.

He couldn't see.

'Watch out!' cried Jack.

'Leave them to it,' said Ghostface. He tensed his sword against Jack's throat, forcing his head back.

The peacock grinned and swept forward, his blade glinting crimson.

Now Jack was scared.

Somehow, half blind and scrambling backwards, Kit parried two killing stabs – one to the throat, one to the heart.

On the peacock's third thrust, Kit's feet moved so fast that Jack lost track. He dodged the blow, then twisted his sword right inside the Frenchman's guard. Their blades squealed, hilts locked together. Kit gave the man a hard shove.

The peacock yelped as he went flying. His flimsy sword skittered away across the cobbles in the other direction.

'Your friend fights well,' said Ghostface. Jack marked the surprise in his voice.

'Yield,' snapped Kit, pointing his sword at the Frenchman. 'Or die like a dog.'

The peacock snatched a dagger from his belt and held it out in front of him with two hands.

Kit cackled. 'What will you do with that? Prick me?'

'Kill!' snarled the Frenchman.

There was an explosion and Kit was knocked backwards off his feet. A cloud of smoke rose up. Echoes banged back and forth across the square.

Kit was clawing at the breast of his doublet.

'You shot me.' Kit wiped his bloody hand across his mouth, and winced. 'With a *knife?*'

Now it was the peacock standing over Kit. A thin plume of smoke was still rising from the handle of the dagger. Jack had never seen anything like it.

'Don't!' he shouted.

'Oh it's too late for that, my friend.' Ghostface said. 'Malpas does not miss his shot.'

'Jack, my lad.' Kit gave a strange and gruesome grin. 'I'm very, very sorry.'

All of a sudden, Jack realized the blade was gone from his throat. He fell to his knees at Kit's side.

Kit took a breath, and it sounded strange – bubbling, rasping. A trickle of blood was running from his mouth. There was a neat black hole in his coat, just over the heart.

'Fetch help! You ain't killed him,' said Jack. 'He can't die.'

96

'Oh, I can you know.' Kit gave a long, slow sigh. Blood was leaking from his mouth, all the colour draining from his face.

'Kit? No! Stay with me.'

'Sixteen shillings – thruppence – ha'penny,' Kit whispered. His eyes rolled back into his head.

'Kit!'

He did not breathe again. Jack shook his body, pounded on it. Kit's head wobbled like a doll's.

'For a drunkard, that was a brave death.' The Frenchman was fiddling with his dagger. Jack marked a tube of dull-coloured metal sticking out from the hilt. A smell of gunpowder.

'Brave,' Ghostface agreed. 'Perhaps a touch theatrical.'

Jack glared wildly from Ghostface to Peacock. This couldn't be. It was all too quick. Who were they? How had they killed Kit? How was there a privy where the cellar stairs should be?

He looked about for help. The square had gone very quiet. People watched – but from a safe distance. Not one of them wanted any part of this.

Jack heard a door opening, and a blast of music. A group wobbled out from the main building beyond the privy, moving towards them – a fat drunk with two giggling wenches on his arms.

'They've murdered my friend!' said Jack. 'Quick! Fetch help!'

Ghostface caught the man's eye, and bowed.

The peacock blew a kiss.

The women turned and ran inside. The man made a strangled noise, and fled away across the square as fast as his boots would carry him. The sky was lightening now, black to grey, and Jack could clearly see the rows of giants' palaces and the marble columns that fronted them.

'Come back!' Jack shouted. 'It's murder!'

The man ran on, tiny as an ant against those towering buildings. Jack's eyes filled with tears. He made a grab for Kit's sword. The peacock kicked it away, keeping his own sword ready.

'I think no. That was no murder,' he said. 'A question of honour. I venged an insult, as my lord will assuredly testify. No one will believe the lies of a—'

'What a prodigious great beetle.'

Jack whipped round. Ghostface was stooping over something small and dark on the ground. The imp. He picked it up between long, elegant white fingers.

'Imp,' said Jack. 'Kill them.'

The imp did not move.

Ghostface's eyes were pale green, with a mocking spark. He gazed into Jack's face, like someone trying to make out a difficult passage in a book.

'Did you just order this beetle to kill me?'

Perhaps the imp was dead. Like Kit. Jack had brought

them through that door. He had killed them both.

Where was Beth?

'The boy is an idiot,' said the peacock. 'His friend was such.'

'An idiot. There's a thought.' Ghostface slipped the imp in his pocket, and pulled out a small golden box. Opening it, he took a pinch from inside and held his fingers to his nose.

'Malpas . . .' Ghostface sniffed hard, tilted his head back, and sniffed again. His eyelids fluttered. 'I ask you, *cher* Malpas: what are we to do?'

The peacock shrugged.

'Why not take him where we take all our most interesting idiots?' said Ghostface.

The peacock gave a short laugh. 'But you do not joke? *C'est sérieux?*'

'Quite serious, Malpas. Where else to take such an obvious lunatic?'

'Very well.' Peacock grabbed Jack under the arm and hauled him to his feet. Ghostface took his other arm. His grip was like a spider on its prey, tight and remorseless.

They dragged him away. Leaving Kit lying dead on the cobbles.

'No! I won't!' Jack tried to break free. 'I'm not a lunatic.'

'No?' said Ghostface. 'How interesting.'

They dragged Jack on across the square. The freshening

sky revealed barrows filled with cherries, oranges and nodding lily-flowers. Standing behind them were carters: women in tattered silks and thick-painted faces; grubby children with baskets full of roses.

They watched Ghostface and Peacock take Jack away and not one of them moved to help.

Big fish, these two. What old Sharkwell would have called big toothy sea-bastards.

They bore Jack on into the far corner of the square where a row of horse-drawn chariots waited, each with a dirty-looking coachman.

And despite everything else, Jack was astonished.

A dozen horse-drawn chariots. Jack had only seen one in all his life: it belonged to the Earl of Essex, the richest man in England. He'd heard the Queen had one too, though he'd never seen it.

Here were a dozen, all lined up in a row.

Again he tried to squirm free, but the grip on his arms was hopelessly tight.

They marched up to the nearest chariot. Ghostface muttered something to the driver, and then Jack was being bundled into a stuffy box with leather-lined seats leaking horsehair.

The chariot creaked as the driver climbed onto his perch. A crack of a whip, a groan of the wheels and they were rattling off, gathering speed into a trot.

'What I still can't make out, is where they came from,' said Ghostface. 'There of all places. Quite the *devilish* coincidence, eh?'

He looked Jack straight in the eye. *Devilish*. What did he know?

Jack didn't speak. How could he, when Kit was dead? Jack had dragged him through that door. He'd brought him to it.

A bubble of grief rose up his throat, threatening to burst.

He turned to the window. They were rolling down a broad street – more of the big stone buildings to either side, all straight lines and sharp points, nothing like London, nothing like anything.

All the time he knew Ghostface was watching him. He felt the man's stare like an ice-cold grip. Peacock had killed Kit, but there was something about this one that scared Jack more.

His calm. The mocking spark in his eyes.

Peacock was holding his weapon, with the blade pointing up. As Jack watched, he unscrewed a stubby barrel set into the hilt, cleaned and replaced it, drew out a tiny powder-horn from a box in his lap, and poured in gunpowder. Next came a bullet, tamped down with an elegant jewelled ramrod.

A dagger-pistol – another piece of madness to add to all the rest.

Ghostface watched Jack all the while, eyes flicking over him taking things in, like a knowing dealer reckoning up horseflesh. Jack's eyes did the same. The man's coat was open at the front, with a solid coating of jewels and gold lace beneath.

A rich man. A man who knew no obstacles. A man who was above the law.

Ghostface was still staring back at Jack. His white-powdered nostrils flared like a wolf scenting blood.

'Why are you dressed like that, Jack?' he said. 'Jack is your name, isn't it?'

A man who missed nothing. A man to be feared.

'Where are we going?' said Jack.

'To Bethlem hospital. Do you know the place?'

Jack didn't blink. Yes, he knew the place – Bedlam, the madhouse, the spoonyard.

Bethlem Hospital was in London. Not here, wherever *here* was.

It was impossible. Mad.

'This ain't London.'

'Are you quite certain? You're not familiar with the sights? If you've not seen Covent Garden before, surely you recognize the Strand?'

Ghostface nodded at the street rolling past outside.

Jack glanced out of the window. This was not the Strand. All he saw was more of those strange giant palaces.

And then, peeking from behind a grand arch, the river – a gloomy surge, swirling and eddying as the tide dragged it down to the sea. The smell, seeping into the chariot, was unmistakeable to any Londoner – dead fish, rotting reeds, inlets choked with waste and offal.

'No,' Jack whispered.

He thought of the dream that woke him that morning. How he'd flown over London and seen all those buildings jumbled together. Huts and houses and strange marble palaces.

And then, as if it was part of the dream, he heard the voice of Dr Dee.

Time runs differently for devils.

Jack forced himself to look up at Ghostface.

'What year is it?'

'What *year?*' Ghostface glanced quickly at the peacock. The peacock shrugged.

'What year . . . ?' said Ghostface, squinting down at Jack.

'Please!' Jack said.

'Remarkable,' he said. 'What year do you think it is?'

'Please,' said Jack. 'Just tell me.'

Ghostface pursed his lips. 'Well, boy, if you really don't know . . .' his eyes narrowed, watching Jack's face. 'This is the year of our Lord, 1792.'

Chapter 8

The carriage rattled fast through empty streets. East, skirting the river, north up Fleet Market, east again; a brief delay at Smithfield, where cattle and drovers still clogged the streets, just as they had two centuries before; out onto Cheapside, onwards to Poultry and then north once more.

Had Jack been thinking clearly, he might have recognized the few buildings that survived from his London – the Temple, a church or two, an old stone well – but he was barely able to think at all.

He certainly wasn't alert enough to notice the most important change.

Ever since he'd got the Alkahest stain on his hand, London had been an itchy city for Jack, prickling with devil heat. But now, through the whole carriage ride from

Covent Garden to Bedlam, his hand didn't so much as twitch.

But Jack didn't notice – and that was hardly surprising.

Kit killed. Beth lost. The imp a dead weight in Ghostface's pocket. Two hundred years had gone by in the single turn of a key.

The year of our Lord, 1792.

Jack couldn't grasp it. Each time he tried his thoughts slid away, like a nimble wrestler greased with hog-fat.

A row of trees flashed past the window, and they passed into open fields. The carriage swept on down a broad drive-way with more trees to either side. Mist hung soft over the grass.

'And here we are,' said Ghostface.

'This ain't . . .' said Jack.

'Bedlam? I assure you, it is.'

In Jack's time, Bedlam madhouse had been a loathsome place – mewling naked wretches huddled under a caved-in roof – a place of filth and starvation with no hope of release. Only the truly mad would ever seek shelter there.

Now, the building rising through the mist was broader and higher than the great hall at Westminster. Its two sweeping wings glittered with a hundred glass windows. The gatehouse alone would have done for an earl.

The carriage settled on its springs with a sigh. The sun

was rising now, streaking the sky with gold. On top of the gates, two marble giants lay sprawled on their sides. One was chained, howling defiance. The other stared upwards with empty, idiot eyes.

Ghostface opened the door and jumped down. The peacock stayed with Jack, watching him.

Jack glared out of the window, wanting to scream like the stone giant. Kit dead, Imp dead, Beth vanished.

His whole world vanished, come to that.

And if he didn't do something sharp, he would be locked up. Bedlam: even prettied up, the madhouse was worse than any prison. The horror of it made him reach for the door – and then he heard a low metallic click, and the peacock's dagger-pistol was out.

'I do not miss, boy.'

The peacock smirked. Jack sank back in his seat.

Soon after that, two large men in matching blue coats came over carrying a chair. They hauled Jack out of the carriage, bound him to the chair by his wrists, and carried him aloft to the gates. Ghostface was waiting.

'So here we must part, my dear.'

'I ain't mad,' said Jack, desperate now.

'Oh? What are you then?'

Jack couldn't answer that. '*Please*.'

'Don't fret. They will keep you safe. You will see me again – depend on it.'

Ghostface smiled, raised his hand and gave a little wave.

The porters lifted Jack and carried him through the gates.

An arrow-straight path, bordered by low, neat-cut hedges, led on to the main building. Neatly trimmed lawns stretched out to either side. Jack could see a few white-dressed figures shambling about on the grass – lady lunatics, taking the air, guarded by more of the men in blue coats. One woman pulled at her close-cropped hair, muttering. Two more followed each other round and round in circles, reaching out to the sky.

A little further off was a single solitary figure. As he drew closer, Jack saw it was another white-clad woman. Her head swung very slowly, tracking him as he passed.

Her eyes were dark and seemed huge in her fine, pale face. Jack could feel her stare brushing his shoulder blades, all the way up the steps and into the palace.

Inside, someone was screaming. The echoes hung in the high marble spaces of the entrance hall, along with a faint smell of steeping cabbage. The porters set him down. Jack felt tiny, like a beetle in a ballroom. A beetle on its back, unable to move.

The porters rumbled out. As soon as he was alone, Jack started working his wrists back and forth, trying to loosen the ropes. His struggles only made the knots bite deeper.

Up ahead of him, a sweeping staircase curved round on itself, leading to the upper floors. To his left and right were two thick-barred doorways. The chamber was bitterly cold, as if all this smooth, white stone were really carved from ice.

Faint noises seeped from behind the doors – a mumbling, rustling hubbub, pierced occasionally by whooping sobs or cackling laughter. Jack's teeth chattered at the cold. He tried to rouse himself, think of ways to escape; but every thought was bleak and flat. He did not know how much time passed before he heard footsteps on the stairs and looked up.

A man was standing at the head of the grand staircase. A long-faced woman in a clean white cap stood behind him.

'What have we here?' said the man.

Like all the others, there was something odd in his accent, something Jack couldn't quite put his finger on. The words were the wrong shape – just like the buildings, just like the clothes.

The man trotted briskly down the stairs, stopped in front of Jack, and leaned in to examine him.

'My name is Dr Isaac Keith. The lady there is my chief nurse, and her name is Damp.'

He was a foxy-looking cove – though from his disordered hair, his nightgown and his stockinged feet, Jack reckoned he'd just been roused from his bed. He didn't look over cheerful about that, either.

The doctor's gaze flicked over Jack's clothes, taking stock. His eyes were hard, like two hammered nails.

Jack stared at the floor, and kept silent. This seemed to amuse the doctor. He allowed himself a wintry smile, and pulled out a piece of paper from his pocket.

'Lunatic boy,' he read. 'Found raving in Covent Garden piazza. No knowledge where he was nor how he came there, and – well! Remarkable! Doesn't know what year it is!' The doctor drew back his head, and stared down his nose at Jack. 'Well? Nothing to say?'

Jack stayed silent.

'Now now,' said the doctor, 'that won't do you any good. You've caught my lord's interest. When my lord wants an answer, he gets it.'

He fingered Jack's ruff. 'Curious get-up . . .' he said. 'Anything to say? Are you an actor, or some such?'

'No,' said Jack.

'He speaks!' said Dr Keith. His nimble fingers went exploring down the buttons of Jack's doublet, undoing, feeling inside. He prodded and pushed at Jack's skull, peered up his nostrils, and peeled back his eyelids to stare deep into his eyes.

'Patient shows no cranial injury; pupils responsive to light. Phiz appears sound: no marks of pox.'

The doctor stared down at Jack as if he was a sum that didn't tally.

'Do you have a name, at least?'

'My name's Jack,' said Jack. 'I ain't mad.'

'Gad!' said the doctor, with a bark of laughter. 'Are you not, indeed? Your case is much graver, then. As my lord says, you are *interesting.*'

Jack looked down at the floor. He didn't like that word.

The doctor cocked his head. 'Odd clothes, queer speech . . .' He gave a brisk nod. 'If you're not mad, you'll know the answer to this: who's our king?'

'King?' said Jack, unable to keep the surprise out of his voice.

'A simple question: who is the monarch, the chief personage of our commonwealth, our noble and most esteemed sovereign?'

Jack had no answer. Queen Bess, dead too. Of course she was: no one lived for ever.

'No? Very well. Damp – the men's gallery. Cell number eight. I'll send porters. Time for my breakfast, I think.'

Dr Keith turned snappily on his heel and went back up the stairs.

While they waited for the porters to arrive, Jack tried to think how to make a run for it when they untied him.

Behind him, he heard the door open. A confused babbling filled the room. The lady lunatics who had been exercising outside were coming back in.

Coming against their will, clearly. The doors weren't even closed behind them before one of the women started screeching like a cat. Another began cursing, high and shrill. Damp's harsh voice shouted for silence, but the ladies didn't stop. They got wilder. Jack heard slaps and punches, the commotion getting fierce. He craned his neck and saw Nurse Damp wrestling with a woman who kicked and screamed and clawed at her face.

This might be his chance, if he could topple the chair. They hadn't tied his ankles . . .

The woman broke loose, running free. She was going for the stairs. Damp bellowed for help. More women were running about, chased by men in blue coats.

Jack rocked hard to the side. His chair fell to the ground. He tried to get his feet up underneath him, but there wasn't enough slack.

Someone grabbed Jack's hand.

He pulled back, and saw her face – eyes blazing dark, pale lips parted – staring down at him out of a frame of tufty, short-cropped hair. A thick smell, dark honey and fiery liquor, wafted off her.

Jack's heart thumped once, very hard. It was the woman from the garden.

'Help me,' she said.

Jack felt a throb of heat pulse through the hand she was holding. The Alkahest hand. As if a devil were near – only now, clothed inside the heat like bone inside flesh, was a cold so deep it made him cry out.

'Help me,' said the woman.

Jack's hand throbbed, cold within the hot.

Where her eyes had been were two holes filled with darkness. A darkness that moved. A darkness that *crawled*.

Jack stopped breathing.

'Help me,' she mouthed again, but Jack didn't hear the words this time. He couldn't hear anything now except for the buzzing in his head.

They dragged her away, but Jack could still hear it. A rustling, and a buzzing, like a cluster of flies trapped against a windowpane.

Flies that were her eyes.

Flies that were the Swarm.

The men's ward was a long, gloomy, high-vaulted chamber. The cells lay off it behind barred doors. Jack didn't struggle as they carried him. He was still mumped with the fear of what he'd seen.

The Swarm had followed him here.

Cell number eight was small and bare. There was a large

112

iron ring stuck in the middle of the floor, with two long chains attached. A half-moon window was set in one corner. A sad clump of straw was piled below it. There was nothing else.

It was bitterly cold.

The two porters bore him down to the floor, holding him by the arms and legs. Jack wriggled, but they were too strong. They crouched there like statues in the middle of the cell, until Nurse Damp and Dr Keith came in. The nurse was carrying a large pair of shears.

'Prepare the boy,' said Keith.

Nurse Damp tested the edge of the shears against her finger, and gave a tight little nod. The porters tightened their grip on Jack's limbs. Damp crouched down at Jack's feet, and tugged off his boots. Then she went to work with her shears. In a flurry of short quick snips, she cut Jack's clothes from his body – first his doublet and shirt, and then his britches and hose.

Damp was fast. Within a minute, Jack was naked.

'Now: ventilate his brains.'

She moved round behind Jack, where he couldn't see her. One of the porters held his head still. Jack could sense the sharp blades of the shears, inches from his skull.

'Now then,' said the doctor, 'when you come to thank me, you will remember that your cure started here: Keith's particular remedy. Fresh air on the scalp, to draw the vapours out. You are lucky, my boy, to live in our present enlightened age.'

'I ain't mad,' said Jack.

'Oh really? Then tell me this. Answer me straight and I'll let you go. Who's our monarch?'

'I don't know,' said Jack.

'Well then: we proceed.'

Damp took a handful of hair and cut, fast and close. The tips of the shears dug into Jack's scalp as she moved on to the next clump. Dr Keith watched as the nurse sheared Jack's head like a sheep. After a while she changed over to a razor blade, working with sure, practised movements as she scraped away the stubble, not cutting Jack above three or four times. When it was finished, the doctor gave a satisfied nod.

'Chain him fast for now.' The doctor patted Jack on his new-shaven head. 'You'll be better soon, you'll see. Reason conquers all.'

He turned and stalked out of the cell. The porters snapped the leg irons around Jack's ankles. Before she left, Nurse Damp threw a thin white shift at his feet.

The door slammed shut. Jack heard the bolt being drawn across on the other side. There was a small hatch in the door, also bolted.

No keyhole. No peace either – through the thick planks

came the rumble of Bedlam at breakfast, shrieks and moans and the rattle of chains.

Jack smelled porridge.

His chains were just long enough to shuffle to the wall beneath the window. The wind whistled in, knifing across his skin.

Shivering, he pulled the shift over his head, and buried himself in the straw. At least it was clean. Slowly he began to feel a little warmer.

He tried not to think of the woman with the flies in her eyes.

He tried even harder not to think of Kit.

Beth could be anywhere out in that strange new London. She wouldn't have been locked up, not her. The shame of being caught made Jack's cheeks burn red. He could hear Kit's mocking laugh already.

Except Kit would never laugh again.

Kit wasn't meant to die. Not like that. Jack should have been used to the taste of death by now, but the truth was it always tasted fresh. Fresh and bitter as unripe fruit.

Beth lost. Kit dead. Everyone he'd ever known dead, come to think of it, and their children and grandchildren too. Even the imp was lost. This was Lud's gift to him – the freedom the King Devil had bestowed. Hundreds of years gone by in a great rushing torrent, and everything he'd ever known washed away.

He burrowed deeper into the straw. When he closed his eyes again he saw another pair of eyes staring back, wide and haunted, with a swarming darkness inside them.

He knew what it was.

Help me, she'd said.

That was a bitter joke, when he couldn't even help himself.

Chapter 9

Grey light on grey stone as London woke up to a cold November morning. Coffee by the pint, stamping feet, and *What's the news, Fred?* Rumours of more horrors in France.

Satisfied, the city blew its nose once, fiercely into its handkerchief, and set about its customary business. By the middle of the morning, seven fortunes would be made and eight lost.

Bedlam, though, was a world apart. Curled up inside his straw, Jack felt a tiredness like he'd never known. Sleep took him, plummeting deep like a stone.

In his dream the storm clouds were black as night. In the canyons between them the wind whistled and howled. Jack flew fast before it. He was looking for Beth – but the city was empty.

Towers of glass, tall as mountains. A thousand ships at anchor in the Thames. Marble pavements, great grey domes, sad-eyed statues in the high places. He searched and searched, but the towers and the ships and the pavements were all empty.

Jack flew over it all, and as he flew it began to fall apart.

Tiny holes at first – but as soon as Jack saw them they were everywhere, shimmering and darkening, joining together. Deadlight dots became lines became cracks, seething over everything. Unshaping, disrupting, ravenous.

Here – a tower tottered; there – a roof collapsed. Where the tower had stood was a hole, not just in the ground but a hole in everything; and the Swarm came boiling up out of it.

Streets crumbled into foulness. The water of the river turned rank. A hot, choking stench rose up. So fast – like watching a corpse rot away in seconds.

Where was Beth? He had to save her.

The triumphant buzzing of a billion flies filled his ears. The wind failed. His wings were too weak. He fell; and as he fell, he saw her – a solitary figure, walking amongst the ruins.

Her face turned up to meet him. A cold face, beautiful and pale as the moon.

The wrong face.

Her eyes were wide and black. She opened her mouth to speak. Flies crawled out over her lips and across her face.

'Help me,' she said.

*

Jack bolted fast awake. He felt panic at first, not knowing where he was. Then he remembered. Where. When. And the panic gripped harder.

Bedlam. The year of our Lord, 1792. *Two hundred years.*

He had to get out. Find Beth and Kit and the imp. Except that was wrong, too. Kit was dead. The grief was worse now, as if sleep had given it time to grow and mature.

Kit was dead, and Jack had brought him to it. For several minutes, that was all he could think or feel. It pressed down on him, like a heavy stone over his heart.

Finally, Jack sat up. Something tumbled off his chest and tinkled across the floor.

Lud's key. The very cursed thing that had brought him here.

Jack snatched it up, dragged his chain to the window and drew back his arm, ready to throw it as far away from him as he could.

He stopped, arm outstretched, heart thudding.

Beth, Kit, the imp – all dead or lost. Dr Dee – long, long dead. The key was the last thing he had – and it had brought him here, and followed him here, and two hundred years had passed in a single night.

Cursed or not, the key was powerful.

Stop panicking.

Think.

119

The window looked out over miles and miles of rooftops, spires, towers and chimneys. Beth was out there, somewhere. Jack was locked up in here.

Get out.

Find Beth.

Find a way home.

Jack waited for his breath and pulse to slow, and then tried the key on his shackles. It didn't fit. He wasn't surprised. This was not a key for opening ordinary locks.

He shuffled back to the corner where his straw was piled. Using the key, he scraped away at the crack where the wall met the floor till he'd made a deep enough groove, then wedged the key down inside it. He piled the straw back on top of it, and sat down to think.

It was simple really. All he had to do was find a way to get these chains off, and then escape. And he had to do it before Ghostface came back.

Jack had hardly begun making his plan when a little hatch in the door snapped open, and a deathly white face looked in on him.

For a horrible instant, Jack thought it was Ghostface come already – till he realized it was some other white-powdered gimblet. This one had painted his lips red, too. He peered in at Jack for half a minute, sneered, and left.

Through the open hatch, Jack heard soft laughter and excited chatter from the gallery outside. A loud voice sang out that 'pastries, hot pastries' were for sale. It sounded more like a theatre audience than anything else.

Strange.

Dragging his chains behind him, Jack limped over to the door and peered out. It had been dark when they bundled him in here. Now daylight streamed in from windows high up in the walls. He was looking out onto a much larger space – a broad, echoing gallery, and a scene of utter madness.

The men's and ladies' galleries at Bedlam were a fashionable meeting-place for all who could secure a ticket. The visitors came to taunt the mad and titter in delicious horror. But most of all they came to flaunt, and flirt and be seen.

At first all Jack could see was strange: shimmering rainbows of silk and three-cornered hats; flour-stained aprons and scuffed workman's boots; powdered wigs and greasy pigtails.

Quickly though, with his sharp nipper's eyes, he shaped out the pattern of it. It really was like a theatre, even if it was awkward to pick the players from the audience here.

As Jack watched and pondered, his face went sly and distant – the same as it did when he was picking a lock, or scoping out a likely gull.

'You new, young fellow?' A twinkly-eyed face appeared at the hatchway, interrupting Jack's study. An elderly man with a jittery smile, dressed in a faded, rust-coloured coat.

His hand scrabbled in his pockets.

'Here's gold,' he said, very excitable. 'Thirty guineas enough?'

He winked, and passed a clump of soggy straw through the hatch, pressing it into Jack's hand.

Not a visitor, then.

'Thank you,' said Jack.

'Aha! You're a quick one, ain't you just?' The man lowered his voice to a whisper, and pointed at the crowd. 'Muscovites. Watch out for 'em.'

'I will.' Jack had a thought. 'Oh, can you tell me who's king?'

'Aha!' said the man. 'Precisely!' He grinned, tapped the side of his nose. 'Who's king, eh? Who indeed, my bright lad! Knew you were a sharp one, *knew* it from the moment I saw you.'

He winked, and tiptoed away. Jack's eyes narrowed as he watched him pass down the gallery. He was a slight man, no taller than Jack. He stopped beside a group of wigged gentlemen, hovering, awaiting their attention. Just for a moment there was no way for them to tell if he was an inmate or just a humble old pauper in a threadbare coat, scraping to his betters. Then he plucked out a clump of straw and began to speak, and the gentlemen roared with laughter.

Looking past him, Jack saw a particularly sad specimen

of a lunatic – a bald, goggle-eyed man who'd torn off his clothes and was capering lobster-naked before a bevy of tittering ladies.

One of them threw the man a penny. He bowed and bobbed and snatched it up from the floor.

Jack hissed like a cat.

'Hey!' he shouted. 'Hey, ladies! Sweet ladies!'

The group were looking over. One of them started in his direction, pulling the rest along with her.

'Well?' she said, peering in at Jack. 'What is it?'

Jack heard giggles from behind her, her friends crowding in for a peep.

'A bold scamp, I declare,' one of them said.

'Well?' said the first lady again. Then, sounding disappointed, 'You don't look very mad.'

'I ain't,' said Jack. 'I'm just . . . a bear!'

He started to throw his limbs about. The chains weighed him down, but that was good if anything – a bear should dance heavy.

'I do declare he looks like one.'

Jack raised his head, and grunted.

'He's quite mad, after all.'

Jack pawed at his chest. He stooped down, grabbed a handful of straw and scattered it over his head.

'How sad,' said the lady.

And then came a tinkling sound, and Jack saw the penny

spinning to a stop on the floor, and he stopped dancing.

'Dance some more, bear.'

Jack picked up the coin.

'I say dance some more, and you'll have another penny.'

Jack didn't look up.

One side of the coin showed a half-naked lady with a spear and a shield. The other showed a fat man with puffy eyes and laurel leaves around his head.

He didn't look much of a king.

In the evening, Nurse Damp and Dr Keith came by on their rounds.

'Now then!' Dr Keith strutted in, perky as a rooster. 'How do you, Jack? I've news! His lordship returns to visit you tomorrow.'

Jack had no intention of waiting in Bedlam for Ghostface's return.

'You know I'm not mad,' he said. 'Take off my chains. Please.'

Keith didn't agree: instead, Nurse Damp set six leeches to Jack's shaven scalp – 'to draw the nonsense out,' the doctor said. Two porters in blue coats held his arms to stop him pulling the foul little beasts off.

The leeches fed. They felt wet and cold against his skin. After much too long, they began to drop away, gorged with Jack's blood. Nurse Damp caught them in a bucket. Dr Keith waited until the last had tumbled down with a soft, wet plop.

'How do you now, Jack?' he asked.

'I . . . I feel better,' said Jack. 'Aye, much better. Cured. You can unchain me now.'

'You may walk the gallery when you show some *measurable* sign of progress,' said Dr Keith. 'So. Tell me now: who's king?'

He shot Jack a foxy look under his brows.

'I will if you unchain me,' said Jack.

'Who's king?'

Jack thought of his penny, safely hidden along with the key – the fat-faced man with the laurel wreath, and the letters engraved on the coin's rim. Beth had only started teaching him to read these past few months, and it had taken him a long time to spell them out.

'George,' said Jack. 'King George the Third – God bless him.'

'Well said!' Dr Keith's soft hands stroked Jack's scalp, poking and prodding every bump in his skull. 'I knew it would be so: the noble leeches!'

'Yes, the . . .' Jack couldn't quite bring himself to call the leeches noble. 'Thank you, sir.'

'Sound science, you see!' Dr Keith patted Jack on the head, delighted with himself. 'Damp, strike off the boy's fetters. Tomorrow you will walk the gallery with the others. See, lad, how progress is rewarded?'

Chapter 10

The next morning after breakfast, Jack's cell door was left open.

Even though his shackles were off, Jack made himself wait. The hours gnawed at his nerves – Ghostface might arrive any minute – but there was no hurrying the plan. Three burly bluecoats prowled about, and two more guarded the gate that led out towards the entrance hall.

He knew he would only have one chance at this. He sat in his cell and tried to distract himself as the visitors slowly began to arrive.

A printseller had set up shop in one corner of the gallery. In a carrying voice he cried up his penny sheets showing the most infamous inmates of Bedlam. Jack soon knew them all by heart: George Brown, the Dulwich black-smith who thought he was a kettle; Sir James Pottinger, the demented huntsman galloping his invisible horse after an imaginary golden stag. The visitors' favourite was wicked Ada Seward, the Lady Libertine, who had been driven mad by her own wild misconduct. She'd taken the devil himself as her lover, it was said; and it was her engraving, 'shewing all nine of her vices', that was asked for time after time.

The story made Jack think of the woman from the garden – the woman from his dream. She was Ada Seward, he was sure of it. All the more reason to get out of here. All the more reason to run, as far and fast as possible.

Even so, it was well into the afternoon before Jack judged the crowd was ripe. Sixty or seventy people in the gallery – visitors mixed in amongst the mad, peeping in at cell doors, chattering in little groups together.

It was time. Jack went over to the corner of his cell, pushed aside the straw and dug out his penny and Lud's key from the groove he'd made. Clutching the key in his left fist, the penny in his right, he sidled out into the crowded gallery.

It felt strange to be leaving the cell. The other inmates mostly ignored him, wrapped up in their private worlds. A fat man wearing a paper crown offered to make him a duke. A flame-haired musician hummed to himself and played an invisible fiddle. Another man stood staring at the wall, his face inches from the plaster. As Jack passed by, he turned.

'Can you find me?'

Jack couldn't meet his mole-ish, blinking eyes. He shook his head, looked away, and saw the Muscovites man, standing alone in the far corner of the gallery, watching the visitors with a look of dark suspicion.

Jack sidled up.

'Muscovites,' muttered the man, speaking out of the side of his mouth.

'I know it,' said Jack. 'Sniffed 'em out meself.'

'Good lad!' He reached into his pocket and slipped Jack a pinch of straw. 'I knew you were a game one the instant I saw you.'

Jack nodded wisely. 'I say they're up to no good. Hatching a plot.'

'Always are,' the man agreed.

'I think it's time for that caper we spoke of.'

'Caper?'

'Scope 'em out. Spy on 'em.'

'But of course! Observe their motions – the very thing!' said the man. 'Oh, you're a likely one, ain't you, ain't you just?' He broke off, narrowing his eyes. 'Speak their lingo?'

'Oh aye,' said Jack. 'All I need now is your clothes.'

'Oh?' said the man. He frowned, and looked Jack up and down.

'Don't you see?' said Jack. 'I need a disguise.'

'Of course!' The man's face cleared. 'Disguise – dissimulation . . . yes, yes!' He nodded, stroking his chin. 'Capital! Come, we'll make the exchange in my chambers.'

Five minutes later, Jack strolled out of the man's cell dressed in a rust-brown coat and breeches, and with a red spotted handkerchief wrapped around his bare scalp. Lud's key lay small and heavy in a pocket of the coat.

He ambled over to the printseller, and exchanged his penny for a sheet on Sir James Pottinger, the demented huntsman, complete with woodcut illustrations. By the time he reached the gate, he looked engrossed – staring down at the sheet, lips moving, occasionally tutting to himself.

He drifted into the tail end of a group who were waiting to leave. He squinted at the sheet, and drew it closer to his face.

The group began to move out. As he passed the porters at the gate, Jack forced down a rising tide of excitement, an urge to run as soon as he was through. Instead, he shuffled along with the rest, face buried in the printed sheet, till they'd reached the cold marble entrance hall with its massive double doors.

The doors were open. The group did not go towards them. They were walking straight across the hall, heading for another barred gate opposite the one they'd just passed through.

Jack could see daylight streaming in, feel the live air of

the outside. He sidestepped, twisted free of the group – steady now, *stroll* out the doors, down the steps into the gardens—

He turned back fast for the shelter of the group, his heart leaping in his throat.

Ghostface was coming up the steps.

Ghostface and Peacock, deep in conversation with Dr Keith.

Jack didn't think they'd seen him. He certainly didn't dare look up to check. He kept his head down, buried himself in the group, and let it sweep him along.

They passed out of the hall, through the barred gate and into another gallery – the ladies' gallery. Lady lunatics on all sides, grinning, scowling, laughing and weeping. One of them lifted her skirts, cackling, to dance a sailor's hornpipe. Someone threw her a coin. Jack's group began to disperse.

Ghostface was on his way to visit Jack. How long would it take them to realize he was gone? Three or four minutes at most, Jack reckoned. Right now they'd be in the main hall still. Give them a minute to pass through into the men's gallery? No: a minute was too much – they might be in the gallery already, they might see he was gone at any moment. He had to go *now*.

Jack turned to leave – and saw her.

It was the woman from the garden. The woman from his dream. Ada Seward, the devil's mistress.

She was locked up in a special, open-barred cell, set up so as many people as possible could see her. She was sitting on her bed, holding a stub of charcoal and gazing down at the floor. There was something impressive in her stillness.

Every inch of her cell walls was covered in drawings. Lines and lines of them – flies and scorpions, spiders and locusts; other things without names, marching around the walls, covering everything.

Ada Seward looked up. Her enchanted eyes fixed straight on Jack. Her fingers fluttered, peeled the air.

'Is it you?' she said. 'I knew you would come.'

Her voice was soft and certain. Her face—

No one else could see this, Jack knew. Only him: only with the devil-sight. His weird eye watered as he glimpsed it; his right hand burned with the Alkahest heat – all except for the black spot at his fingertip, which was stone, icy cold.

Her madness was alive. Beetles crept and twitched across her face. Moths hovered at her lips. And her eyes. Her eyes were not there at all. Where they should be, was nothing but thick black clusters of buzzing, creeping flies.

She came towards him, whispering.

'You! Are you Him? No, I think you are not. I think you are here to shut Him out. There is power in you. I see, I see, I saw . . .'

Jack was dimly aware of people turning to look. He

heard titters – they were enjoying the show. Ada Seward advanced towards the bars of her cage.

'She likes you, boy,' someone said.

Jack knew he should be running – Ghostface would come, someone would realize who he was – but instead, he found himself walking up to the bars. Walking to meet her.

Something had taken control of his feet.

It had power.

She came on slowly: closer, closer. The awful, shuddering creatures swarmed across her face, struggling against each other.

Against *her*, Jack thought.

Living stitches bound her mouth with trembling black threads. She was moving slower now. Fighting hard. Her hands gripped the bars, and she dragged herself forward, knuckles white with the effort.

Her face was inches away – bone pale, beautiful as the full moon, and *cold*. Her lips parted. Her breath clouded in the freezing air between them.

'Help me!' she whispered.

Cold-hot in his hand – cold at the fingertip, hot everywhere else. Boiling cold, frozen heat. Somehow they were both getting worse, and worse. Jack clamped his teeth against a scream.

His hand shot out and clutched the woman's face.

The swarm inside her squirmed at his touch. Flies buzzed

with hate. Her head jerked from side to side under his hand; and then they vomited out of her – out through her parted lips, out through her nostrils, out through her eyes like flaming tears. Jack shut his eyes. His chin flopped down against his chest. In the crowd behind him, someone screamed.

Time ran away and hid.

When it was over, they were both kneeling on the floor. Her face was resting against his hand. The hot-cold feeling was gone. His index finger was numb at the tip, and the whole of his arm was tingling.

Jack glanced at his hand, then stared with a growing horror.

The black spot had spread. The tip of his index finger now looked as if he'd dipped it in ink. Dark spider lines webbed out across his palm like blood rot. Black on red. One curse on top of another.

Ada Seward looked up at him. She blinked hard, once, like someone shaking off a bad dream.

'You made it go away,' she said. 'How . . . ?'

'There, you young dog!'

Jack was spun round as the blue-coated turnkey seized him by the shoulders. 'Meddle with the lady, would you? I'll—'

The man went rigid. His hands rose from Jack's shoulders, clutching at air.

A maggoty speck of blackness was crawling along his

133

upper lip, squirming its way into his nose. He fell to his knees.

Beyond him, the Swarm was everywhere. The bits that had landed on the walls or the floor were already beginning to fade, shrivelling up like salted slugs. But where they'd landed on the living . . .

The crowd were still gawping down at Jack and Ada Seward. No one but Jack could see the Swarm – wriggling beetles; blind, hungry grubs; twitching flies – frantically searching for a new home.

They raced across clothes and skin. They wormed in through ears and mouths and nostrils.

All Hell broke loose.

A woman in a red silk dress carefully set to shredding her bodice with her nails.

Her daughter clutched her mother's skirts and screamed for her to stop: the woman punched her in the face.

A grand old matron crouched beside them on all fours, rubbed against the mother's legs and licked at a puddle on the floor. She raised her head, arched her back and mewed like a cat.

Jack clambered to his feet, heart hammering. The Swarm was loose. He didn't want to see what came next.

'Wait!'

It was Ada Seward. She was reaching through the bars. The turnkey was writhing on the floor in front of her, clutching at his teeth. He'd dropped his keys; they were just out of her reach.

'Please . . .'

Her eyes darted down at the keys, then back up at Jack. 'Please.'

Jack kicked the keys through the bars. The turnkey stood up all at once like a puppet, and screamed in his face. His breath was cold, and foul. His eyeballs were filled with crawling blackness.

Jack ducked past him, but there was no end to the horror. Nightmare snatches wherever he looked. The victims raved and tottered, fleshed in their own particular terrors.

The woman in the red silk dress was clawing her own throat bloody.

A circle of children knelt over something on the floor, giggling to themselves as their arms rose and fell.

A wigged and powdered gentleman turned to his wife and bit her in the neck.

At the end of the gallery, people were struggling to get out. A frantic band of porters and nurses were pouring in the other way, trying to sort the mad from the sane. They were seizing the lunatics, throwing them to the ground, holding them down. They were bringing in chains.

Jack dove headlong into the scrum. He pressed himself in between two panic-stricken bodies and lowered his head.

A porter came barging past and collared a white-robed woman just behind Jack. Of course – this was the ladies' gallery. They wouldn't be looking for male slackwits. The doorway was close now, and once through it the crowd wouldn't stop: they'd stampede all the way out of here, carrying Jack with them. A gap opened up and he could actually see the open doorway, and the marble hall beyond it.

Jack froze.

Standing just beyond the door, observing the chaos, stood Ghostface. Their eyes met. He raised an eyebrow. He pointed at Jack, and shouted an order.

Someone grabbed him. This was it. No escape now, and they'd lock him up double fast after this . . .

Someone was weeping. Not a porter or a nurse: it was Ada Seward. She was wearing a long brown cloak over her Bedlamite shift, and she was weeping. She pulled Jack close, hiding his face, and stumbled towards the door.

'My husband!' she wailed. 'My husband! Oh – your father, my poor boy – they've murdered him!'

She held Jack tight, swirling him up in the protection of the cloak. He felt hands on his back, but they were pushing him on, helping him through.

'Thank you! Oh Lord! Please – doctor – my husband! They've—'

The crowd surged around them, carrying them onward.

They were out in the hall now. Jack peeked out from under the cloak: behind them Ghostface was searching through the crowd. Up ahead, two bluecoats struggled at the great double doors, trying to get them shut.

They didn't stand a chance. The panicked crowd surged past them.

Jack and Ada were out, running down the path towards the open gates, the cold air stinging Jack's lungs. Ada's hand in his.

'There they go!' a voice roared behind them. 'The woman and the boy! Fifty guineas to the man that catches 'em!'

Ada was gasping for breath as they rushed on through the gates and into the fields beyond.

Behind them, Bedlam raged and roared.

Chapter 11

They ran across the fields, through a thin, damp mist, ghostly shapes pursuing them. Shouting. Gaining ground.

Jack grabbed Ada's hand and ran faster. His own hand was still tingling, jangling . . . no time to think on it now. The shouts behind sounded very close.

Something big and grey loomed up, grew and sharpened into a row of houses.

'Here,' said Jack, diving into the first alley that offered – and then into an even narrower, grimmer way. Ada's palm felt warm, clasping him tight, her pulse fast beneath the skin.

His toes squelched and slipped in cold black mud. He'd forgotten what it was like, going barefoot.

'Where – are we going?' Ada panted.

Jack shook his head. Breath spent talking was breath wasted.

Left, right, and he was losing his bearings. He could hear heavy splashing feet – one turning behind? Two? The mist and the mazy turns played games with sound.

They came out into a long, paved yard. A doorway dark and yawning, a cart leaning on its shafts outside. No one watching – empty sacks in the bed of the cart – prime cover.

'Here! Down.'

Jack pulled Ada in beside him, dragging the scratchy hempen sacks on top.

The footsteps were close now, pounding off the stones. Ada was gasping for breath. Jack's heart was going like hammers.

'Who are you?' hissed Ada.

'Shh!'

They heard shouts. The footsteps clattered into the yard. Closer. Clatter-echo. Boots on paving.

And then the sound of them fading. The boots were going away.

'What *happened?*'

Jack thought of the shrieking Hell they'd come from – the Hell he'd unleashed from inside her – and shook his head. 'Not now.' He peered out from beneath the sacking. The yard was empty. 'Come on.'

They were still a long way from safe. Jack chose a path

that led away from the one he thought the pursuit had taken. Ada was muttering as she loped along, head down and breathless.

'Something happened. Something happened, something happened . . .' She looked at Jack. 'You. What did you do?'

'Wait. Hear that?'

Was it the sound of boots again? Jack couldn't be sure – couldn't even be sure if he'd heard anything at all, over the blood-thunder in his skull.

But now he could hear other noises, too – noises that called to him like water to a gasping fish. Rattling wheels, a woman scolding a child – a crowd. Lights up ahead, soft in the mist.

'This way.'

They ran out into a broad street, busy with foot traffic even on a miserable evening like this. Jack caught Ada's wrist.

'Slow. Walk.'

Walking was safer now. In this crowd, they were just two walkers amongst the rest. Jack's breath came easier. He caught himself thinking that they might be safe, and then remembered the Fourteenth Law: once you'd been scoped you didn't stop. Not until you were salted away by friends who'd deny you'd ever been born.

That was all very well when you had friends, had a

Family with Laws to protect each other. But Jack was quite alone here. The nearest thing he had to a friend was a beautiful lunatic who until today had—

Had what?

Had the Swarm inside her.

Jack glanced sidelong at Ada. She caught him looking.

'Those people,' she said. 'What did you do? I don't remember, it's all dark . . .' she shuddered. 'But then those poor people. I remember that.'

'You asked me to help you,' he said.

'Did I?' She frowned, then nodded. 'I think . . . yes.'

Ada's face was set, eyes staring straight ahead.

'You did help me,' she said after a while. 'I thank you. I can help you in return – you don't want to go back there, do you?'

Jack shook his head hard.

'Of course not,' said Ada. Then, half to herself, 'Where can we go?'

'A friend?' suggested Jack. 'Someone who can hide us?'

Ada nodded slowly. 'Yes,' she said. 'There's someone. Though we've a long walk, to reach his house tonight.'

Up ahead, a church bell was ringing. And here was the church itself, a dark grey shape in the mist. A big old church . . .

Ada peered at him curiously. 'Where are you from? I can't place your voice.'

141

Jack didn't answer. He could have said London – this *very same* London. But he didn't.

He was staring up at the church.

It was St Helen's, Bishopsgate. There was no mistaking that squat, sandstone fortress, even if they'd slapped an airy little spire on top.

St Helen's meant the Lasher. Jack clenched his hand, steeling himself for the burn. The Lasher was a devil, bound inside a stone statue from ancient times, deep beneath the church crypt; and it was one of the bad ones. The first time Jack came across it, he'd felt as if a bullwhip had been cracked across his palm: the pain hadn't gone away for days.

Now, though . . .

No Alkahest heat; no sign of the Lasher at all. Only the numbness in his finger, and the strange tingle where black faded to red.

He slowly let his hand relax.

'Hey,' said Ada. 'Hey!'

Jack blinked.

'Hey, it's them!' She took his hand and dragged him into a stumbling run.

'What?' said Jack.

'There, it's them, come on!' she said, and Jack looked back and saw them: three or four bulky bluecoats.

Beth would have known to keep walking, but it was too

late for that now: they were running, and the men were running too.

'Too far,' Ada panted. 'Never reach him.' She glared wildly about, veered left, then changed her mind and dragged Jack towards a turning, off to the right.

'Where are we going?

'Another friend – used to live this way. Hope she does still.'

The next moments passed in a desperate blur. They barely kept ahead of the pounding boots behind. The streets were against them, no matter how many twists and turns they made; and with the hunt in clear sight there was no point trying to hide.

At last she plunged into a quiet, empty street – wrong, wrong, thought Jack, this was a dead end – and then they were running straight for a smooth expanse of brick. Except here was some ivy, here was a doorway half hidden in the ivy, the ivy whipping at his face as Ada dragged him through it.

'Friend,' Ada muttered between breaths. 'Hide us. If she's here.'

The doorway led into a dingy yard, a square formed by the soot-streaked backsides of narrow tall houses. Ada dragged him straight across it to a back door – unlocked – and then straight up a pitch-dark flight of stairs to the second floor.

The door at the top was locked. Ada rapped on it. 'Kitty?'

There was a window on the landing, looking out over the yard. Through it, Jack saw the Bedlam bluecoats, running in through the ivy-covered door. One of the men spoke, and they spread out, each one heading for a different house.

'*Kitty!*' Ada hissed. She threw herself against the door. It didn't even rattle.

Jack looked at the door, and prayed it was locked and not bolted. The lock looked simple enough – though he hadn't practised the Black Art in months, and he had no tools . . .

Lud's key. Jack pulled it out of his pocket. It was no proper darksman's tool, too thick for fine work; but fine work wouldn't serve now, there wasn't time.

He jiggered the key's copper tip into the lock. Downstairs, someone banged on a door. Jack heard sleepy curses greet the disturbance. They'd soon move on, move upwards . . .

No: forget them. Forget everything except what's inside the lock. Remember Mr Smiles, poor old murdered Mr Smiles.

Gilks and picks, my ladderoon, all aspire to the station of a finger. Feel *the lock* – palpate it, I say – *stroke it as you would a blushing cheek.*

Lud's key was more like a thumb – thick, stronger than a finger, not so good for feeling things out, but very good for leverage. This lock had a square-section tumbler, he could feel that much. If Jack could find the right angle . . .

There. Wedge the key against the tumbler. Grip. Downstairs the voices – but he mustn't think of them.

Grip – and twist. If the tumbler snapped now, it was over. Jack twisted harder. The metal loop of the key bit into his fingers. Footsteps on the stairs now.

The lock turned. Ada was ready on the handle. She pushed, they tumbled inside, Jack eased the door shut behind them – softly now – and bolted it.

They were in a small stuffy room that smelled strongly of damp stockings. Cracked plaster on the walls, crumpled drifts of clothes in the corners, an immense canopied four-poster bed. A woman lay on the bed, sprawled back with her head to one side, as if she'd just been thrown down hard. The damp stockings were hanging over the fireplace. A few embers glowed in the grate – and along with a guttering candle on a table by the bed, provided the only light.

Ada put a finger to her lips, went over to the bed.

'Kitty,' she whispered.

No response. Ada picked up the candle and shone it in the woman's face.

'*Kitty.*'

Jack heard a heavy step on the landing, and then a hammering fist on the door behind him.

'Kitty it's me, it's Ada.'

145

Kitty screwed her eyes shut and moaned. She was very pretty, and she was either dreaming or drunk – her face slack and flushed, her eyes heavy. Her nightgown was very thin, and open at the front.

The hammering at the door continued.

'Don't like the galloping boys,' said Kitty. 'Tell them to stop.'

Ada shot a despairing look at Jack. 'Kitty, *you* must tell them. Wake up, for God's sake.' She put down the candle and gave Kitty a hard shake. Kitty pushed back indignantly.

'Who d'you suppose—' she said, and then Ada clamped a hand over her mouth. That did it: her eyes woke up, and she froze.

'*Shhh*,' said Ada.

Kitty gave a tiny nod.

'There's a man at the door,' Ada whispered. 'He's looking for me. For us.' Kitty's eyes moved to Jack, and widened. 'We're not here, you understand?'

Kitty didn't move.

Jack saw the handle turn, and then the door creaked as someone pushed against it.

'Open up! Open up in there!'

Ada took her hand away from Kitty's mouth. Kitty, still looking at Jack, gathered her nightgown up around her throat. She got up out of the bed.

'You two – in here,' she whispered.

Jack tiptoed over to the bed and climbed in, Ada pulling the sheets over them both. The bed was still warm. It smelled of sleep.

Ada took his hand, holding tight. He could feel her breath, hot and ticklish in the darkness.

Jack heard the door open. He tried to picture it. The Bedlam men at the door, the golden-haired beauty in her nightgown.

'What is it?' Her voice was soft and sleep-rumpled – just right, thought Jack. 'I was sleeping.'

Jack pictured the Bedlam bluecoats blushing, taken aback. That nightgown really was very thin.

'What is it?' Kitty's voice began to tremble. 'Please, you're scaring me . . .'

'Par'n, miss.' The voice a little hoarse. Ada squeezed Jack's hand, and he squeezed back in agreement: all well so far. 'Escaped lunatics, is what it is. Came this way: you see anything?'

'I told you, I was sleeping. What lunatics? Are they dangerous?'

'Wery dangerous, miss.'

'Oh dear, how terrible! But you will protect us, I hope? Please tell me you will.' A little catch in her voice now, and Jack had to admire the way she was playing it: the damsel in distress. Beth could hardly have done it better.

'We will do our utmost, miss.'

Jack imagined the bluecoats drawing themselves up a little straighter, very well satisfied with themselves.

'Please do! Why, I can hardly bear to think of it, raving fiends on the loose . . .'

'Quite so.' This was another voice, an older, drier-sounding man than the first. 'And if you should happen to remember anything . . . anything at all . . . there's money in it. Handsome reward, for any information leading to their capture.'

'I only wish I could help,' said Kitty.

Jack heard the door closing – footsteps on the landing – footsteps on the stairs, going down.

He breathed out. Ada let go his hand and pulled back the sheets.

Silence. Kitty still standing by the door. And then, unbelievably, she giggled.

'Ada, you scared the life out of me. I really thought you had come to murder me.'

Ada sat still, eyes narrowed, listening for the men outside. Jack was pretty sure they were safe here for now.

'How did you get in?' said Kitty. 'How did you get *out*? I heard they had you chained . . . I mean, I . . .' She stammered to a halt.

'Didn't come to visit me?' said Ada. 'Don't fret, I wouldn't remember if you had. I don't remember any of it, right up—'

She glanced over at Jack. 'Up to today. Do you think they've gone?'

The question was for Jack, and he nodded.

Kitty cleared her throat. 'Who is your friend? He's very quiet.'

'He is, isn't he?' said Ada, with a considering look at Jack. Her eyes were deep pools in the candlelight. Kitty was pretty, but Ada . . . those eyes in the pale face, the dark tufts of hair, her warmth against his body . . . Jack felt a slow blush spreading up from under his collar.

Ada laughed. 'I don't even know your name.'

Chapter 12

The hunt fanned out across London. Within the hour, small boys were posting notices up all over town: fifty guineas offered for the safe return of the runaways.

As night drew in, the escaped lunatics were the talk of every coffee house, tavern and potshop from Limehouse to Tothill. The betting – as ever – was heavy, the market fixing rapidly at three to one against their staying out another day. The odds lengthened further when it became known that the notorious thief taker, Captain Wilde, had offered the services of his bloodhounds.

Sitting on Kitty's bed, wrapped up in her blankets, Jack and Ada had no notion of the toasts being drunk to their derring-do.

'Move over Jack, there's a lamb.' said Kitty. 'Tell me,

how'd you get in here? I thought the door was locked.'

'Oh, you should have seen it!' Ada laughed. 'Jack figged it easy as an apple.'

'So you're a thief, are you?' said Kitty. To Jack's surprise, she wriggled in closer, and patted his arm. 'Well, I am an actress, and Ada's a lunatic, so you're in good company.'

'Actress?' said Jack. It was out before he could think about it.

'Yes, well,' said Kitty, 'I don't know why you're so surprised. I am tolerably well known, I believe.'

'Aye,' said Jack slowly. The idea was so very strange, a woman on the stage. 'No. I mean – I'm . . . not from here,' he said. That was true enough; and Ada was nodding, believing him.

'I thought your voice sounded odd,' she said. 'West Country, is it? How did you end up in Bedlam?'

'I don't know.' True, again.

'What happened? Before we left. When you helped me. How did you do that?'

Jack hesitated. 'I don't remember. Like you said, before: it's all dark.'

'Like I said before,' said Ada. She was frowning again, looking at him with that considering look. She was too close up: they both were, pressing in on him with their soft bodies and their questions. Jack slid down onto the floor. 'Fire's dying,' he said. 'Mind if I give it a stoke, miss?'

151

'Oh please do,' said Kitty. 'Useful as well as quiet: a perfect youth, Ada, I do declare!'

'Hmm,' said Ada. Jack could feel her watching him as he bent over the hearth.

'You really don't remember anything?' said Kitty. She was asking Ada, not Jack, and he was glad of the distraction. 'Nothing about that night, at the Hellfire Club? The way we found you, out in the square – it was too terrible – raving, *howling* like a beast . . .'

'I . . . no, I don't remember,' said Ada. 'Something happened. Something too horrible for my mind to bear. Or recall.' Her fingers twisted together in the sheets.

'You'd rather not speak of it,' said Kitty.

Ada shook her head. 'I must, though. I must find out. Do *you* know anything?' she said. 'You were there, weren't you?'

'You were wandering out in the street,' said Kitty. 'No one knew how you got there, or what had happened. Oh, there were rumours – there always were with you and Ravenscar . . .'

'So you think it nonsense?'

'Don't you?'

'Yes,' said Ada. Then, more firmly, 'Yes. He would never harm me. I was going to him tonight, before we were waylaid . . . I was going to ask his help. For Jack, too. I owe you that much,' she said, turning to Jack. 'Ravenscar's the man I spoke of before. The friend who could hide us.' She smiled, eyes narrowing. 'In fact, he can do better than hide us. He's a powerful man – if he sees I am cured, and I tell him you helped me, he'll arrange matters. No going back to Bedlam. No more running for either of us.'

Jack nodded. It sounded good – too good maybe.

'Well,' said Kitty, 'with those wolves out for you, you must stay here tonight. And tomorrow I will fetch Ravenscar myself. I know exactly where to find him, too – at the Theatre Royal. He has a new flame, that little actress, Artemisia Devine. Remember her?'

Ada nodded.

'She plays the lead in that play of yours,' said Kitty. 'Ravenscar never misses a performance.'

Ada looked a little taken aback. Jack felt the same way, though for a different reason: that play *of yours*, Kitty had said. Women playwrights was even stranger than actresses.

Kitty got down off the bed and reached underneath, pulling out a small wooden box.

'If you *are* staying,' she said, opening the box to reveal a neat line of tiny bottles, 'I happen to have a *leetle* drop of something good to drive away the terrors. I declare I am a heap of nerves after my rude awakening, and I shall take a drachm or two regardless.'

'Spiritus?' said Ada, with a sudden, alert look.

'Yes,' said Kitty.

She sorted through the bottles, holding them up to the candlelight and frowning as one by one they turned up empty. Finally she found one with a few drops remaining.

'Here,' she said. 'Really, Ada, if you knew the monstrous expense of it nowadays . . .' She fiddled with the stopper. 'Since I stopped being invited by Ravenscar, I've had to rely on one jumped-up chit after another, selling watered-down Spiritus for five shillings a drachm . . .'

The stopper came off. Jack's right hand twitched, as if someone had struck it with a small but heavy hammer.

Moving with greedy haste, Kitty put the bottle to her lips. As she swallowed, Jack's hand twitched again, harder this time, then settled down to a steady, pulsing warmth – the Alkahest coming awake – all except the blackened part, which stayed as numb as ever.

He looked with the devil-sight, just to be sure.

Scraps of light, skeins of shadow, coiled under Kitty's skin. A strange fever glowed in her eyes. Visible only with the devil-sight – but this was not the swarm. This was something he'd never seen before.

Kitty was passing the bottle to Ada. Before he could think, Jack was reaching across to stop her.

'Why, Jack, whatever is the matter?' said Ada.

'You shouldn't . . . it might be dangerous,' said Jack.

'What do you know about it?' said Ada, looking

suspicious now. 'I could have sworn the Spiritus Mundi was a closely guarded secret. Certainly not known . . . wherever it is you are from.'

'No,' said Jack. 'I mean . . . just, after today, what happened . . .'

'So serious,' said Ada, her gaze softening. 'So earnest, Jack. I am flattered that you care so. But this . . .' She held up the bottle. 'This mixture is a gentle one, I assume?'

Kitty nodded. 'Gentle and soothing, even if it is three parts water.'

'Well then,' said Ada, and raised the bottle to her lips.

'No!' said Jack, but it was too late. She had drained the few drops that remained in the bottle, and the strange flecks of light were already spreading beneath her skin.

Jack stared hard at Ada. The flecks were something devilish for sure – but nothing like the foulness before. Jack had to admit she looked well on it: the hollows in her cheeks were filled out, the shadows beneath her eyes had disappeared.

'Whatever are you staring at, Jack?' she said, and giggled. 'So *earnest*, I do declare. Like a baby goose.'

Jack blinked. That made them both laugh even more. It was a raucous sort of laughter – but not mad.

Or if it was madness, it was of a merry kind. For an hour or more they egged each other on, planning hilarious new ventures: Ada would write a play about Bedlam; Kitty would play the lead lunatic; their fortunes would be restored.

To Jack's relief Ada didn't ask any more tricky questions. She seemed to have forgotten he existed. Jack melted into the background and tried to understand. Ravenscar came up often: he was the one who was going to make it all happen. They didn't speak of the dangers, the men still hunting them out in the night. The Spiritus, as they called it, seemed to cure them of fear.

It didn't cure Jack. With Ada and Kitty distracted, he'd time to examine the blackness on his hand. He pinched a fold of skin sharply between two fingernails, harder and harder until, with a stab of alarm, he saw that he'd drawn blood. He felt nothing. The black part was utterly numb. He peered at it, trying to see if it was still spreading.

Whatever he'd done to cure Ada, it had cost him dear.

The merriment died gradually. Jack noticed Kitty glancing at the bottle, her fingers twitching, and with the devil-sight he saw the lights in her eyes were dimmer than before.

As Kitty's glances grew more frequent, her chatter dried up. Ada quietened too – though she seemed drowsy rather than nervous. Kitty kept scratching at her arms and her neck, as if she had fleas.

At last, after a long and pensive glance at the bottle, Kitty interrupted.

'I could take another sup, what do you say?'

Ada frowned and smiled at the same time. 'Why Kitty, you temptress.'

'Well?' Kitty's voice sounded forced. 'We'll need money, I'm short just at the moment, but I know where to get more . . . I can be back in five minutes.'

'Money, Kitty? We only escaped Bedlam today – we don't have money!'

'Couldn't Jack the Thief steal us some?'

'Come,' said Ada. 'Why, Jack will think us a pair of opium eaters. And I must sleep tonight. Come, Kitty, ain't you tired too?'

Jack saw Kitty knit her hands together and press them down into her lap.

'You're quite right,' she said. 'Time to sleep like good little girls.'

'Come, Kitty . . .' Ada reached across to her and stroked her cheek. 'Come, you're tired. Let's be warm together. Warm and sleepy, yes?'

'It's very well for you,' Kitty muttered. 'Just because I'm tired, doesn't mean I want to sleep . . .'

'Hush,' said Ada. She pulled up the sheets and snuggled down inside. Kitty shot a final glance over at the bottle, then allowed Ada to pull her down, coddle her up.

'Won't you come to bed, Jack? All lovely and warm . . .' Ada looked at him over Kitty's shoulder. Her eyes were dark slits, the last dying motes of devil light spiralling deep inside. She blinked, very slow and catlike.

'I – no. Thanks. I mean, I'll see to the fire.' Jack lurched round to face the fireplace. Behind him, he heard a drowsy giggle and a rustle of sheets. His cheeks felt hot.

Ada giggled. 'So serious. A little . . . serious . . . pup. Don't worry Jack, we're not going to ravish you.'

Jack really didn't know what to say to that, so he said nothing – didn't even look round. Another laugh from Ada, and then he heard the rustling of sheets and blankets as the women made themselves comfortable.

He found some logs in a box by the fire. He put one on and poked at the embers, watched the flames lick up. His ears adjusted to the quiet, and soon he could hear the thump of his own heart, gradually slowing, and Ada's and Kitty's breathing, slowing too until one of them started to snore. Jack heard Ada muttering softly, talking to someone called Tom, and he knew they were asleep.

Jack sat and held his right hand in front of the fire. No matter how close to the flames he held it, the blackened part remained numb. He didn't think it was spreading any more.

The black had appeared after his first encounter with the Swarm. Then it had grown after his second. Perhaps if he could avoid the Swarm in future, it might fade, or at least stay the way it was.

A very thin hope. The truth was, he didn't know. He didn't know what it was, or what it might do to him.

He sat there in front of the fire for a long time. He felt afraid, and melancholy mournful. It was a long time before he became aware of the noise.

It was a light tapping at the window shutters, such as a small branch might make in the wind. There was something wrong with it though – too rhythmical for a branch . . .

He went over to the window, with a quick glance towards the bed. Ada and Kitty seemed sound asleep. He eased the shutters open a couple of inches – it was full dark outside now – and then he saw what was outside the window and it was all he could do not to shout out for joy.

A small black shape was crouched on the windowsill, outlined in moonlight. 'Ma . . . gic . . . boy!' croaked a scratchy, familiar voice.

'Imp!' Jack reached down and plucked the softly glowing beetle from the sill. 'Imp! Imp! You wily shaver! You wonderbug! You . . . haha!'

He had to force himself to keep his voice at a whisper – had to force his feet not to trip into a delighted jig.

The imp flexed its legs, and sighed. Its shell flickered red, warm and dim like a tired smile.

'You're all smashed.' Jack traced a long crack across its right wing case.

'Pcha! Bird-scars!' The imp looked up at Jack, and froze in alarm. 'Ghastlook master – clix-clox top-fur!'

Jack rubbed his scalp ruefully. He still hadn't got used to being bald.

"S'only hair. What you been about, Imp, leaving me all this time?'

'Great voyage, and mecktick warrings, magic boy. Here'est . . .' And then, in a voice that was still weak and scratchy, and in its own cussed way, the imp began its story.

The leap through time had fuddled the imp much worse than Jack. The first it remembered was waking up in Ghostface's pocket, rolling along in the horse-chariot, miles away from Bedlam.

'Shame-fillingst! Gone from master, gone from home. Ve-ery sad for little shuklet.'

'You know now, though? Where we are?'

'*When* we are, yes-yes? Same placings, different whiles . . . what a naughty shuk is that satyr!'

'You knew it could do that?' said Jack.

'Nix kennit.' The imp shook its feelers. 'Mecktick madsense. Here in this placetime, London city is too-too great-big, nix? *Millions* big. Very fretlick to find boymaster.'

'Aye, I can imagine,' said Jack.

'And lokmok man, too, is lost, nei?'

Jack swallowed.

He couldn't say it.

'Boymaster?' said the imp, this time with a tremor. 'Where is lokmok please?'

Jack looked down, and shook his head.

'Dead?' said the imp.

Jack nodded.

The imp went black all over.

'Aye, I know,' said Jack. He hadn't wept for Kit, himself. He didn't want to do it now. 'Come on, Imp, tell me how you found me, eh?'

'But lokmok . . .'

'He's gone. We're still here.' It was the kind of thing Beth would say. It didn't help much. The imp was still mourning-black – but it stopped asking about Kit.

'Go on,' said Jack. 'How'd you find me?'

'Much-times wandersearcht, but no glimmer beglintet. Until *this* day, and cometh great uproaring perilsome reekings: master ist dangewrack, master ist burning with mecktick devilkind.'

'What time?' said Jack. 'The reekings, when'd they happen?'

'After midstday. Before dark, shortly.'

'And you found me then?'

'Flew straight thereto, but then boymaster gone. Seeing lights and chasers, following here. But master not letting admittance.' The imp swivelled its eyes over towards the bed, then rolled them back at Jack. 'Master is finding new lovey-doves – two rumpled ladies, naughty master make tearsheet tumblings!'

'It's not . . .' Jack stopped, as a thought struck him. 'Did you smell that stuff they drank?'

'Tsa!' said the imp. 'Hellstuff!'

'But not . . . What you call it, Beez—'

'Nix, *nix* to name such, I say already once!' said the imp. 'Why asking now?'

'Those reekings of yours, what brought you to me: that was the same thing. The Swarm. Same sort of stuff, anyway.'

'Veritlick?' The imp saw the black spot and glowed lemon yellow with alarm.

'Aye, only it was in her, see? I drove it out. With my hand.'

Jack held out his hand. The imp went from yellow to white. 'Foulness, master! Lumpenface boy, to touch! Death is there, death is coming . . .'

'I ain't . . . it ain't spreading any more,' said Jack, trying to sound surer than he felt.

'Nay! List and hist, if even smallest part of *Him* be here, we must be gone! Homeward, awayward! Hope find doctor to make curings!'

'We'll do it,' said Jack. 'Ada says she can help me . . . then we find Beth . . . and I have the key.' It sounded unlikely, even as he said it. And he was leaving out the worst of it.

Even if they did find Beth, they'd still be leaving Kit behind. Dead.

'We'll find our way,' he said.

'Goodly,' said the imp. 'Sad days, magic boy. Sad and fretlick ... death and confuse. But better now near master.'

'You know . . .' Jack smiled, 'it's better now for me too, Imp.'

Chapter 13

'**W**ake up, Jack.'

Jack woke slowly, stiff, bleary-eyed. Ada was crouched over him. She looked scared.

'What?'

'I thought I heard a sound.'

'What?'

'And Kitty's gone.'

'So?'

'Last night. She's changed. Did you see how she craved the Spiritus? And she'd spent all her money: I'm afraid she'd do anything to get more.'

'Like what?'

'Remember what the man said, last night? Rich reward for our capture? She's gone, and there was a sound . . .'

Ada was already looking over at the door when Jack

heard the boots. Heavy boots on the stairs. More than one pair.

Jack sat up fast. By the time he was on his feet, the boots were just outside the door.

There was no time to run. The door flew open, and a file of Bedlam bluecoats charged in.

'*Balkutt Yayn!*'

The imp was halfway across the room before the first man had cleared the doorway. It went straight for his face. The man bellowed, slapping at it, stumbling back into the man behind him. They crashed to the floor.

Ada stared aghast at the immense beetle, flashing battle-red as it disengaged and swooped in for a second attack. So did the third bluecoat, framed in the doorway.

'Quick! Window!' Jack wrenched open the shutters with a squeal of damp-warped wood.

A draft of cold air rushed in. Jack dragged Ada to the window. Below was the roof of an outhouse, reducing the drop to a single storey. Good.

A Bedlam bluecoat was waiting there too, smiling up at them. Not good.

Jack craned his neck and looked up at the roof. The eaves started only a foot above the window, but they overhung the wall a touch as well. This would not be easy.

Jack glanced back into the room, and saw one bluecoat in the doorway flapping madly at his face and screaming.

His two friends were struggling to their feet. The imp was a flashing red blur.

'Going up,' he said to Ada.

'You're not . . . ?'

Jack nodded, jumped up on the sill, forcing his body to relax – remembering Mr Smiles, instructing him in this very dodge, months and centuries ago. He'd always hated climbing.

'Yes.'

He grabbed for the lip of roof. Getting a good grip with his elbows, he kicked hard off the sill. His feet dangled in space for a moment. He heard a shout from below as he pulled himself up.

He looked down. Ada was white-faced, poised on the sill. From inside came muffled thumps and oaths.

'I can't!' said Ada.

'Don't look down. Take my hand!' Jack called, reaching down. Ada grabbed hold, and latched on to the lip of the roof with her other hand.

'Now push!' said Jack, leaning back and hauling with all his might.

Ada floundered. Her hand slipped on the wet slate. Her feet scrabbled for purchase. Jack felt himself sliding towards the edge.

'I'm falling!'

Jack was pulling with all his might, but he couldn't take

her full weight. His fingers ached. He slipped another inch.

'Hel—oh!' said Ada. 'What's that?'

'Ladypushink!' The imp's voice, from below.

Ada's weight slacked off so fast that Jack – still pulling – fell backwards onto the roof. Ada sprawled half on top of him.

'Hazzat!' cried the imp.

'What! Is! Happening?' hissed Ada. 'Something pushed me!'

'Up, quick,' said Jack.

The bluecoats were at the window. Down in the alley, Jack heard the slap of heavy boots; and worse, much worse, the baying of a dog.

He gripped Ada's hand and scrambled over the ridge of the roof, out of sight of the hunters. The roof they were on was part of a long terrace. Jack scrambled off towards the far end, keeping his head below the ridgeline.

The imp swooped down and perched on Jack's shoulder.

'Hardlick hunt a-coming, boymaster!'

Ada's eyes stretched wide. '*What?*'

'Later!' said Jack, scanning ahead, already worrying about how they would get down.

They scurried as fast as they could across the slippery slate. Ada slipped once and nearly fell, but Jack steadied her. As they reached the edge of Kitty's building, Jack heard a shout behind him and saw that the bluecoats were up on the roof.

There was a five-foot jump to the next house. And a thirty-foot drop.

'Can you—' Jack never finished his question: Ada launched herself across the gap, bold as an alley cat.

'Come *on!*' Ada was already on her feet. Jack jumped. He landed with a clatter, off-balance. Behind them he heard the bluecoats' boots rattling on the tiles.

Ada led off across the steep slope.

As he crossed the ridgeline, Jack's heart sank. The new building ended abruptly. Twenty-foot gap to the next. And no way back. The bluecoats were steeling themselves to make the jump.

'Trapped!' Ada cast about, looking for a way out.

The imp shot from Jack's shoulder down over the edge of the roof. A moment later it swooped back, trailing a washing line behind it, shirts and smallclothes fluttering like flags.

In a blur, the imp whipped the line around a chimney, tying it off with a sturdy knot that left it taut as a bowstring.

Jack saw the imp's idea at once. His stomach pitted hollow. The washing line led down at a steep angle to a balcony on the opposite building. Slide down to it, and you could hang and drop from the balcony to the ground.

'Sharp work, Imp.'

A thump sounded as the first bluecoat made his jump.

Jack grabbed a shirt, wrapped one end around his fist and looped the other over the imp's line. He looked down. Thirty-foot drop to the ground – a killing drop, and only a washing line to preserve him.

Before he could change his mind, he jumped off the roof. For a terrifying moment he was falling.

'Kzaaa!' the imp cried, as the line dipped, dipped . . . and held.

Before Jack had time to realize it was working, he was crashing into the balcony rail on the other side. The blow shook him from skull to ankles. He bounced and grabbed on, hauling himself to one side to make room for Ada.

But Ada hadn't jumped. She was fumbling with a pillowcase, trying to loop it over the line as Jack had done. Already the bluecoats had crested the ridge behind her.

'Jump!' shouted Jack.

Ada cast one panic-stricken look over her shoulder.

A bluecoat dived down the slope. The imp whirred straight into his face, a dark red blur. Jack heard the man's scream, choked off hoarse – as Ada pitched forward into space.

She slid down, swinging wildly, barely hanging on. She slammed into the balcony, and gasped. Up above, the imp sliced through the washing line, cutting off the pursuit.

Jack slung himself down to the ground.

'Drop!' he said.

Ada let go, and fell straight into his arms. Her weight knocked the breath from his lungs. He floundered on his back, Ada on top of him. She was heavier than she looked.

The bluecoats on the roof shouted for help. Jack heard answering halloos rise up nearby, along with the dreadful baying of a bloodhound on a nice fresh scent. *Their* scent – and the hunt was much too close.

Ada heaved Jack to his feet. Each breath was agony, but there was no time. They ran for the narrow ways, feet slipping in the mud. Ada picked an alley at random. It branched hard to the right.

Jack let his feet take over: one, two, driving through the mud. Never hesitate – take the turnings, no matter which way – left, left, right and they were out into another open court. Four grimy paths, more gutters than alleys, led off like spokes on a crooked compass.

Where now? The dog's barks were getting louder. The imp flew down and landed in Jack's coat pocket. Jack took a deep breath, and gagged. Stabbing through the usual gutter vapours came the rancid stench of steeping fat. For a horrible moment he couldn't take another breath.

Ada started off again, but Jack clutched her sleeve.

'S-stay! Smell!' he gasped, eyes swimming. 'Smearmongers!'

He pulled Ada down the smelliest of the lanes. They

passed several turnings, but Jack ignored them, chasing the stink. It grew worse as the lane grew narrower.

Up ahead was a low brick wall, oily black smoke roiling up over it. Jack didn't falter. Ada's hand was tight clenched in his as he pulled her on, running hard for a dirty wicket gate.

They burst through it at a gallop. They smashed through long lines of candles hung out to dry. Shouts rose up behind them. Strings of hot tallow dried on Jack's face. They plunged through swirls of greasy smoke, rising from the heavy copper cauldrons.

Ada was retching from the stink of boiling fat. They swerved past gaping smearmongers. The smoke thinned, and they were through an open door and into the gloom of a warehouse. Beyond the stacks of bones, skins and firewood, Jack saw daylight.

'There!'

They ran out into a busy street. Jack didn't look back. He wriggled and pushed, driving them deep into the traffic.

'Wait!' Ada was gasping. 'Can't breathe!'

She bent over, choking. A coachman bellowed at them to move on or be trampled.

'Come on.' Sucking down gulps of fresh air, Jack dragged Ada across the road. He let the flow of foot traffic sweep them along, out of sight of the smearmongers' warehouse. Ada coughed and coughed.

'Lose them?' said Ada, red from coughing.

'Think so.' Jack spat the taste of greasy tallow from his mouth. 'Stay chary, mind.'

His blood was still thundering when he allowed himself to look back. No sign of the bluecoats. No sign of the dog. The sun was driving broad golden slabs through the steam from the milling crowd. The street was uproarious busy: bellowing bullocks, creaking wheels, the cries of the vendors hawking chestnuts and cabbages. Hoots of laughter swirled from the jostle around a puppet show.

'Hit 'im! Rip 'im. Grind 'is bones!'

London was awake, and Jack was in the thick of it again. He felt sharper than he had in months.

As if by magic, his eye hooked on a fat purse. Its owner was the picture of a country coney: a pure gaping gift, his attention all places except where it should be – his pocket, where the purse bulged heavy and unguarded. Before Jack had taken another step, he'd already scoped his line of approach, the nip itself, and three different routes of escape. A left-handed nip – Jack didn't trust his right, with its numb index finger – but even left-handed should be easy with a yokel like this, grinning like a baby at the puppet show.

Didn't he know any better? Jack was surprised to feel a flare of pity for the gull – lost in wonder at the strangeness of the town.

It didn't stop him robbing him blind. He brushed past.

His hand dipped swift and sure. The coney didn't notice a thing. Neither did Ada.

They crossed the street and ducked into a dark doorway.

'I can't – believe – Kitty! And you . . . you . . .' At last Ada got her breath back. 'You, Jack! What *is* that . . . creature?'

The imp twitched.

'Pleased to acquaint, mistress.' The imp poked its head out of Jack's pocket, and waggled its feelers. 'Apexdrum-corporal Arcathonn Tufrac Anael-kra Calzas Baraborat Mecktic – *Eie Eia* – of the Sixth Circle, Wegrizkov sigil, Awkwardest Legion, Great Duchy of Samaz.'

'I just call it Imp,' added Jack.

Ada's mouth was hanging open. With a great effort, she drew it shut again.

'Ada Seward,' she said. 'Enchanted to meet you.' She turned to Jack. 'An *imp*? Truly?'

'Veritlick!' the imp chirped.

'That's what it is,' said Jack.

'As to say, a small sort of devil. That talks.'

'Aye.'

'It saved us! There was I, thinking we could trust one another – and now you turn out to be . . . what? A young savant, with a magical beetle? I am quite astonished, I declare.'

Jack looked round at her, surprised: Ada was finding this funny.

She hoiked an eyebrow at him. 'Well?'

'What?'

'*What*, you say? Your *talking beetle*, that's what.' Ada nodded down at Jack's pocket, and snorted. '*What*, indeed.'

Jack took a breath. Two steps and he could be gone. He should do it, now: she'd never believe the truth. And she had her great lord to help her, and Jack had his own business. Running about London with a half-mad lady who'd recently played host to Beelzebub was definitely not a part of it.

Ada glanced again at Jack and began to laugh, full and hard.

Without knowing quite why, Jack began to laugh too.

'Stop!' Ada choked. 'No . . . don't . . .'

For a few moments neither of them could talk. Jack hadn't laughed that hard for two hundred years – when Beth had brought him that soup.

Jack realized with a stab of guilt that he had hardly thought about Beth since escaping Bedlam.

Ada wiped her eyes and gave him a funny, half-questioning look.

'Well, Jack? You've rather a lot of explaining to do.'

Beth. He'd come here to find her. Ada was nothing to him.

He should have run a minute ago, before they'd laughed like that.

Ada tutted. 'Make up your mind, Jack. If you'd really rather quit me than tell me, then go. If not, we should get out of sight before those bloodhounds catch up with us.' She looked out into the road, eyes searching, and then her hand went up. 'Hack!' she shouted.

A passing horse chariot swerved across the road, and pulled up beside them.

'Well?' said Ada. 'Are you with me? If you are, I'll need the truth. What are you, Jack?'

Jack was half stunned that you could just wave down a horse chariot; but it wasn't just that, stopping him from turning away.

She laughed like a barmaid; she summoned a chariot like a queen; she loped through the streets like a wolf . . . Two wolves, that was what they were, running from the hounds.

He found himself nodding.

'Good,' said Ada. 'We lunatics must stick together, you know.' She winked, and turned to the chariot.

Chapter 14

The inside of the chariot smelled of bacon, pipe smoke and straw. Jack settled back against the bench and closed his eyes, letting his body sway as the horse lurched into a trot. It was like being in a cosy, well-caulked boat.

'So,' said Ada. 'Devils. Tell.'

Jack didn't know where to begin. He shuffled his feet against the chariot floor.

'You can't tell anyone else . . .' he began.

'No, of course not. They'd have us back in Bedlam in a trice.'

'Right. So . . .' Jack looked down at the imp. It gave a little shrug of its wing cases.

Jack took a deep breath. 'First thing, I didn't tell you true, before, where I was from. I'm from London . . .'

'You certainly don't sound—'

'Aye, that's it. I'm from London, but not this one. I'm from . . . two hundred years ago.'

Jack looked sideways at Ada, half expecting her to laugh: either that or call him mad and kick him out of the chariot.

She didn't laugh. She didn't say anything.

'You believe me?' said Jack.

A slow nod. She was staring straight ahead, staring inward, as if some vast landscape were opening up inside her head. There was wonder in her look, plenty of that – but no disbelief.

'Right,' said Jack. He hadn't expected this. 'So. Was . . . a devil brought me here.' Ada caught her breath. Jack paused, still waiting for her to call him mad. But she didn't.

He pressed on. 'This devil – first it took my friend, see, and then I came after, looking for her. But it was the devil did it.'

'The devil did it,' Ada said. 'Two hundred years, by God! Time, yes: we always thought time—' She blinked, and her eyes sharpened, looking curiously at Jack. 'But *how*? If devils do this, why are there no others like you? We'd know about it, wouldn't we?'

Jack shrugged, impressed. It was a good, pointy question, and he'd never even thought about it. 'I don't know. I think this one devil . . . took against me. I stole it, see?'

Ada gave a single astonished whoop of laughter. 'You stole it? You're a *devil thief*, then? Is that how you acquired your – your *imp*, too?'

Jack shook his head. 'Imp's a different story. Long story. Imp used to belong to a sorcerer – only, no, he was a devil too, turned out . . .'

'Devils everywhere!' said Ada.

'Only round me,' said Jack. Then he shook his head again. 'No, that's not right; they are everywhere, all over the place where I come from. Here I ain't seen so many. They're bound into things – old things. Buried under the ground, mostly. Best place for 'em . . .'

The imp gave an indignant squeak.

''Cept you, Imp,' said Jack, patting its shell.

'Buried . . .' said Ada. Her eyes darted from side to side, still with something of that inward look – like she was reckoning up some figures only she could see. 'My stars,' she murmured. 'If only Tom knew of this.'

'Hey, no!' said Jack. 'He won't know, cos you're not telling anyone, remember?'

'Of course. No – you have my word.' Ada waved a hand impatiently. 'Lord, how to explain . . . you see, people now, people like me – we don't believe in all that any more. Devils and magic and so on. What Tom and I—'

'Who is he, this Tom?' Jack interrupted.

'My oldest friend.'

178

'Is he Ravenscar, then?' said Jack. 'The one's going to help us?'

'Oh no!' Ada laughed at the idea. 'Tom is . . . no. That's not the kind of thing . . . if we'd a broken clock, or an unknown spider, or a question about the nature of light, why then – Tom, yes. To get these dogs called off our trail . . . Tom is a dear lamb; but for this, we want a man of the world. Ravenscar.'

'Tom, though: he knows devils are real, does he?' said Jack, trying to understand. 'That's why you want to tell him?'

'Not a bit! Him least of all!' Ada grinned. 'I think it must be fate that's brought us together, Jack.'

'Aye, or something worse.'

'No no! You see – oh! Where to begin? See, a few years ago Tom and I discovered a chest full of dusty old papers in his grandfather's attic. The most marvellous, peculiar trove. They belonged to some ancient great-great uncle of his – a man of your time, hah! And they were all about *devils*.' Ada shook her head in wonder. 'Can you credit it?'

Jack didn't understand. 'So – you did know about 'em then.'

'We didn't believe it, that's the thing.'

'*K'rstr'mph!*' said the imp, with a flash of purple indignation.

'Why didn't you?' said Jack.

'Believe?' Ada snorted. 'Of course we didn't. It was all far too medieval. But the more we investigated, the more we saw there was *something* in it. Something real, behind the superstition.'

'Shuklet is no superstition!'

'I beg your pardon, noble Imp,' said Ada. The imp ruffled its feelers, pleased. 'Of course I see now we were utterly wrong. There we were, dashing about London after these buried devils of yours – always old things, ancient things . . . We didn't believe in *magic*, so we came up with all sorts of theories: something accumulated over time – some sort of charge, or force – it was so exciting, the feeling of discovering something new, and unknown, and *real*. You see, they did have an effect. Made me feel quite peculiar . . .'

'Aye, they do that.'

'So we dug them up, conducted experiments . . .'

'You dug them up?' said Jack.

'Yes.'

Jack swallowed – thinking about what the satyr had done to him on being dug up. Digging up lots of devils sounded alarmingly stupid. No wonder Ada had had the Swarm in her . . .

'Is that when you started going mad?' he said.

'Oh no. We were at it for months and I was quite sane the whole time, I'd stake my life on it. No. It happened all at once, at the Hellfire Club.'

'The Hellfire Club,' said Jack. 'Like you were talking to Kitty about, last night.' He leaned forward. 'What did they do, to make you mad? Hellfire, right? Devils? Tell me, I swear I'll keep it secret.'

'Steady, Jack.' Ada was shaking her head, trying to smile. 'I really don't remember what happened, but . . . no. I can see why you'd think it, but the name's a joke: it amuses Ravenscar to be always so wicked.' She chuckled again. 'Lord Ravenscar ain't leading a coven, I assure you.'

'But it was a devil, made you mad. I know it.'

'How?'

'When I cured you, I pushed out a devil, or – bits of one,' said Jack – remembering the flies in her eyes, the spider stitches binding her lips. 'It was something I'd seen before. A devil, a big one, called B—'

'Str'krmphk!' said the imp. 'Nix to name it, master!'

'Aye, well, it was a bad one. Nearly did for me. Nearly did for you too, by the looks,' said Jack. 'And this Ravenscar of yours is part of it? And we're going straight to him, are we?'

'No – I see your objection, but you're mistaken. Ravenscar isn't like that.'

'You sure?'

'All that hellfire stuff: he was playing a game, he never believed in it. That's what he does. What we both did.' Ada laughed, a melancholy-mad sort of laugh that Jack didn't like. 'Some of the others, perhaps . . . if I could only remember who was there . . .' She shook her head. 'I'm sorry, Jack. It's all a blank, that whole night—'

'Hoi!' A shout from outside, and a rap on the roof. 'Drury Lane! Close as we get. That'll be eighteenpence.'

'Eighteenpence we don't have,' Ada muttered.

Jack dropped the purse he'd stolen out of his sleeve, enjoying the look of surprise on Ada's face. He passed it to her and she paid the coachman what they owed.

They jumped down into ankle-deep mud. Ahead was a narrow passage between two overhanging houses – a broad passage, ten feet wide, but crowded to choking. Burly men shouted their way through, carrying great big boxes on poles, while wigged and powdered faces peeked out through little windows. At the entrance, a carriage had jammed in the mud up to its axles.

All around them were an army of street girls and promenading gentry, hawkers and barkers and nippers on the prowl. The London parade, in all its glory. Jack recalled *his* Drury Lane – the muddy, hedge-lined cut he'd strolled along, four days and two centuries past – and whistled softly.

Ada pressed forward into the passage, pulling Jack by the hand. They emerged into a cobbled yard, packed and babbling. Jack closed his eyes and sniffed deep. There it was – sweat and perfume, booze and tobacco, roast nuts and armpits – the familiar tubwrack stink of the London theatre. There was even a pamphleteer.

'I give you Ar-Te-Misia DEEEE–wine, suh-pwised in her petticoats, tupp-hence apiece!' The pamphleteer waved a sheaf of papers in Jack's face, ran hard up against Ada's glare and ducked out of sight.

'Pff,' muttered Ada, in a distracted sort of way. 'Surprised in her petticoats, my foot!'

As with all buildings in the new London, the Theatre Royal was enormous, grand, and the wrong shape – more like a fairy keep than a theatre. Golden lamplight blazed from every window.

'You sure we can find your lord in there?' said Jack.

'I've no doubt.'

'You sure we *want* to?'

Ada pursed her lips, and skirted round to one side, avoiding the crush at the doors. 'This way's more private.'

She led him to a narrow passage down one side of the theatre. At the far end was a green door. A looming old gent with bushy side-whiskers bristled like a badger as they drew near.

'Not you. Not 'ere. Snudge off, hedgebirds.'

'So fierce, Musgrove? Don't you know me any more?' whispered Ada, flicking back the hood of her cloak.

The man blinked once, very hard.

'It's you, miss! Miss A—'

'Hush.' Ada laid a hand on his arm, and kissed his cheek. 'I'm not here.'

Musgrove blushed bright red. 'Nary a word, nary a stray syllabub, mistress, will pass my lips.' He pressed his finger against his nose, and winked.

'The boy is with me.'

'Then he is wery welcome.' Musgrove pulled the door open and stepped aside. They ducked beneath his arm. The corners of his mouth twitched as he fought down a grin.

'It's a thrice-plied joy to see ye well, Miss A!'

His whisper boomed so loud he might as well have shouted; but no one noticed. They'd entered straight into the working part of the theatre: bustle and mayhem, everyone far too busy to care who or what they were.

Ada led Jack through baffling branching corridors, past dressing rooms and half-costumed actors – two men carrying a wooden horse, surpassing lifelike – and into a long room filled from floor to ceiling with racks of costumes. Ada picked a plain green dress for herself, and began changing her clothes right there in front of him. Jack looked away, blushing, until she called out that it was his turn.

'Boots . . . breeches . . .' she said, handing Jack several pairs of each to choose from. Finally she tossed over something that looked like a dead spaniel pup with a silk ribbon attached.

'What's that for?'

'A periwig. Just the thing for the bald-headed man of fashion. Pop it on.'

Ada moved on to a rack of coats, and picked out a long black one with silver stitching and waistcoat to match. The imp nearly exploded with joy as Jack put them on. It buzzed and bustled all about him, doing up buttons and fastening ties, until Jack was tightly encased in his new outfit. He was hanging the mud brown coat of the Muscovites man up on the rack when he felt something small and solid. With a jolt he realized he'd almost forgotten Lud's key. He fished it out, tucked it in his waistcoat pocket and buttoned the pocket down tight.

'How do I look, Imp?' said Jack.

'Entklessent!' cried the imp. 'See how master be primped, all fine and dashlick!'

'Ready?' said Ada.

'Ready,' said Jack. 'Back in my pocket now, Imp, and stay quiet.'

'Nix to make pocketsbulge,' the imp growled. 'Spoiling and ruination of master's looks. Shuklet will not do it.'

It flew up onto Jack's head and went quiet.

'Imp?' said Jack.

Silence – a silence that somehow struck Jack as crafty.

'Imp, what're you up to?'

He felt a prickle on his scalp, over and above the itching of the wig; his right eye twitched. The wig rose from his head, twirling its side-curls in delight.

The Goliath beetle tumbled lifeless to the floor.

'Ack! Ack!' said the imp, hovering in the air in front of Jack. 'Nowly am veriwig periwig!'

Ada was staring. 'What on Earth . . . ?' she said.

'Oh, aye,' said Jack. 'It can do that. Well, Imp, I hope you're happy now.' He tucked the beetle shell into his shirtsleeve. The curled-up legs scratched against his wrist.

'Happlick-snapplick,' the imp crowed.

'Is this . . .' Ada frowned. 'Is this a common feature of devils, then?'

'Nix!' said the imp, very pleased. 'Onelick I, of all devilkind. Hand of boymaster made it – Reverse Bind, shiftlick shuklet am I!'

'Well, a talking wig,' said Ada. 'I hope you'll stay quiet in public.'

'As master commandst,' said the imp. It swished its ribbon back and forth like a silken tail.

Ada led them on again, out of the dressing room and up a narrow spiral staircase. They passed a number of green doors. From behind each one came the unmistakable, merry murmur of a crowd settling in for entertainment.

Ada was counting doors; at the fourth she stopped climbing.

'Ravenscar's box is through here, but we aren't dressed for the Circle. So. Keep your eyes low, step aside for all comers, and they'll think we're servants. We'll be invisible.'

She was trying to sound encouraging, but Jack could tell she was wound tight. Something was nagging at him – a feeling that he was missing something that should be plain and obvious.

The green door felt like a trap.

'One more thing, Jack: if you want to keep your secrets it's best you leave the talking to me. Lord Ravenscar dearly loves a mystery, and God knows you are one. You must call him "my lord", and you must bow to him. Then keep quiet.'

'Wait,' said Jack.

Lord Ravenscar loves a mystery. Aye, and Lord Ravenscar was a mystery, too much of one – suddenly, going into the theatre seemed like the most barmy-pated foolishness.

But Ada didn't wait. She pushed through the door.

'Courage, then!'

They came out into a crowded, curving corridor with numbered doors along one side. They kept their heads down, threading their way through rustling silk and frothing lace, powdered faces and murmured civilities. Just as Ada had predicted, none of the Quality even glanced at them. Bright lamps burned on crimson silk-lined walls. It was dizzying, discomforting. Very hot.

'Almost there.' Ada took Jack's hand and squeezed it. 'Don't worry, Lord Ravenscar won't eat you.'

The nagging feeling gnawed stronger with every step. They broke apart, sidled crabwise around a woman in four-foot-wide skirts. Just beyond her was another of the numbered doors, this one open.

'Listen, we're almost there. We can—' Ada stiffened, and stopped.

A little group of men were standing next to the doorway. One of them turned to face them. Ada gripped Jack's hand in warning, sharp and urgent, the nails biting deep.

'Jack – it's him!' she gasped. Her lips pressed white. 'I've made a mistake; Christ, I remember it all, I—' She turned away, trying to hide her face.

She was too late.

They'd made a mistake, for sure and certain.

The man stepped forward, rouged lips curving into a hard and frosty smile. His sallow, powdered skin looked parchment thin. It clung tight to his skull, almost transparent. Pencilled eyebrows arched up his forehead till they were almost lost in the immaculate curls of his wig.

It was the Frenchman. Peacock.

Kit's killer.

Chapter 15

A worm-thick vein was throbbing in Peacock's painted forehead. Jack watched it pulse, twice, before the man spoke.

'This is most *convenable*.' Peacock was still smiling, but his eyes were cold as winter puddles.

Jack's surprise was already changing into a horrible sense of aptness.

Kit's killer: the same as put the Swarm into Ada. It reckoned up. The Swarm had followed him here – and Peacock was its servant.

Ada had his hand in a death grip. Jack tried to tug her away, but she was all clenched up with fear, like a rabbit cornered by a fox.

Peacock raised an eyebrow at her, advanced one leg and gave a perfectly measured bow.

'I 'ardly expected—' said Peacock – before another man pushed past him, a big man with a rosy face and dark eyes, elbowing Peacock out of the way in his eagerness.

'*Ada!*'

'Tom! Yes, it's me, I-I'm so happy to see you!' Ada's smile looked painted on. *Tom*, Jack thought – the friend she'd spoken of on the way here. Peacock was looking at him in lip-curling irritation. Good: anything that thwarted Peacock was good.

'But – but . . .' said Tom. 'It *is* you! What are you doing here?'

Jack thought Tom might swing Ada off her feet, but he stopped himself, took her hand gently, and bent to kiss it.

Others were beginning to take notice.

'Ada? Ada Seward?' gasped a wigged and ribboned lady. She nudged the lacy gimblet standing next to her, who nearly tumbled over in surprise. The whispers spread in waves through the corridor.

'. . . *really her?*'

'. . . *fifty guineas' reward.*'

'. . . *in chains only yesterday—*'

Tom glared about him, as if he would challenge the next person who spoke. The whispers faded.

Tom ushered Ada in through the little numbered doorway. Ada's hand was clutching Jack's, pulling him along with her. Peacock took three quick mincing steps – and now he was standing behind Jack, very close behind him, and something sharp and hard was pressing into his back, just below the ribs.

'Do not think of departing,' he murmured in Jack's ear.

No escape. Confined space, knife at his back. Jack struggled to fight down panic.

They entered a small, dark box-room, curtained with red velvet at the far end. Behind Jack, Peacock closed the door with a soft, final-sounding *snick*.

'*Alors*. All our mysteries together,' said Peacock. 'As I said, *convenable*.'

'By all that's—' Tom rubbed his face. 'How can you be so cold, Malpas? Ada! Is it really you? I still cannot credit it.'

'And yet here I stand,' said Ada, with a little laugh. 'Tom, this is Jack. He helped me escape. Jack, this is Tom, the friend I told you about.'

Tom seized Jack's free hand and pumped it up and down. 'My dear, dear fellow – if you helped Ada, that makes you my newest friend too!'

He was certainly an odd companion for Peacock Malpas. His coat sleeves were stained with ink, his collar was askew, and his thick brown hair stood out in tufts. He had a starry-headed look about him – the sort who'd stand a-contemplating while you nipped his purse strings. A lamb, Ada had called him. Aye, but a big man for all that, and her oldest friend – and anyone could see he worshipped Ada.

Jack wondered what Malpas might be doing right now, if Tom wasn't here.

The Frenchman was looking Ada up and down, cold and assessing.

'So you are entirely yourself, again, *mamselle?*'

'All except my memory,' said Ada. 'That, I'm afraid, is a sad blank. The last I recollect is a week before my . . . illness came on.' Her nails pricked into Jack's palm, signalling the lies. Malpas pursed his lips and let the silence draw out.

Ada remembered it all now, she'd remembered the very moment she saw Malpas – and Jack feared that Malpas knew it, too.

'Now.' Ada drew herself up tall, like a queen addressing her troops. 'Will you offer a lady a seat, or must I take my own?'

'Forgive me!' said Tom, blushing, and drawing out a chair.

Ada pulled Jack down onto the seat next to her. Now they were sitting up against the velvet curtains, with Malpas at their back. From the other side of the curtains came the busy hum of a settling crowd.

'A shame, that you remember nothing,' said Malpas. 'We 'ave all been so curious, as to the cause of your *malaise*. Some very strange rumours were circulated . . .'

'Come, Malpas, don't badger her. Of course – we were

concerned – but Ada, my dear, dear Ada . . .' Tom seized a wine bottle from a table in the corner. 'The joy of seeing you again! It is too good – Cured! – Let's drink on it!'

'I will gladly take a sup of wine,' said Ada.

'Jack, you'll drink with us?' said Tom.

'Yes, sir.'

'Good fellow – and call me Tom. To Ada's renewed health!' As Tom made his toast, a bell sounded outside.

'I believe, *mamselle*, your play is about to begin,' said Malpas.

'Never mind the play!' said Tom. 'In the name of all that's human, Ada, how did you get here? How did you escape that dreadful place?'

'There's plenty of time for that,' said Ada. 'Let me see the show.'

'Are you quite sure?'

'She said she was.' Malpas stepped forwards and drew the velvet curtains.

Jack was not prepared for what was on the other side.

This wasn't like the theatres back home. Jack had known that already, from the outside; but this . . .

The box-room was actually a balcony: beyond the parapet was a thirty-foot drop. More balconies arced out to either side, crammed with faces. High above, a thousand winking candles hung suspended from a dome wreathed in gold. Below, where the pit would have been in an ordinary theatre, rows of benches were filling up with spectators. The stage was very wide and tall, hidden for the moment by a giant curtain. Just in front of it, a deep hollow held a band of musicians. They were striking up a tune, but no one was listening.

Word was spreading, heads were turning, necks craning. Everyone was trying to get a look at Ada. Painted faces cracked with wonder. Eyes goggled. Beehive wigs quivered and swivelled. The last time Jack had felt so many eyes on him, he was riding in a wagon to Red Lion Fields – to the gallows.

From the other direction, he felt Malpas's stare prickling between his shoulder blades.

Ada gave the gawpers no countenance. She held her head high, and stared levelly out at the stage.

'My dear, I do wish you'd sit back a little . . .' murmured Tom.

'Why should I hide?' said Ada. 'This is my play!'

'Ada, come—'

'They've seen worse, at Bedlam!'

Ada was blazing up fierce and proud – and Jack thought he understood why. If she feared Malpas, then she was right to make an exhibition of herself. He couldn't do much with two thousand people watching.

With a blare of trumpets, the heavy curtains swept aside.

The stage was lit up bright, and furnished to resemble

the inside of a grand house – astoundingly thorough – nothing like the bare boards of the theatres Jack knew – but the audience hardly marked it at all. Half of them still gazed up at Ada; the rest kept up a steady stream of conversation.

Two actors ambled onto the stage. Jack could hardly hear them over the buzz of the audience.

'I am so angry at how they pursued you, Ada,' said Tom, knitting his fingers together. 'As if you were a nothing but a low criminal. I had tried myself . . . but they would not let me take you. Scoundrels!'

'Don't think of it,' said Ada. 'We're safe now.'

'Did you really jump from a roof?'

Ada described the chase. Tom followed every detail wide-eyed, gasping and muttering from time to time. All the while, Jack was aware of Malpas standing behind them, sipping his wine.

Trapped. Help might be close by – if Ravenscar really was in the theatre – but how to summon it?

Jack was sure that Tom would help them, so far as he could. But Ada couldn't just ask him to fetch Ravenscar: that would mean leaving them alone with Malpas.

So Jack would have to do the fetching. But how to find Lord Ravenscar, when he had no idea what he looked like?

How to escape the box, with Malpas at the door?

On stage, the next scene was assembling itself. Jack looked back over his shoulder. Malpas's cold eyes were there to meet him. The Frenchman was tipping something into his wineglass from a tiny crystal phial. Something that made the stain in Jack's hand pulse warm and soft.

Malpas sipped his wine. Deep within his eyes, something awoke, and stirred.

Jack turned away fast.

One of the actors made a grand gesture with a staff, and a hammering thunderclap rang out.

The crash was so loud it shook Jack's teeth. It silenced the audience too: everyone was looking at the stage now, and Jack could feel the anticipation, a hush in the great hollow space.

Something like a star was being lowered over the stage.

With a single, trembling note from a fiddle, the star began to get brighter. It was actually a sort of hanging seat, Jack could see now, lit up from behind with powerful lamps; and now everyone could see the figure sitting there swinging her legs – a girl, tall and slender, silhouetted against a light so bright the curves of her body showed clear through the gauzy gown she was wearing.

A universal silence greeted this vision. Jack stole a quick glance behind him, and saw that even Malpas was staring at the girl. His eyes were wide open, pupils dilated. Dim wisps of light trailed circles deep inside them.

As if it was the most natural thing in the world, Ada leaned in close to Jack and pointed at the stage.

'Interval soon,' she whispered. 'I'll make a scene. Find Ravenscar.'

'Where?'

Ada turned from him, laughing out loud.

'Don't be silly! No, that is the famous Artemisia Devine. I hear even Lord Ravenscar waits outside her dressing room between acts.' She flicked a wink at him – but Jack noted this with a slim, fleeting corner of his attention.

The girl on stage had advanced right up to the lamps at the front. Now her face was visible, and the audience was pinned.

It was a good face in itself – strong, sharp rather than pretty; but the way it was set now, words like 'pretty' didn't enter the matter. The girl's face blazed forth and held the theatre rapt; a face that could snatch your heart with a single smile, break it with a frown.

He'd seen her do this many times before. She'd always been a master of it – making her face to fit the lay, weaving a character from the set of her shoulders, the turn of her jaw, a single darting look from under her brows. She was famous for it – guller of a thousand gimblets; drover, gentlewoman or fishdaughter as the lay demanded – the Destroying Angel in person.

Beth.

Chapter 16

The rest of the act passed in a bright blur, with Beth at the centre. The audience was spellbound, watching her every move, hanging on her every word. Jack didn't follow the story. As soon as her face first showed, he hadn't had a single thought except that this was impossible. Beth was a sharp one, but this, here, after less than a week?

Impossible.

She looked different. Of course she looked different, she was dressed in gauze, painted up to look like a goddess.

Still, and beneath the paint – different. A different way of working her face, a different stance. She was playing a part, of course. It was always hard to tell with Beth. But still, she looked older – and her shape, too – though maybe that was the clothes . . .

Jack caught himself watching the slim outline of her legs, clearly visible through the flimsy gown. He thought of the hundreds of other eyes doing the same. He remembered what Ada had said about the great Lord Ravenscar, waiting outside her dressing room door.

His cheeks felt hot.

The curtain fell. The audience thundered their delight.

Ada gave a faint sigh and slumped sideways in her chair. As she sprawled onto the floor, Jack came sharp awake. Here was the scene.

'Ada!' cried Tom. He knelt down beside her, cradling her head. She was panting, her eyes closed, her chest heaving. 'What is it?'

Jack hadn't got up yet, but he was ready to spring. Ada was playing her scene well. Her eyes came open now, the lids fluttering; her lips moved feebly.

'I don't . . .' she said. 'I can't . . .' She gave a quick gasp, and her hand went to her throat. 'Water!'

'Don't stand there preening, man!' Tom glared up at Malpas. 'Fetch it.'

'Assuredly,' Malpas smirked, and crossed to the table in the corner.

Jack took his chance. The instant Malpas' back was turned, he was moving. In three steps he was through the door. He didn't look back, worming his way through the crowded corridor till he reached the green door leading to the stairs.

It opened, and a man slipped out with a teetering tray of wine bottles. Jack darted in behind him, quick as a shadow. He jogged down the stairs, passing first one door, then another. Here came another tray man.

'Who're you?' said the man.

What was Beth's new name?

'Message for Miss Devine,' said Jack.

'That so?' said the man. 'Who from?'

'My master,' said Jack, thinking fast. 'Lord Ravenscar.'

'Heh-heh-heh,' said the man, with a leer and a wink. 'Thought you looked a bit roguish-like. I ain't seen you before, have I?'

'I'm new,' said Jack.

'Quite the education for a saucy young lad, I'd fancy, his lordship's service. Message for Miss Devine, eh?' The man leered afresh. 'I'd give her a message or two, if I were 'is lordship!'

Unnameable fears eeled up in Jack's mind.

'You've missed your road for Devine, anyhow. You want next up – follow the broad passage, on past the stage and you're there.'

Jack hurried up and through, into the shadowy vault behind the stage. To his left was a painted backdrop rigged up with ropes and pulleys. To his right, the backstage rambled out, a cross between a warehouse, a painter's studio and a carpenter's workshop.

There was enough bustle here for Jack to pass unchallenged. At the far side of the stage was another broad corridor, crowded with costumes on hangers and props laid out on tables – and here was the door, just as promised. A sign pinned to it read: *Miss Artemisia Devine.*

Jack didn't see anyone waiting there who might be Lord Ravenscar. He felt a coil of wig hair tickle his cheek.

'Here be lovey-dove,' said the imp.

'Can't you just call her Beth?' said Jack. Now he was here, he felt a strange reluctance to open the door.

'Ahem,' said the imp. 'On occasion of tender refinding, I sing.'

'No.'

'*Ooh, lost was lovey-dove, frecktlick lost*
In placetime far away.
Boymaster went to find . . .'

'No singing.'

'*But firefly lady Ada seeing,*' the imp carried on in a low croak. '*Shuklet said his heart was fickle,*
Nearly nearly was beglimmert,
But master has found his lovey-dove
At last.'

'That don't—' said Jack.

'Only with help of shuklet,' added the imp.

'That don't even rhyme,' said Jack.

'Not all poetics must to rhyme,' muttered the imp. 'Song to rhyming, tsa. But master commandet: no song.'

'Well,' said Jack, 'just be quiet now.' He raised his fist and knocked on the door.

'Go!' Not Beth's voice. 'No visits!'

Jack tried the handle. It was locked.

'Begone, wretch, *allez*!' The same angry, foreign voice.

'It's me. It's Jack! Beth, are you—'

A crash and a curse, followed by quick scampering footsteps.

'*Mamselle, non!* Your powder! 'Ave a care!'

The door was flung open.

'Jack?' A strange woman stood before him. Her face was covered with thick white paint. Her lips, reddened to a bright ruby, trembled.

The eyes were Beth's – wide clear eyes the colour of wet flint – softening now, welling up . . .

'It's you.'

Jack's throat was too tight to speak. He nodded.

Beth slapped him hard on the cheek.

'Ow!'

With a choking noise, she grabbed him and dragged him close. Jack felt the greasy stage-paint on her cheek as it pressed against his.

The imp started humming, very quietly, in Jack's ear.

'I thought you'd never come,' Beth whispered. 'I'd given up.'

'I came as quick—'

'Quick!' Beth punched him in the shoulder, pushing him away. 'You dare call that quick!'

'I was locked in Bedlam,' said Jack.

'Bedlam? For *ten months?*'

'What?'

'Count 'em! Ten!'

'But . . .' Jack blinked. 'We went in right after you. Been – four days at most . . .'

'*Mamselle!* For shame!' The foreign voice interrupted. 'Your little *tendresse* is most affecting, but ze curtain is five minutes.'

Beth half turned. Behind her stood a slim, severe older woman, hefting an ivory-handled powder puff like a cudgel.

'Not now,' mouthed Beth, shaking her head a touch, then glancing at the maid.

Jack understood: *careful in front of this one.*

'*Mon dieu,* but look at your face! You are ruined, miss!'

Beth patted her cheek, where a whole streak of paint had come off onto Jack. 'Swive it,' she muttered. 'Jack, get inside.'

She ushered Jack in, bolting the door behind him. 'Right,' she said, 'now what?'

'Ziss will not wait.' The maid grabbed Beth by the hand and dragged her into a high-backed chair. Beth's face was reflected in a large mirror on the dressing table in front of her. It disappeared in a cloud of powder as the maid went to frenzied work on her wig.

'Scrubadub, primple, swab and puff!' the imp whispered approvingly.

Jack's eyes darted about the dressing room, trying to get his thoughts in order. The walls were plastered with cut-out scraps of paper saying things like 'Devine Strikes Again!' and 'Artemisia, London's Latest Toast'. The floor was covered in a comfortable clutter – discarded stockings, open jars of ointment, piles of half-read books and manuscripts. Posies stood out everywhere – more posies than vases. By Jack's foot, a dozen red roses drooped in a chamber pot.

She had a mess and a maid.

She was in a play. She knew her lines.

She had all London sending her flowers.

Ten months . . .

'So,' said Beth, catching his eye in the mirror. 'Here you are.'

'Yes.'

'At last.' Beth scowled, then shut her eyes as a fresh powder cloud exploded in her face. 'Listen, Jack. This . . . you shouldn't be here now. I'm expecting someone.'

'Lord Ravenscar, you mean?' said Jack.

Beth's eyes snapped open.

'That's prime if you are,' Jack added, somewhat flustered and not quite knowing why. 'I'm looking for him myself.'

'Cease parlay,' said the maid. 'Ziss paint must go onto ze smooth, still cheek.'

Beth composed her face. The maid set about touching up her paint.

'So,' said Jack, 'I thought we might go to the Raven later on. Remember that old place, times we used to have? Seems ages now, don't it?'

There was long pause while the paint went on. Jack watched Beth's face in the mirror. It was perfectly still, impossible to read. Then with a final dab the maid leaned back to view her handiwork, and gave a quick pecking nod.

'Of course I remember,' said Beth, speaking carefully so as not to crack the new paint.

There was a brisk triple rap at the door; a short pause, then two light taps.

In the mirror, Jack saw Beth's eyes go suddenly wide. She licked her lips. 'Ballocks,' she muttered.

The maid pushed past Jack to unbolt the door.

'I mean,' said Jack. 'That's what you want, ain't it?'

'Of course,' said Beth. Her voice sounded strange. 'It's only—'

Behind her, the door swung open.

'What *do* women want?'

Jack knew that voice.

He turned.

The maid stepped back from the doorway and went still as a statue.

'Well?'

A glittering man, black coat crusted with gold, diamonds bunched at his throat, was standing in the doorway. Powdered and devilish, eyes like pale jewels, a tiny black heart dotted on at the cheekbone.

He stepped into the room, glanced over at Jack – and stopped for an instant, eyes widening a fraction.

'Why, Lord Ravenscar,' said Beth.

Jack didn't know what his own face looked like in that moment. A picture of shock and horror, most likely.

Ravenscar.

Ghostface.

One and the same.

'The oldest of riddles, Devine,' said Ravenscar. 'I do hope you weren't about to answer, and spoil the fun.'

He floated past with a swish of exquisite velvet coat-tails, paying Jack no more mind than if he'd been a chair or a chamber pot: aside from that fractional flare of the eyes, no sign he knew him at all.

'Master,' breathed the imp in Jack's ear. '*Shiny*, master!'

'What . . . does Devine want?' Ravenscar took Beth's

hand and bowed low, brushing his lips over her knuckles. 'So very many men would like to know.'

Beth's eyes darted from Ravenscar to Jack, and back again.

'Shiny glitterman,' breathed the imp. 'Mecktick, *mecktick* raiments. Oh, for master to be so primplick.'

Ravenscar reached into the inner pocket of his embroidered coat and pulled out a ruby necklace. He leaned in, hands clasping Beth's throat, snapped the chain together and stepped back to admire the effect.

'Blood and snow. Delightful. Someday soon I shall see you all in red, Devine.' He nodded, quite certain. Still he took no notice of Jack, utterly unruffled by whatever monstrous chance had brought them together again.

Except – Jack thought – it wasn't chance, was it? A monstrous *mistake*, was what it was. He'd come here to find Lord Ravenscar – and now here he was.

Jack couldn't take his eyes from the rubies at Beth's throat, and the pretty blush spreading there beneath her powder. *Someday soon I shall see you all in red.*

He made a promise to himself then and there: Lord Ravenscar wouldn't be seeing any more of Beth, all in red or otherwise.

'Ack! Ack!' whispered the imp. 'Not only boymaster be fickleheart. See what a loverman Prettylips hast entweezelt!'

Some small, regular part of Jack's mind was still rolling

along. It marked that Ravenscar was tall, and rich, and devilish handsome; that the price of one of his diamond shoe-buckles could buy a street of houses; that he carried himself as if doubts were something reserved for other, smaller people.

He saw Beth's fingers brush the jewel. He heard her bring out her thanks – her very fetching, very pretty thanks.

She had been here ten months.

Jack looked down to hide his dismay.

'Jack, you seem quite changed tonight,' said Ravenscar, without glancing round. 'The worthy Dr Keith triumphs again?'

'Aye, thassit,' Jack mumbled. 'Leeches.'

'You've met?' said Beth, unable to mask her surprise.

'Indeed,' said Ravenscar. 'And so kind of you too, Jack, to bring Miss Seward back to me. I gather her wits are quite restored.'

'A-aye, milord,' said Jack.

'Fascinating,' said Ravenscar. 'And now here you are again. We share a taste for sable-haired beauties, 'twould appear.'

His mouth gave a little twitch, almost a smile – and Jack thought of Ada, and the horror he'd seen inside her.

Behind Ravenscar's shoulder, Beth was mouthing something: looked like *careful* was in there somewhere. *Careful*, that was precious.

Jack knew what he had to do.

He ran.

Ravenscar didn't even try for a grab. Jack heard a soft chuckle, cut off as he slammed the door behind him.

He piked and shimmied through the backstage bustle, sprinted down the corridor, bounded up the stairs three at a time. On the fourth floor he pushed through the green baize door.

He had to warn Ada. She'd made a mistake all right, coming here to those two – Ravenscar and Malpas, Ghostface and Peacock – killers, Swarm servants, two of a kind . . .

The corridor was mostly empty. The door to the box was open. He could see Ada standing, leaning over the balcony. He ran in through the door.

The Alkahest heat blazed up in his hand, stopping short at the numb black part. Jack looked round, saw that the box was empty except for him and Ada.

'Ada,' said Jack.

She turned, her head jerking awkwardly like a badly handled puppet.

'It's happening again,' she said.

The imp quivered and clutched at his scalp. 'Hellstuff,' it said. 'Much hellstuff, master!'

His right eye was watering, swimming into devil-sight. He looked at Ada and saw what burned inside her –

hellstuff, Spiritus – but nothing like before, with Kitty. Not just sparks now, but a firestorm of shocking blue, rose, livid green streaked with black – the flames swirling like leaves whipped up by a gale.

'Who did this?' said Jack.

Ada shook her head. 'It's coming,' she said. 'I . . . Oh God!'

Jack felt his right index finger go from numb to deathly cold. Cold against hot, the two feeding off each other, unbearable. He staggered, fell to his knees. Behind Ada's eyes, the storm of flame changed to a flat white light.

Ada reached up and clawed at her own face, leaving a trail of bright red streaks.

'It's coming,' she said.

In the centre of the light something was growing. Tiny dark specks. Getting larger. Getting *closer*. A triumphant buzzing rose up somewhere on the edge of hearing – shrill, grating, filled with an unutterable hate.

'I can't . . .' said Ada. She turned, and lifted one leg over the parapet. 'It's coming, and I can't . . .'

'Stop it,' said Jack.

'You don't understand, it's happening again. Worse this time. Can't fight it any more . . .'

'No, stop it, STOP!'

But she didn't stop.

She lifted her other leg up onto the parapet. Jack reached forward, grabbed hold of her skirt.

She jumped. The hem of her skirt tore off in Jack's hand.

A deep sea-roar surged up from the pit below.

Jack heard steps behind him. Malpas. Here out of nowhere, as if he'd been hiding behind the door.

He glanced over the parapet, turned to Jack, and pursed his lips.

'Oh dear,' he said.

Jack forced himself to look.

Ada lay directly below him. All around her was a circle of empty floor, an island in the jostling sea of heads, some of them struggling to see her, some to get away. She lay very still. Her head was at a strange crooked angle on her neck. Her face looked like something ugly made out of wax.

She was gone. Jack had seen enough dead people to know the difference.

Things began to happen very quickly, though to Jack they all seemed slow, like swimming in treacle.

Tom came in, and ran to the parapet. He croaked some words out, Jack couldn't hear what. His face was red and wet with tears. He grabbed Jack by the shoulders and started to shake him. His mouth moved, trying to speak, but only sobs came out.

Then Lord Ravenscar was there, and Tom stopped

shaking. Ravenscar went to the parapet, looked down at what lay below.

'The boy,' Tom was saying. 'The boy was – I only left her a moment . . . and he . . . he . . .'

Ravenscar turned to Jack, his white face tight, one nostril trembling very slightly.

'What have you done?'

Chapter 17

It was Malpas who dragged Jack out of the theatre, gripping his neck in a chokehold. Each time Jack tried to twist free, his breath was cut off. By the time they reached the lobby he'd started seeing stars.

Lord Ravenscar's chariot was waiting for them in the street. It was a big one, gleaming black, with four black horses in harness. A pair of lackeys in black and gold livery stood to either side of the door, one of them holding it open. Malpas shoved Jack inside and shut the door on him. Jack went for the opposite door, but it was locked and shuttered.

'Quick, Imp,' he said. 'Ope it.'

The imp lifted off his head, flew down to the lock.

The first door opened again. Lord Ravenscar stepped inside and shut it behind him. The imp flopped to the floor.

'You've lost your wig,' said Ravenscar.

Jack bent to pick it up. He thought of launching the imp at Ravenscar. It might give him time to get past him and out into the street – and then what? Straight into the arms of Ravenscar's lackeys, and Malpas with his dagger-pistol. Did Jack think the imp could tackle all four? He did not.

He put the wig back on his head. The ribbon twitched against the back of his neck.

'Dreaming of escape?' said Ravenscar. His cold grey eyes regarded Jack. 'You will not, I assure you.'

Ravenscar didn't say anything more after that. He banged on the ceiling, and with a crack of a whip they were moving off.

The black carriage beetled north, leaving old London behind as it moved away from the river. The houses here were big, stone-fronted mansions, square and stern and new.

It began to rain. The ride was deathly silent. Ravenscar stared at Jack. His powdered face was ghost-white, expressionless.

Jack didn't know where to put his eyes. If he closed them, he saw Ada's broken body on the theatre floor. She'd known her danger. She'd asked for his help.

But he hadn't. He'd gone straight to Beth, and now Ada was dead, and Jack was in bad trouble.

Aye, trouble, but *Ada was dead.*

The hurt was too sharp to hold for long. Jack swallowed

hard, shoving down the great bubble of remorse that was rising in his throat.

Beth's voice. Thieves' Law: no moping, no looking back. Save your own skin.

All that felt hollow now.

Ravenscar House lay at the heart of a grand new development, streets and squares laid out fresh over the fields north of the Oxford Road. Lord Ravenscar had overseen the entire project, which was designed with the latest scientific principles in mind. The drains, the hospital, and the bright street lamps were all thoroughly modern. Even so, the architects had had to make some strange compromises when it came to the construction of Ravenscar House itself.

For one thing, once the building was completed Lord Ravenscar had ordered them to burn every copy of the plans. There were secrets inside that he wanted to keep very quiet.

'Here we are, milord,' the coachman called, as the carriage slowed to a halt.

Flecks of freezing rain stung Jack's face. Ravenscar propelled him out of the chariot and into the arms of his waiting servants. The coach lamps cut bright cones through the gusting sleet, lighting the way to the front doors. Jack saw dozens of windows glowing down from above.

Once he was inside, no one would know or care if he

came out again. A powerful man, Lord Ravenscar. A man who could do as he liked, and never mind the law.

The servants marched him up to the doors, Ravenscar striding ahead. Jack tried a sudden twist as they were mounting the doorstep – and before he knew it his wrist was pinned high behind his back, his arm half out of its socket, the pain sickening.

'You're his lordship's guest now. Mind your manners.'

The doors swung open. A lackey bowed low as Ravenscar swished in, his footsteps clicking brisk on marble slabs. Jack went in stumbling and faint with pain. He felt the imp tense against his scalp.

The doors slammed behind him. Servants all around now. Too late to use the imp. The moment had passed so quickly, and now he was shut in, trapped in Lord Ravenscar's private domain.

Candles blazed down from all sides – enough light to fill a cathedral. Now there was nowhere to run, the men relaxed their grip. Jack's arm dangled limp by his side, his shoulder throbbing.

Ravenscar was walking towards a broad, sweeping staircase straight ahead. He turned and beckoned to Jack. For a moment, in the candlelight, his cold white face flickered dark and demon-hot.

There was nothing else to do but follow.

The staircase curved back on itself, twisting up towards

the domed roof fifty feet above. Jack's eyes travelled up as he climbed, past blank-eyes marble statues and gilded columns, to the painted ceiling. Dim naked bodies in a fire-wracked sky, only half human: bat wings and cat faces, goat legs and serpent tails. Jack felt the imp tense again. He remembered the way it had looked the first time he'd seen it, before it was bound – part dog, part dwarf, part child. He remembered the satyr.

These were devils on the ceiling – devils and hellfire.

Jack was suddenly sure this was the place where Ada went mad. The idea brought fresh stabs of pain. Ada at Bedlam, saying *help me*. The chase through London, her hand in his. Her dead face: it still didn't seem possible. Jack had never known anyone so alive.

He tried to put it out of his mind. What mattered now was the way it looked – that Jack had pushed her to her death. And the way it looked seemed far more likely than the truth – flat white light in her eyes; a Swarm that ate up sanity. No one would believe a word of it.

Except Ravenscar, said a cold voice deep inside. What if Ravenscar knew very well what had happened to Ada? What if Ravenscar knew much more about the Swarm than Jack?

This was the house of hellfire. Jack was in deep water, icy and black, with silent horrors gliding in the fathoms below.

They climbed the stairs and circled round an upper gallery, through echoing rooms furnished in gold and glinting black. More paintings – devils and torments and howling lost souls. Ravenscar never looked back. He knew Jack had no choice but to follow.

At last they arrived in a windowless chamber with mirrored walls and delicate gilded chairs. Ravenscar produced a little box, black lacquer inlaid with gold, and snapped it open. He turned to Jack. With his thin, white fingers he took a pinch of powder from the box. He raised it to a thin, white nostril. He sniffed sharply.

'So.' It was the first word that had passed his lips since he'd first climbed into the carriage. 'Why did you push her?'

'I didn't do it,' said Jack.

'Tush.' Very soft was his voice, perilous soft. 'My friend is dead. I will have the truth out of you: the whole truth, willing or not.'

Willing or not. Torments, then. Jack had seen men, back in his own day who'd been put to the torment – broken, pitiful creatures.

What could he say that would save him? Nothing came: his mind was all gummed up with Ada. She was really dead. He had failed her.

The longer the silence lasted, the worse he felt, and the harder it was to speak.

A knock on the door made him jump.

'Enter,' said Ravenscar.

A footman opened the door and announced, 'The Chevalier de Malpas, and Mr T-*urgh*!'

Tom smashed past the footman, going straight for Jack, hands clutching for his throat. Jack just had time to raise his arms before Tom was upon him, grabbing his wrists and bearing him down to the floor.

'Control yourself,' said Lord Ravenscar.

'No, sir! Dead, sir! Dead – murdered – I'll have my vengeance!'

Tom loomed close, red with murderous rage, his breath hot in Jack's face. Now he had both Jack's hands pinned in one of his, and the other was at Jack's throat. Jack squirmed. Something hot splashed on his face. Tears. Tom was crying, even as he throttled him. Vengeance: fair enough. Ada was dead. Tom was the only one who seemed to feel it.

'It wasn't me,' Jack said, loud as he could with his throat squeezed half shut. 'I tried to help her, I'm not the one who . . .'

Tom's grip tightened, choking off the words. Stars in front of his eyes, a rushing in his head, thick pounding of blood, an ache as if his brain would burst . . .

Then Tom was off him. Ravenscar and Malpas had him by the arms. Tom struggled at first and then the strength drained out of him and he was staggering down into a chair.

Ravenscar gave Tom a little pat on the shoulder. His

eyes never left Jack. Malpas leaned over and whispered something in Ravenscar's ear. Deadly cold, these two. Tom might want Jack's life: Jack could understand that. What did Ravenscar want? What did he know?

'The one who what?' said Ravenscar.

Jack shook his head.

'You said, it wasn't me. I'm not the one who . . .' Ravenscar raised his eyebrows, spread his hands. 'Who what?'

'Made her jump,' said Jack. He forced the words out, hating himself. Better to be like Tom, venting his grief, than to talk of it like this, all cold-blooded.

'Meaning someone else did?' Ravenscar tutted. 'Find a better story than that, boy: you were the only one there, we all saw it.'

'I didn't do it,' said Jack.

'Then whom are you accusing?' said Ravenscar.

Jack's eyes flicked over to Malpas, standing behind Tom's chair. The Frenchman's face was blank, unreadable. No fear of discovery there. No: because when Malpas killed people, Ravenscar helped him get away with it.

'She jumped,' said Jack. 'It's the truth!'

'Truth?' said Ravenscar. He paused, savouring the taste of what he was about to say. 'Oh, but even if it were, we'd not have scratched the surface of the *truth*, now would we?'

'Don't understand,' said Jack.

'No? But you positively *seethe* with unanswered

questions,' said Ravenscar. 'You leap out of Moll King's privy, clad like something out of Shakespeare. You talk to beetles. You don't know what year it is – but still you contrive to break out of Bedlam amidst the most sensational scenes of riot and madness. You steal my mistress, elude my pursuit, only to bring her straight to me. Whereupon you push her to her death.'

Jack felt a deathly tiredness creeping upon him. There was no story that could compass this, Ravenscar was right.

'Strange enough yet?' Ravenscar held up one finger. 'No! For there is more. Earlier this evening, just before Ada's death –' Tom's shoulders shook, but Ravenscar sailed on – 'you pay a visit to my good friend Artemisia Devine, with whom you appear tolerably well acquainted.'

'Your *good friend . . .*' Tom's voice was low, but Jack caught the look of pure, unguarded hatred he shot at Ravenscar.

Either Ravenscar missed this, or he chose to ignore it.

'See, I have a notion we now approach the centre of this whole unhappy business. You do not deny that you are acquainted with her?'

'No, milord.' Jack hung his head, defeated. Here was the final straw, and he had almost forgotten it: he'd left Ada to die, everyone thought he'd killed her – and he'd dragged Beth into it too. Everything he'd done to find her – to rescue her, as he'd thought – had ended in disaster.

Jack blinked, and felt the tears spill out of the corners of his eyes. 'I was . . . looking for her.'

The imp stiffened. The silk periwig ribbon brushed quickly at the back of Jack's neck – a quick one-two, back and forth.

'And?' prompted Ravenscar.

Jack heard light footsteps approaching the door.

'She's . . .'

'What is she?'

'She's my . . . I'm her . . .'

'Brother!'

The door swung open behind Ravenscar, and Beth swept into the room.

Her eyes found Jack. For the barest instant he saw her relief; then the mask swept down, and now she wasn't Beth at all, but Artemisia Devine – quite at home in her paint and powder, a very smart package, a stranger.

Ravenscar's ruby necklace twinkled dark at her throat.

'Don't gape so, brother,' she said, speaking with the clipped, Frenchified tones of this London – only a little lazier, a little drawlier. 'Ravenscar. Gentlemen. My condolences.'

Tom's tear-stained face was turned towards her, gaping in astonishment, but she swept by him without a glance.

'Devine.' Ravenscar bent low and brushed his lips over

her fingers. 'I thought you might come. The second half was cancelled, I collect.'

'*Quelle dommage,*' said Beth.

'The pity of the world, my dear. I bitterly regret any lost chance to see you perform.'

Beth laughed. 'You are a cold devil, Ravenscar.'

'On the contrary,' said Ravenscar. 'I have been having the most *heated* conversation with your – brother, did you say? It seems he pushed Ada to her death.'

'But . . .' said Beth, 'but what makes you think he did that?'

She looked utterly astounded. She stared hard at each of the men in turn, turning from one to another in bewilderment.

Beth – thank Christ – Beth Sharkwell, cool as you please, sweeping in, taking charge. Jack felt an urge to throw himself at her feet and clasp her by the knees.

'Why, we all saw—' Malpas began.

'Saw what?' said Beth. 'There are a thousand-odd witnesses at the theatre who *all saw* her jump, quite unassisted. They are printing up the broadsheets as we speak.'

Tom gave a low moan. Malpas was shaking his head. Ravenscar was looking at Beth, his expression unreadable.

'Well, my lord?' said Beth. 'What exactly did you see? I'll wager it wasn't Jack pushing her.'

'No . . .' said Ravenscar. 'He was there, but . . .'

'But if the boy didn't push her, why did she jump?' Tom burst out.

Jack saw Malpas glance up, suddenly watchful.

'Why?' said Beth. 'There's a good reason that lunatics are locked up, sir. It's for their own protection as much as ours. Only a *day* ago this poor lady was in Bedlam.'

Wrong, Jack thought. She hadn't been mad, even at the very end. She'd known what she was doing. She'd jumped because the Swarm was coming, and this time she couldn't fight it.

Jack looked over at Malpas. Their eyes met, and Malpas's narrowed.

Malpas knew. Jack was sure of it.

He prayed that Beth could get him out of here, and then immediately felt ashamed of himself. *Save your own skin.* Ada had done the opposite.

'A thousand witnesses saw her jump,' Beth continued. 'I am told the coroner's verdict is a foregone conclusion. But you assume that my poor idiot brother . . . well, this is most uncharitable.'

'Your poor idiot brother,' said Ravenscar, in a slow, musing sort of voice. 'Well, this is quite a tale, Devine. I've always wondered about your origins, and now I meet your family!'

There was a glint of knowing in his eye now – the same

that Jack had seen in him from the first; a man who knew more than you did, always . . .

'Tell me more, my dear,' said Ravenscar; and Jack felt his heart high in his throat, because if Ravenscar had been looking at him that way it would have frozen his tongue.

Beth was blushing. Jack could believe it, even of her: she'd met her match, she couldn't talk her way out of this one, she was blushing like a liar caught in her lie . . .

And then she began to speak, and Jack realized she was entirely in control.

'I . . . really, Ravenscar, this is a most unfair advantage. I do hope this will remain between us . . .'

Ravenscar raised his eyebrows, and said nothing.

'Well then. Jack is my brother, and I won't be ashamed of him.' (Though her blushes told another story, Jack thought.) 'He's been quite addled in his intellects, ever since he was kidnapped as a child. Kidnapped by a smuggler, if you can believe it.'

'A smuggler?' said Ravenscar. 'How romantic.'

Jack looked at Beth – almost as unbelieving as Ravenscar.

'Yes, and what's more romantic still, an *Italian* smuggler. Well, half French, I believe. Called Udolpho.' She gave Jack the tiniest of nods. 'He was taken as a little boy.'

It was their old sham story. The one they'd worked up to cozen the *magician* Udolpho.

Jack saw what Beth was playing at.

'Took me in his boat,' he said. 'Pa was fishing for sprat.'

'Poor Father,' began Beth. 'He was always a dreamer . . .'

And they were off together.

Despite a few stumbles, Jack remembered his lines – not too well, because he was meant to be the idiot brother after all, but well enough. Beth brought the whole tale out as polished and perfect as the first time she'd told it – the wreck of their family's fortune, the death of their mother, Jack's capture, and the perils she'd undergone to get him back. She followed Jack's lead when it came to explaining what had happened in the last few days. They wove their stories together; and whenever Jack faltered, Beth was ready with an easy line or a laugh at his flickering wits.

It was a good story. There was no doubt that Tom was taken in. A lamb, Ada had said, and though Jack had just seen him roused to fury, he believed her now: Tom was gazing at him with pity in his eyes.

But Malpas's eyes were as narrow as ever, and still as a snake's; and Ravenscar's white face was cold and hard as bone.

'You are remarkable, Devine,' he said at the last, shaking his head. In a flash, Jack remembered Udolpho saying exactly the same thing. 'To have kept all this secret for so long.'

'I'm ashamed of him, you see.'

'Hey,' said Jack.

'Hush, dolt,' said Beth. Then, to Ravenscar, 'You understand why I'd rather this stayed between us. He is but a poor rude creature. More fit for the attic than polite company.'

'And yet he is your kin,' said Ravenscar. 'Remarkable.'

He was leaning back, watching Beth's face with a sort of amused admiration. His eyes travelled down the length of her body, then back up again, coming to rest on the ruby necklace at her throat.

Beth's eyes were bright, staring right back at him; but there was an artful blush spreading beneath her powder. At least, Jack hoped it was artful.

He was certain of two things: Ravenscar didn't believe them; and Ravenscar wanted Artemisia Devine much more than he wanted Jack.

'It grows late,' said Beth. 'I will take my brother now – I hope you understand there's no use questioning him. He is quite muddled.'

'Oh I see a muddle,' said Ravenscar. 'But – no use? I wonder. I'm sure I could think of a question or two . . .'

'But you must permit her, my lord!' said Tom. He started up from his chair. 'After what . . . My dear boy . . .'

He stumbled over and pumped Jack's hand between both of his. 'I beg forgiveness. I have done you a terrible injustice.'

'No matter now,' said Jack.

'In my grief, I know not what – I wanted to do such things, I wished you such harm – for Ada's sake . . .'

Jack saw the tears spring out in Tom's eyes as he spoke her name. He felt something respond inside himself – and now his own voice was trembling. 'I know,' he said. 'I knew her too, see?'

'Lord! That's nobly said.' Tom turned to Beth. 'To think what I would have done . . . how can you ever forgive me, Miss Devine?'

Beth swivelled her head an inch in his direction. Tom was much taller than her, but somehow she contrived to look down her nose at him.

She sniffed. 'Sir,' she said, 'if you'd broke his neck, I should scarcely have forgiven you. Since you have not, I fail to see how you could possibly offend me.'

'Charming,' said Ravenscar. 'Quite charming. Sisterly devotion: I like to see it. You must certainly take him, Devine.'

'Thank you, my lord.'

'On one condition,' said Ravenscar, his smile broadening. 'I play host here, tomorrow night. You will grace me with your presence.'

'You are mighty bold, to presume . . .'

Jack glanced over at Beth.

'Oh yes.' Ravenscar smiled lazily. 'Bold as gold, Devine: we are alike in that. Now do you want your brother or not?'

Beth hesitated; then she curtsied, still holding Jack's hand. Ravenscar bowed.

They descended the stairs. Beth's face gave nothing away. Jack didn't mind. His whole body was trembling now. He could hardly believe he was out of that room.

Outside, a footman handed Beth up into a dainty little chariot drawn by a team of matched white horses.

'Whip up, Jenks!' called Beth. 'Come on Jack, step in. We're going home.'

Chapter 18

Home. The word sang inside Jack's head as he tottered into the chariot, wrung out with grief and shock and relief. Home: Ravenscar might think he had them in his power, but not even Ravenscar could know about Lud's key – and as long as the key worked, not even Ravenscar could follow where it would take them.

He unbuttoned his waistcoat pocket, and pulled out the key.

And then Beth turned from the window to look at him, and the good feeling went away.

'What in piss-tarred Hell was that, Jack?' She was angry. Why was she angry? 'You've . . . Ada Seward dead, and . . . Christ, but you've had a busy time, ain't you? Took me ten months to get where I am, and you tumble all down in a trice!'

'What d'ye mean, tumble all down?'

'Never mind,' said Beth. She took a deep breath – drawing herself in.

The imp chirped in Jack's ear. 'Skapings, eh – and shukdoor speedward?'

'That's right,' muttered Jack.

'What's that?' said Beth.

'Just the imp. Imp wants to go home too.'

'Ah – I'd quite forgot your creature.' She frowned. 'Where's it hiding?'

'Hazzat!' hissed the imp, raising up from Jack's head and waggling its periwig curls.

'Huh,' said Beth, taking in the imp's new appearance with a quick jerk of the chin. 'Ahoy there, Imp.'

'Hoylick, pretty-lips,' said the imp, settling back on Jack's head.

Outside the driver cracked his whip, and they were in motion.

'Fine chariot,' said Jack, trying to make conversation, still trying to work out what was wrong. 'It yours?'

Beth gave a single nod. 'And they're called carriages, not chariots.' She was still angry.

'Look,' said Jack, holding up the key. 'I've got the key, so . . .'

They both stared at it. Jack wished it would change shape, or glow, or do anything to show its power. It lay there, cold and heavy in his hand.

Beth gave a short laugh. '*I've* got the key, Jack. I'm going to lock you up in my attic, just like I told Ravenscar. That way you won't tumble aught else.'

'Tumble . . . what d'ye mean?' said Jack. 'I've got the key. *This* key. We can leave, now, tonight. Long as it works again . . .'

Beth was shaking her head. Jack didn't understand.

'What?'

'We're not leaving tonight. I'm taking you home. My home.'

Her voice was flat. Her eyes wouldn't meet his. 'I've been thinking, Jack. And I've decided.'

Jack waited, but she didn't go on.

'Mayhap forlorning for glitterman,' whispered the imp. 'Probable, tsa, for such a glintick.'

'Beth,' said Jack.

'What?'

'We can't—'

'I can,' said Beth. 'I've thought on it.' Now she looked up, hard and proud. 'Wait till you see my house, Jack. Coming here? Best thing ever happened to me.'

'But you said.' Jack paused, trying to take it in. Staring at the jewels around her neck, as angry thoughts began to whisper louder and louder inside. 'You said, at the theatre, you'd come.'

'Aye, well. I've thought on it.'

He still couldn't bring himself to look at her face. He didn't need to: he could hear it in her voice. She was pulling away from him, drawing herself in, hard and stubborn.

'Made up your mind, have you?' he said.

'Jack. Look around you. What do you see?'

Jack said nothing.

'Riches,' said Beth. 'What're we doing, riding in a carriage, eh? You ever even seen one before you came here?'

'Aye,' said Jack. 'Earl of Essex's.'

'Aye: once, haply. How many you seen this past few days? Riches, Jack – London's rich now, England's rich, we own half of *India*. Richest men in the world live in London these days, and all the richest of *them* are falling over each other to line my purse. I don't even have to cheat for it. Same old tricks, but now it's on the stage, out in the open, and everyone loves me for it! It's perfect. Come on, tell me you don't see it.'

Jack scowled. He could see it, all right: Ravenscar's rubies, a prize that could have cost her neck back when they were thieves. What had it cost here? What had the carriage cost, the velvet cushion he was sitting on, the house they were going to?

'What about the Law, Beth?' he said. 'You'd remember which number, I don't know, but what it says is nothing comes free. You remember that one?'

'Number Four.' Beth rolled her eyes. 'So I go to dinner

with fat old lords, wear something flimsy, what have you. Easiest living I ever heard of . . .'

'What about Ravenscar? He ain't a fat old lord. He's dangerous, he—'

Beth shook her head, hard. 'I can wrangle Ravenscar,' she said. 'He's sharp, aye, and dangerous to his enemies, but – he likes me. Not just like that, either. Listen: after I came through that door, I was on the cozening lay, scraping by, hand-to-mouth-like . . . one day he sees me gulling a gimblet gent, friend of his . . . sees right through the lay, but did he cry beef? No! He saw what I could do. He *saw* me. Gave me my start, on the stage . . .'

'Oh, well, so you owe him, then. What's he ask in return?'

'I'm in no one's pocket, Jack.'

'He buy you this carriage?'

'And what if he did?'

Now Jack looked her in the eye, and the look she gave him back made him stop short.

After all he'd gone through to find her – left Ada to her fate, to her *death*, gone running straight to Beth – for this?

Everything fouled up, everything ruined.

'We're here,' said Beth, as the carriage slowed, then halted outside a pretty little house – wrought-iron railing out front, ivy and roses growing up the wall. She led him in, a servant sweeping the front door open while the coachman rattled off to wherever she had her stabling – Jack thinking it through now, the riches, all the people and property she must control – and then gaping, unable to help it, as he saw the inside of Beth's house.

'Sheeny shiny glintick *shiny!*' breathed the imp in his ear, overcome with awe.

The hallway was the colour of white wine, with shimmering patterns woven into the stuff covering the walls; Turkey carpets on the floor; a tall mirror where Beth glanced, checking herself before leading him on up the stairs. A maid hovered in the background, scurried off when Beth nodded to her and said, 'Coffee for two.' Once the maid was gone, Beth turned to Jack. 'Careful what you say when she's about. Ravenscar pays her, I'm pretty sure.'

'To spy on you,' said Jack. 'Nice cage he's got you in, ain't it?'

'Oh for such a cage for a shuklet,' said the imp. 'Polish and swish, all day for shinies . . .'

Beth had reached the top of the stairs. 'Jack?' she said, stopping in front of a door up there, her hand on the handle. 'I pulled you out the mire, back at Ravenscar's. You're in my house. I'm giving you coffee.'

'Whatever *that* is,' said Jack.

'Point *is*, Jack,' said Beth. 'Be civil.'

She put on her Artemisia Devine voice for that last bit, all cut and polished like expensive glass. Jack hated it.

'Come on,' said Beth, opening the door. Jack followed her into another jaw-dropper of a room. The walls weren't gold like the hallway: they were a dull powder blue, with silver patterns; pictures hanging here and there; a marble statue of a girl with a bow and arrow, wearing a sort of kirtle round her waist and nothing else. The face on the statue was Beth's, no mistaking it.

Jack looked away, blushing. Beth was sitting down on some kind of silken couch. She didn't seem embarrassed. Maybe it was normal, here, to have naked breasts all over the place. He remembered the suit of gauze she'd worn in the theatre, showing off her body. Even what she was wearing now – walk around the old London dressed like that and she'd be taken up for whoring, locked in Bridewell.

'Like what you see?' said Beth. Jack stared at the floor, feeling the heat rise through his cheeks.

'Oh, the carpet's to your taste, is it?' Playing with him, the same bantering game she'd played with Ravenscar.

Jack didn't want to play. He wanted to go home. He'd been better off out in the cold, even – on the run with Ada.

Ada had cared for him. Ada had needed him.

'Which are you now, then?' he muttered.

'Eh?' said Beth.

'I said which are you now, Beth Sharkwell or Artemeesia whatchermaycallit?'

'Devine,' said Beth. 'And it's Artemisia. After the goddess. Artemis the huntress.' She nodded at the lewd statue. 'That's her – or me, if you prefer. See the likeness, brother Jack?' She was taunting him now, switching between the two voices.

'I ain't your brother,' he said.

'What are you, then?'

Before he could answer there was a tap on the door and the maid entered, carrying an elegant silver pot on a tray with two tiny cups. 'Coffee, *mamselle*,' she said, setting the tray down on a little table beside Beth's couch.

'Thank you, Jeanette,' said Beth. Then, when the maid was gone, 'Won't you try some coffee, Jack? Come on, sit. Don't be a moonlicker.'

It sounded enough like the old Beth for Jack to sit down.

'Here's how it is, Jack,' she said, pouring steaming black liquid into the two cups. It smelled good. 'I *am* Artemisia Devine now, and I got there by way of *being* Beth Sharkwell. Same thing I always did – playing at different parts, cozening all and sundry. Christ, if they'd let girls on stage back home I'd have tried this years ago, made my fortune.'

She held out one of the tiny cups. The handle was so thin Jack thought it might break off in his hand.

He raised it to his lips and stopped. His hand was on the coffee cup. It was hot from the steaming stuff inside, but that wasn't all. There was another heat, a prickly heat that went bone deep – a heat that only Jack could feel, only in his stained hand . . .

Beth was raising her cup to her lips. Jack shot forward

and pushed it away. Steaming black coffee splashed across her front.

'Ow, bloody Hell Jack, *what?*'

Jack was staring into his own cup – staring with the devil-sight now, seeing what was in there as tiny motes of light, flickering different colours.

Spiritus.

'Who gave you this stuff?' he said.

'What are you talking about?' said Beth. She was swiping coffee off her front, the lace of her dress and the swell of bare skin above it. Her face was red with anger.

'This – this coffee, who gave it you?'

'It was a gift from Ravenscar. What's your point – you think I go to bed for a sack of coffee beans?'

Jack shook his head, thinking no, but maybe for a house and a carriage and jewels and servants . . . but that didn't matter for the moment.

This was the stuff that drove Ada to her death, and Beth was drinking it by the pot.

'There's something in it,' said Jack. 'Something bad.'

'What, you mean the Spiritus?' Beth shook her head, disbelieving. 'You scald me and ruin a perfectly good dress over a few drops of Spiritus? What, you think girls shouldn't drink, is it?'

So she knew. She knew what Ravenscar had given her, and she drank it up anyway.

'It's bad,' said Jack. 'It's devil-stuff – it's what killed Ada.'

'Ballocks,' said Beth. She picked up the silver pot again. 'Jack, you don't know the first thing about it. How could you – only been here five days.'

'I know what it did to Ada,' said Jack.

'Oh aye?' Beth was pouring herself another cup. 'What d'you know about Ada Seward? Me and her – very different, Jack. Very different. Me?' She held up her cup. Jack was ready to knock it out of her hand, if need be, but she didn't go to drink yet. 'This is like a cup of beer of an evening. With Ada, it was like downing ragwater by the pint – at that Hellfire Club, where I never went because I know what goes on there. I flash my eyes and get rubies for it, she lets Ravenscar pluck her for nothing. I know what lay I'm playing. She didn't even know what a lay is.'

She raised the cup. Jack grabbed her by the wrist.

'Don't say that about her,' he said. 'I won't hear it.'

Beth didn't struggle against him. She looked at him, dead cold. 'You won't?'

Jack took the cup away from her. She didn't try to stop him.

'Jack,' she said, her voice perilous sweet. 'All I have to do is ring a bell, and strong men will come and throw you out into the street. Is that what you want?'

Jack didn't answer. He didn't trust himself to speak – didn't know if he'd scream with rage or burst into tears

– those things she'd said about Ada hurting him sore. But worst of all was the way she didn't listen. She never had. Beth knew it all, and what Jack said was always rumpskuttle, worthless.

'Now I've been drinking Spiritus regular,' she was saying now, 'the past three months or more. All the girls at the theatre do it. Settles the nerves, they say, though mine don't need it. I drink because I like it. I've always done as I liked, case you'd forgotten. You think I've changed so much?'

'Aye, you've changed,' Jack muttered.

'What, the old Beth Sharkwell wouldn't take a drink if she liked it?'

'Not that.'

'What then?'

'All this,' said Jack. 'Living here, like you're his pet bird . . . cold and false, through and through. He's got you addled, calling it Spiritus, but it's bad, it's devil-stuff – ask the imp, Imp'll tell you . . .'

The imp stiffened against his scalp. 'Shuklet no part of this quarrel,' it said.

'Aye, wise shuklet,' said Beth.

'But Spiritus is of hellkind,' the imp added.

'*Thank* y—' said Jack, before the imp chimed in again.

'But lovey-dove nix addle-pate, methinks.'

'Thanks, Imp,' said Beth, with a look of sour triumph. She looked down from the wig to Jack's face. 'I see where

240

you're tending, Jack. You don't think I'm addled, you think I'm a whore. How else could a *girl* get so much, eh? That's what you been thinking ever since you got in my carriage.'

'Ain't it the truth?' Jack heard his own voice, hoarse and strange. Now he was too angry to stop. 'Who paid for the carriage? House and servants, what, they give you all that for acting pretty on the stage?'

Jack felt the imp clutch at his scalp in alarm.

'Aye, that's the way you think,' said Beth, very soft and calm. 'Dirty fancies, from a dirty little boy.'

Something was changed. She was no longer Beth. Now she was Artemisia Devine through and through, and Jack was a clod-hopping fool – her idiot brother from the country. And he was afraid, too – of what, he didn't know. Only that he couldn't answer her, or meet her eye.

'I saw you, watching,' she said. 'In the theatre, when he gave me this.' Her hand brushed the rubies at her throat, then trailed across the soft skin there. 'Aye, and many another time. Did you want to touch me here, too?' Her finger lingered on her breast, the skin red where the hot coffee had splashed. 'Art *jealous*, brother Jack?'

She laughed, soft and mocking.

'At least with Ravenscar 'tis an honest chase,' she said.

Jack stood up, still clutching the cup. He didn't know if the stuff in the coffee would make her mad, or make her love Ravenscar, or what. All he knew was that he couldn't stay here a moment longer, locked up in this jewel box with Artemisia Devine, her soft laughter and her scornful voice.

'I'm going home,' he said. 'Real home, all the way. Stay here if you want: give you joy of it.'

He blundered to the door, wrenched at the handle – and then he was stumbling down the stairs, out the front door, out into the night – gasping with the cold, walking fast away.

He wouldn't run. Wouldn't give her the satisfaction. Go to the door at Moll King's, make it work: leave her to Ravenscar, if that's what she wanted.

He hadn't even told her about Kit. Jack swallowed hard, and walked faster. What did she care about Kit? What did she care about anyone but herself?

Kit and Ada, both of them true friends. Both dead now, and Jack was weeping in gusts, choking out sobs, hunched over as he walked. *No moping, save your own skin* – but that was Beth again, Beth all over. She didn't care. She never had.

Leave her to Ravenscar.

Let her learn the hard way.

Chapter 19

The streets were empty and dark. Gusts of wind blew dead leaves along the pavements. Melting sleet turned the roadway to slushy mud.

Jack had wept himself dry. He kept up his pace, concentrating on putting distance between himself and Beth.

Art jealous, brother Jack? Her laugh. Her scorn. The terrible things they'd both said.

The imp was no help. As he rushed out of her door it had whispered, 'Master has lost his love,' in a hushed, stricken voice. No more after that, apart from the odd dusty sniffle.

The streets grew narrower – little boxy streets made up of little boxy brick houses; here and there a tottering old relic of Jack's own time. Very dark – the sort of streets where blades and cudgels lurked. Jack began to get a feeling up and down his spine, a scared, out-of-place feeling. This was not a good place to be lost.

That was the trouble with rattling around in carriages: you forgot the turnings, lost your own trail. He was pretty sure Ravenscar's carriage had carried him north from Drury Lane – they'd have hit the river otherwise – but with no landmarks and no sun to steer by, that was no help either.

What else, then? He ought to have felt a devil or two by now. Sure, he was outside the bounds of the old City, but even so: there were devils outside the walls too – at Smithfield, at Whitefriars, at Old St Giles. If he could find just one he knew, he'd have his bearings.

But – strange, when he came to think of it – he felt no tingle in his finger, no shiver in his eye. Not now, not last night either: it wasn't just the Lasher that was missing, it was all of them.

Jack glanced at the black spot on his finger. He'd never thought he would miss the devils of London, but now he did. He wished he were at Moll King's – wished it done, and over.

'Coeee, champion!'

'Who's for a game of Rantum Scantum?'

Two women stumbled giggling into his path. They had white faces and brown teeth. One wore a hat with a bird on it. The other had a wig that teetered high above her head. It had a clock in it, with a cracked face. The hands said half past five.

'Where's Moll King's Coffee House?' said Jack.

'Whyever would you want that dreary old ken?' said clock woman. 'Moll's yesterday's shout, lovey.'

'He's not from Town, is he Bets, talking queer like that? Poor little fing.' Bird woman winked. 'Bide a spell with Betsy and me. Get a scrub in the *ban-io*. We'll have a grand old romp, I promise.'

Jack might not be from their town, but he knew a sharpies' trap when he saw it.

'Just tell me where it is,' said Jack. 'Please.'

'Oho! Please, is it? And in that sad little voice.'

'Lost your sweetheart? Don't waste our time, little man.'

'But—'

'We only go with gallant bucks, such as knows what a lady wants.'

'That's right, cock robin. Sod off. Oh, oh! Feeling dolorous, are we?'

Jack didn't even have the fire to fight back. He turned away.

'Don't cry, little shrimp.'

'She'll only break your heart again.'

The women howled at Jack's discomfort. Their cackles followed him away down the street.

It was a long walk before he saw a friendly face, and even then he nearly missed her. All else was so changed that it was a miracle Jack saw the statue at all.

St Bride hadn't aged well. Her chin had grown a lichen beard, and her nose was gone. At first Jack couldn't believe it was the same statue – no river, no Holborn Bridge, and instead of standing high up above the street, St Bride was now bricked into a wall at eye level.

The eyes and mouth were the same, though. Sad eyes, with streaks of damp like tears across the cheeks; lips parted in a strange, uncertain smile. At her feet was a flagstone that had been lifted, recently, and put back askew. Jack crouched down, and tried to lever it up. It was too heavy, but – there, echoing hollow beneath the ground, was a faint rushing of water, and the age-old stench of the Fleet River.

He frowned. Why brick up a river? The answer came at once: because it was untidy. Because it didn't fit in with this new, squared-off London.

Poor old Fleet.

Jack remembered the last time he'd stood here, and how he'd heard the kissing cup's whispers, and ignored them. Everything might be very different if he'd kissed Beth then – before she'd come here; before she'd changed. He tried a squint of devil-sight, but there was no sign of the kissing cup. Vanished, just like all the other devils of London.

Funny how you could miss something you'd thought you

hated. Funny how you could hate someone you'd thought you loved.

Jack struck out along Holborn. He walked faster, sure of his way now, though his heart felt blacker than ever. As he went further west, he began to see more foot traffic, lighted windows, people gathered inside to drink and laugh and dispute. Jack stalked past them all, hunched over, fists clenched in his pockets.

No point dwelling on might-have-beens. Moll King's Coffee House, and home through the shithouse door. Sooner done, the better.

After the darkness of the streets, Covent Garden was squinting bright, blazing with torchlight and bonfires like a magic king's courtyard. Rows of windows, glinting between the great stone columns, framed a whirl of comings and goings – gold-trimmed lords, scarlet soldiers, painted women on the prowl; smells that Jack had never smelled before; words he'd never understand.

All of it was foreign. All the wrong shape. He could see why Beth loved this place. It only made him hate it more.

Jack slumped into the riot with his head cast down, heading for Moll King's Coffee House. As he came closer, he saw that Moll's was quieter than the other day. No people stumbling in and out; no music or laughter from inside. He walked around to the shithouse at the back, half expecting to see bloodstains on the spot where Kit had fallen. There weren't any. The cobbles there had all been dug up – the muddy ground still showing trowel marks where it had been smoothed over, the stones stacked neatly to one side, ready to be laid back on.

Perhaps they'd buried Kit right where he fell. Kit's body lying shallow in the cold earth, never to dance again: Jack shook himself, shuddering out the thought.

The shithouse was empty. Its rotten door stood half open. Jack shut it, felt for the keyhole. Lud's key was cold and dead as ever – no leaping in his hand, no shape-shifting like before.

'What do we do, Imp?' he muttered. 'How'd it work?'

'Master to 'bandon lovey-dove? Ecktlick?'

'Stow it, Imp. It's how she wants it.'

The imp sighed, and gave a tiny shrug atop his scalp.

'She said it, didn't she?'

Quickly, before he could change his mind, Jack put the key to the lock.

Nothing happened. The key didn't even fit the keyhole, no matter how much he twisted and turned it.

Nothing: and when Jack tried the devil-sight, still nothing. No sign of the satyr, no magical door, no way out.

His stomach was churning. He saw Beth's face again. Cold as ice. Sneering her contempt.

This place was a nightmare, and now there was no way out.

'Sir?'

Someone plucked at his sleeve. Jack whirled round.

It was a boy. A ragbottom, rumpskuttle linkboy.

'Please you, sir,' said the boy, 'I've a message.'

A trap, Jack thought immediately.

'Message for me?' he said, scanning the shadows, looking for the men who would snatch him.

'Message for whoever came trying to lock the privy with a key that didn't fit.' The boy rolled his eyes. 'I didn't make it up. Thought he was a mad-run gent, me, but here you are.'

'What?' said Jack. 'Who?'

'The rummagent cove,' said the boy. 'Got a message for you. Says, he owes you money.'

Still a trap, Jack thought: the old Sharkwell Family used this same opening in a half a dozen lays – 'this cull owes you money' – luring you in to be cozened . . .

'What money?' he said.

'Sixteen shillings, thruppence ha'p'nny,' said the boy promptly.

Beth dabbed at her neck, wiping the day from her face with a sponge. The maid busied herself with eyelets, stays and ribbons. Her deft fingers unwrapped Beth like a parcel. Her sharp eyes watched her face in the mirror.

Beth made sure the spy had nothing to tell. Artemisia

Devine was as cool and collected as any other night. She yawned, and asked for her shawl.

And as Beth wrapped it around her shoulders, a thousand stabs of anger prickled inside her, as if someone had dragged a thorn branch through her guts. She wanted to scream.

'Leave me. I will go to bed, now, Jeanette. I am exhausted.'

'*Bonne nuit, mamselle.*'

Beth lay awake for hours. Her fury at what Jack had said, at his contemptible jealousy, was mixed with a small, but growing doubt.

Was he through that door already? Gone again? Come to her after all this time, and then gone in a day?

Beth tried to tell herself she was well rid of him.

At last, she gave up on sleep. She lit a candle from the smouldering embers in the grate, rolled herself up in a blanket and sat down in the armchair by the window. She ran her eye around the room. Everything was exactly as it had always been.

So why did it seem tainted?

Over the past ten months Beth had gathered many possessions, but the things she was most proud of were all here, in this room. On the mantle was the pasteboard tiara she'd worn when she played Ariel. Next to it, tied in red ribbon, were a few dried roses from a bunch she'd caught during her first standing ovation – for Aricia in *Phèdre*.

Tacked to the wall was her favourite print: it was a fair likeness, not too prettified, nor deformed by hasty draughtsmanship. The artist had drawn Beth as a giantess, standing tall over all the theatres of London. At her feet tiny figures roared and cheered, acknowledging her triumph. The title was *The Conquest of Art*.

'Art, Jack: see that?' She imagined him standing right there: she could see him, scrunty and shy – or gormless, depending on your lights. 'Same arts I always had, only this time I practise 'em honest.

'No cozening. No *whoring*, Jack.'

Sure, she'd milked her admirers as best she could. All the actresses did that. Jack was right about one thing: no one ever got rich on Drury Lane wages.

Restless, Beth got to her feet, and went across to her cupboard. As she'd done many times before, she ran her hand down the rail, pulling the dresses out, one by one. Some were gifts – some worth more than she cared to think – but they were hardly worn, and she passed over these quickly. For hanging alongside them were her treasures. She loved them all equally: the beautiful gowns she wore now as a leading lady, back through junior goddess's robes, and little sisters' muslins, to the milkmaid and shepherdess dresses in crude smocking. Every part she'd ever played was hung in here.

They told their own story.

Hanging at the far end was another gown. This one was made of grey wool, somewhat tattered – though in pretty good condition for two hundred years old. She had never washed it.

Sometimes, when she was feeling especially lonely, Beth had taken that dress and buried her face in it, and imagined that she was back home.

She did it now. The smell was still there: a mix of wood-smoke, beer, lye soap and sweat. It brought her old life rushing back, all at once. It brought no comfort.

Instead, Beth felt a surge of disgust at what she was become: an infant, clutching at a rag. She was always being asked to play this snivelling kind of woman – and she hated it. She turned those parts down, now.

Unbidden, a phrase from her old life rose to her lips.

Moany's next to coney, and coney gets caught.

What was so fine about home anyway? Plague, lice, and the Slubber. All gone now, and Jack gone with it. And good riddance.

She dropped the dress to the floor. She would throw it out tomorrow.

Chapter 20

The linkboy led Jack away from the square and through a twist of backways to a tumbledown court haunted by thin cats and thinner people. He left Jack at a door, telling him to go up to the third floor and knock six times.

The staircase was dark. A fug of tobacco smoke was wafting down from above – from the third-floor room. When Jack knocked, the response was immediate.

'Out! *Sprodzh!* Out, all out! Business attending!'

Jack tensed, all his fears flooding back; but it was too late to flee now. The door flew open, and out spilled a trio of giggling gimblets, all crooked wigs and clattering court swords. One of them gave Jack a doubtful look.

'Is *this* your business, Margrave?' he trilled.

From within came the booming voice once more.

'My business is my business, younglet! This is house of Rasmanovic, and I say *out!*'

A man appeared in the doorway, and fetched the gimblet a hearty kick upon the arse. With a squawk, he followed his friends down the stairs.

A candle was thrust forward in Jack's face, dazzling him so that he only caught a glimpse of the man behind it. But a glimpse was enough.

Those mustachios. That devilish dancing grin.

'Kit?'

'Jack!' Kit hugged him tight, lifting him up off his feet.

'Lokmok!' The imp flew from off Jack's head, and planted a dusty kiss upon each of Kit's cheeks.

'Is your beetle in that wig?' said Kit.

'Yes.' Jack let himself be swung into the room, utterly aflop. He blurted out the first question that came. 'Who's Rasmanovic?'

'An itinerant Polish nobleman I cooked up to explain my ignorance of language and custom.'

It *was* Kit. Only Kit would play it so high. Still half dazed, Jack took in the scattered state of the room – bedroll in corner covered in papers and tobacco ash, dicing table strewn with coin, furniture overturned – and watched as the living ghost set a chair upon its feet, wincing a little as he did. His hand was bandaged where Malpas's sword had cut it.

'Sit down, Jack.'

'*Tsk.*' The imp swirled amongst the squalor, muttering disapproval, straightening and tidying.

'Is that a tear I see in your eye?' said Kit. 'How touching!'

'I thought you were dead,' said Jack, sinking into the chair.

'Yes, I thought my death played most affectingly – the young hero mourning his beloved mentor, the blood, the *whispered* last words . . . all just as I intended.'

'Intended. *Intended?*' Jack was still trying to work it out. 'He shot you!'

'Yes,' Kit gave a patient nod. 'When I'm mended, I will challenge that cheating swine to a duel, and I will kill him dead.'

'Gut him!' the imp crowed. 'Full joyment for such!'

'But . . . you . . .' Jack shook his head. 'He *shot* you.'

'So it would seem, so it would seem. He certainly knocked the fight out of me. If I hadn't died on the spot, he'd have killed me for sure.'

Kit reached down into his shirt and brought out his leather-bound debt ledger. It had a singed hole running right through the middle of it.

'All those debts, Jack. I shall wear them over my heart always, for luck. You helped of course – you always were an easy gull.'

'An easy—' Jack felt he should be angry, but all he could do was laugh: Kit, here in front of him, the same old Kit. 'I thought you were dead!'

'It was very touching. Why, the way you bravely held back your tears, I nearly wept myself. It made the scene.'

'I wasn't acting!'

'Well I was, and I stand by the choice. When you're dead, no one troubles you.' Kit cocked his head to one side. 'You were left alive. How have *you* spent the last few days? I note with interest that you've lost all your hair. Doesn't suit you at all.'

'I was locked up in Bedlam and leeched daily,' said Jack. 'After that I was took up for murder. And then . . .' He stopped. He wasn't ready to tell the rest.

'So,' said Kit, 'I was left for dead, but I patched up pretty swift. Then I recruited a capable guide – that's Vincent, the lad who watched for you. I've been touring the city. It's quite marve—'

'Marvellous?' said Jack. 'Poxed, you mean.'

'Pish to your pox! Why, it's the roaringest place I've ever seen! Sugar-bounteous, flying on coffee, freighted down with gold! Albion rules the world, boy, and the more knowing amongst her sons live fat and greasy on the profits! And I tell you, Jack, I am as knowing as the best of them.'

Kit picked up a pair of dice and rolled them across the table. Two sixes.

'Even in this golden future, fools are still easily parted from their money.'

'If they fall for your old langrets, they're worse than fools.'

'My dear, I've had the most absurd run of luck.' Kit laughed. 'And, listen well: I have a new Plan to make all our fortunes.'

He tossed up his dice, caught them on the back of his hand, and grinned triumphantly. The man was infuriating.

'You know this is all your fault, Kit.'

'Fault? What of it! If fault it be, to—' Kit snapped his fingers. 'Never mind poetry. By God, Jack, I've a stratagem to . . . what? Why so glum?'

The imp sighed.

'You didn't find Beth?' Kit stared intently into Jack's face. 'Or you did . . .'

Jack shook his head.

'Come on, out with it, I'm afire to tell you my Plan.'

'Master has lost his lovey-dove,' said the imp, settling mournful on Kit's shoulder. The room was already, amazingly, quite neat. 'Master make very dumbkop blatherings of illest words,' it whispered in his ear. 'But lokmok ist artlick, wordly cunning – haply help to rectify?'

'What's this, Jack?' said Kit. 'Go on, tell all, I can't have it from a wig – no offence, Imp – I may be wordly cunning, but I'd rather have the tale in plain English.'

He reached into his coat and pulled out a flask, uncorked it and handed it to Jack.

'Drink this. You'll find it bitter, but stimulating.'

Jack eyed it doubtfully, then looked again, with devil-sight; but there was no gleam of Spiritus. He took a sip. It tasted acrid – but after a moment he felt a fire spread through his stomach, and with it a new strength and spark. 'What is this?' he said.

'Coffee. Just another Wonder of the Age. Ain't it brave? Now tell me everything.'

Jack told him – everything, from being taken to Bedlam to the fight with Beth. Kit sipped fitfully from his flask as he spoke. When the story was done, he passed it back to Jack and motioned for him to drink again.

'Courage, Jack – courage and inspiration,' he said. Jack didn't see why, after the tale he'd told, but Kit was smiling. 'You've been through a lot these past few days, and you're grieving for this poor dead Ada, but as for Beth: I see your problem, and I have the solution ready to hand. I have a *Plan*.'

'Ha-ha, *cunning* lokmok!' crowed the imp. Despite himself – perhaps because of Kit's wondrous drink, perhaps because of the bubbling glee of his grin – Jack chuckled too.

All could not be quite lost, with those mustachios twirling in his face, those curling lips ready to spill their plans.

'Well, Kit?' he said. 'Tell us, then.'

Kit waved airily. 'Your fears about this Ravenscar I dismiss out of hand. Very sad about Ada, of course, but we'll be out of his reach soon enough.'

'Aye, but what about Beth? And the key don't work, I told you.'

'As for the key, I have an explanation. As for Beth – well, Jack, you've fouled your hawse there, I'll grant, and you've only yourself to blame – but I think I see a way out.'

'What?' said Jack, sitting forward. 'I know I spoke chuff, aye, but – she wouldn't listen. She'll never agree . . .'

'*Of course* she won't,' said Kit. 'Quite right too. Think, Jack, Ravenscar's just the sort of chicken Beth loves to pluck—'

'He ain't no chicken,' said Jack. 'He's dangerous, Kit.'

'Dangerous, rich, devoted to her – well then, all the better. Do you understand nothing of women, my boy?'

'Nix-naught,' said the imp. 'Master spoke spundle, not primplick like Ravenslord.'

'Thanks, Imp,' said Jack.

'But your periwig has the right of it,' said Kit. 'Frankly, if I were in Beth's shoes, I'd choose the same. The prize goes to the bold, lad. Here you come, blundering in with your churlish jealousy . . .'

'I ain't jealous.'

'Oho!' said Kit. 'Not jealous? Absurd! A blind pigeon could tell which way your passions tend. And why not? Fine upstanding nimble-witted girl – and that's why you need to polish up.'

Jack shook his head. 'She won't listen . . .'

'To you as you are, no she won't,' Kit interrupted, snapping a finger in Jack's face. 'But how if you were – changed?'

'Changed how?'

Kit leaned across the table, so that the candle cast deep flickering shadows in the hollows of his face.

'Changed . . .' he began. One of his mustachios caught fire. He pinched it out, sneezed on the fumes and carried on as if nothing had happened. 'Changed, Jack, into everything Ravenscar is, and more.' He leaped over to his bedroll, rummaged in the straw and came out with a sheaf of papers. 'Lord, the tales I had to spin to get my hands on these – but it was worth it. Immense wealth . . .' He brandished the papers in Jack's face. 'Wealth to make Ravenscar look like a mere . . . a mere fishmonger.'

Kit raised the papers high above his head in triumph – and now he was off again, hopping about the room, even more excited than before.

'Merchant adventurers, Jack. You're familiar with the idea? No? Easiest way to make your fortune while sitting down. Now I've been going through the lot – every ship that made a whomping great fortune in the last two hundred years. England does herself damn well at sea, it turns out. And I've worked out the whompingest whomper of all. The *Honourable East India Company.*'

Kit intoned this mysterious name with a deep reverence.

Jack blinked.

'Don't you see it, Jack? Don't you see what we have here? Come! There's no time to waste.' Kit danced over to the door, and flung it open. 'No time to waste! Except we have all time in the world! Don't you see?'

'No,' said Jack.

'It's simple! In our day you can buy a share of this company for a few shillings. Now – why that same share is worth tens of thousands of pounds.'

'How?'

'The miracle of merchant adventuring, lad. It's as if they made thieving legal. England's shaved half the globe in the past two hundred years. It's truly astounding.'

'No, no. How do you buy something in *our day*, Kit. If you hadn't noticed—'

'Oh,' Kit waved his hand. 'We use your key, of course.'

'What?'

'Of course! Why not? It's already led us to two different destinations, ten months apart. Why not more? Why not – anywhere? Any*when?*'

Jack lapsed into silence, overwhelmed by the sheer scale of Kit's lunacy. This wasn't the first time he'd come up with a Plan to get rich using devils. If Jack hadn't listened to the last one, he'd be home and happy with Beth.

'We will be so rich that we will wipe ourselves with gold leaf!' Kit's vision soared higher and higher. 'No: stap that – gentle eunuchs will swab us down with emeralds! We will bathe in jewels and chuck 'em away, like so much chaff! We will return here, flush with company shares, buy up the entire country and make your sharp-eyed girl a second Queen Bess!'

'Kit—' Jack tried to interrupt, but Kit was in full flight.

'It is within our power to be the richest, ripest villains ever to stride the wastes of time!'

'Stay,' said Jack. 'This is your lay: you want to go to the past and buy shares in a *ship*? And then you want to come back here? Are you drunk?'

Kit shrugged. 'Perhaps, a little.'

'No, Kit,' said Jack, reaching forward and grabbing him by the arm. He could see the shape of it, what Kit was saying – and this merchant adventuring might even work, in outline – but there was a big blank space in the centre. 'The key. The key don't work here, I checked at the privy door. And I ain't seen any other devils here, either.'

'Ah,' said Kit, nothing daunted. 'Yes, I was going to tell you about that. That door won't work until further notice, and I know why; *and* I know what to do about it!' He clasped Jack's arm. 'Dark doings afoot, Jack. Someone's been stealing devils, and *I* know where they've put them. Or rather, young Vincent does. While he was watching for you, he saw them dig up the satyr. He'll take you to them in the morning.'

Kit smiled down at Jack.

'You need to sleep now, my sweet young darksman – for come tomorrow it's time for you to do a little house-breaking.'

Chapter 21

The next morning Jack and Vincent set off early. They walked north from Covent Garden through a grubby tangle of dank narrow streets, very quiet at this time of day; then turned left along a busier way that Vincent identified as the Oxford Road. The buildings here were bigger, smarter; and when they turned north again, and they got bigger and smarter still, Jack began to feel a creepy recognition.

'Here's the spot, cully,' said Vincent, as they rounded a corner into a broad, imposing square.

Jack, stopped; looked about him; looked again and sighed.

Vincent was pointing at a big grey building that took up one whole side of the square. On the other side, directly opposite, rose the broad sweep of Ravenscar House. The dark red brick of the mansion had a looming aspect, even in daylight.

He should have known it would be like this. Wherever he went, Ravenscar was there to greet him.

'Well . . . g'luck,' said Vincent. The next moment he was gone, and Jack was alone.

The windows of Ravenscar House looked down on him, sickly pale in the winter light. Jack shivered, turned his back on the cursed place, turned his mind to the task in hand. Stealing the satyr. Again. Another Plan of Kit's, and again Jack was bearing all the risk.

He could see two ways into the devil thieves' house. The front door – Jack shunned front doors on old instinct – and a servants' entrance, reached from a sunken area at the front of the building.

As he strolled along the frontage, Jack fingered Lud's key around his neck. He was half hoping for a twitch, a sign that the satyr was near.

It didn't move at all.

Beth would not have approved. No: Beth would not even be here. Jack could hear her preachy voice listing all the many ways this was a very stupid lay: he was not only running blind but solus too; he was fishing for a fetch he wasn't even certain was in the building; he didn't have a back way out if things ran foul. By Beth's standards, this was hardly a plan at all.

A madcap Plan is better than none. That was Kit's rule – that he'd made up over breakfast, after three cups of coffee.

Jack was trying very hard to see it that way. Mad, that was certain: there were more holes in Kit's Plan than a rabbit warren. The loon had one thing right though: if they were ever going to get away from Ravenscar, and Malpas, and this nightmare, wrong-shaped London, they needed the satyr. Kit took it for granted that the satyr really would make the door at Moll King's work again. Jack hoped he was right.

'You ready, Imp?' said Jack.

'Tsa!' said the imp, quivering.

'We pull this off, I'm buying you a hundred silver spoons.'

'Hundred! One *hundreds.* A*hax*'hoo!'

'So settle, and do what I say.'

'As magicboy commandset.' If a periwig could ever salute, the imp did it then.

Jack slipped down the narrow stairs to the servant's entrance. The door at the bottom was locked.

'Ope it, Imp.'

The wig snapped off his head and settled against the door handle. It went limp and dropped to the ground. Jack heard the sound of bolts sliding back.

'Done, master,' said a creaky voice, as the door swung open.

Jack went inside, into a dark, empty passageway and a smell of freshly baked bread.

He bent down and held the wig against the door. After another heartbeat's pause, the curls shivered back into life.

'Well done,' said Jack. 'How you feeling?'

'Spruce and sprightlick.'

'Good.'

Jack blinked into devil-sight. He peered all about him, up and down. Nothing. So: it was the hard way then. Jack padded towards the staircase at the far end of the passage.

He passed a door. From behind it came the busy clatter of a kitchen. Opposite was a row of hooks, with coats and smocks hanging off them and boots tucked in below.

Jack glanced at the door, shed his coat and hung it on one of the hooks. He was just pulling a smock over his head when the kitchen door slammed open.

'That you, Sid?'

'Yeff,' said Jack, hoping that the smock would muffle his voice.

'Late again!' The voice chuckled. 'Got some loaves for Miniver's ward. Take them up, then back here at the double.'

Jack writhed inside the smock, keeping his face covered.

'All well, Sid? Need a hand?'

'No: I'll just . . .' Jack shoved a hand into a wrong sleeve, and kept up his writhing.

Another chuckle, then Jack heard something being laid down on the floor, and the kitchen door swung shut.

He poked his head out through the neck hole.

A large tray covered in small, steaming loaves was waiting on the floor for him. Jack shrugged his arms into the sleeves of the smock, thinking fast.

What was Miniver's ward?

What were devil thieves doing, baking so much bread?

Did kitchen boys wear periwigs?

That one was answerable, anyway. Jack stuffed the imp down inside his shirt, picked up the tray and went upstairs.

He stopped at the first floor. He was in a clean white corridor that smelled of soap and fresh paint. There were open doors leading off it: through one he saw a row of beds. A boy with thin, sickly legs was being led along beside them by a man with eyeglasses. The man was counting each step.

'One, two, three . . . very good, Ben. Steady now.'

Something was written above the door in letters of brass. Jack spelled out the letters one by one.

I-N-F-I-R-M . . .

Infirmary.

That was like a hospital, Jack knew. What could a hospital want with the satyr? Jack shook his head: worry about it later, when he wasn't trying to rob them.

He took a few steps down the corridor, wondering where to start looking.

The imp clamped hard against his chest.

'*What?*'

'Can'st not feel?'

Jack closed his eyes for a moment. Everything seemed normal; but then he felt it, a faint scratching in his stained hand, like a pin dragged across the palm.

'Where's it coming from?' he said.

'Aloft!' the imp replied, impatient. It tugged him back to the staircase.

Halfway up, Jack heard two men coming down towards him. He fixed his eyes on his tray. The men ignored him.

Jack's hand led him up two more floors. The scratch became an itch; the itch turned to heat, steadily building with every step.

'This one?' said Jack. The heat was stronger now: they were getting close.

'Onwards thusly,' said the imp.

The walls on this level were still white, the floors scrubbed painfully clean. The only difference was that all the doors were shut. Jack stole forward, feeling exposed.

The heat in his hand led him to a door at the far end of the corridor.

He set his tray down, put his ear to the keyhole and listened. A low, moany, murmury babble came from beyond – hard to make out.

Jack pushed at the door. As soon he touched it, a

coldness sprang up in the black spot on his finger – in what he was starting to think of as the dead spot. Only it wasn't quite dead, was it? Couldn't be, to act up like this . . .

Cold in the midst of heat. The two feeding off each other. Jack swallowed. He could feel his heart beating fast in his throat.

He pushed the door open and saw a long room, with patients in rows of beds lining each wall. All of them were strapped down tight to the beds. They were muttering, singing, cursing to themselves, lost in their own private worlds.

None of them had noticed Jack.

'Ready, Imp?'

'Onwards, master!'

Jack slipped inside. He was close now, he could feel it in his hand – but the wretched cold was still throbbing alongside the heat.

At the far end of the room was another door. Jack took a few steps towards it – then stopped dead.

The old lady in the nearest bed was licking her hands and mewling like a cat. Jack recognized her. She was the old matron from Bedlam.

He switched into devil-sight. His eye travelled along the row of beds, recognizing others from Bedlam – warders, gawpers, men, women and children – and recognizing something else, too.

Jack stopped breathing. This was what the cold meant. There was something hellish here, but it wasn't the satyr. It was inside the people on the beds. Before that, it had been inside Ada.

Flies in their eyes, filthy creeping things beneath the skin of their faces.

The Swarm.

The cat lady snapped forward. Her face was awful, contorted, snarling. Something furred and spined and many-eyed lurked inside her mouth.

The man next to her bucked up rigid against his straps. One by one, the rest of the Bedlamites did the same. Heads snapped round to face Jack. Moans turned to howls, howls to screams. The cat lady hissed, throwing specks of spittle at him. The thing inside her mouth writhed. The man beside her threw his head forward, teeth snapping at thin air.

'Lord is *coming!*' he screamed.

Jack heard shouts in the corridor outside.

'Swift master, endwards!'

Jack didn't need prompting. He ran down the aisle, stumbling between the double row of beds. The Bedlamites strained for Jack, thrashing against their bonds.

He went through the door at the far end at full tilt, shoving it closed behind him. Darkness: he could still feel the throbbing in his hand. More hot than cold now.

He was trembling all over. Outside were running feet

and urgent voices. People in the infirmary: not the Bedlamites, but others, summoned by the screaming.

He was trapped in here. Unless there was another way out.

'Can you light up, Imp?' he said.

The imp rose into the air, giving off a soft, yellow light. A luminous periwig: it looked solemn, like something in church. Jack felt the beginnings of a crazy panicked laugh juddering up inside him.

Don't start. Beth's voice, and somehow it calmed him. He breathed out, long and slow. The trembling got less, though his hand was pulsing hot as ever.

Jack looked about. He was in a small, windowless space – more cupboard than room – walls lined with shelves. To his right were dozens of wooden boxes of many different sizes. The shelves to his left were filled with hundreds of tiny bottles, made of thick, whorled glass. The stuff inside the bottles twinkled with a devilish light.

'See, boymaster! What hellstuff ist?'

'It's Spiritus, Imp.'

Lots of it. Kitty would have been delighted to find herself here. But not Jack: he wanted the satyr, not this cursed stuff.

He opened the nearest box. No lock on the lid. Inside – sawdust. Jack scrabbled through it. His hand brushed something hard and cold. He lifted it out.

It was a large silver cup with two handles, the silver blackened with time. Jack recognized it.

The kissing cup, from Holborn Bridge. He remembered the loose flagstone by St Bride's feet, last night.

They'd dug her up, and brought her here. Along with how many others? He looked up at the shelves. There were more boxes than he could count.

A devil for each box. Dozens of them . . .

Jack felt different things start to slide together in his head. Devil thieves – this place, right opposite Lord Ravenscar's mansion – Ada and Tom, Ada and Ravenscar . . .

'Master?' said the imp. 'Quickens be a-searching!'

'Aye.' Jack nodded. This was going to be hard, with so many other devils about . . .

Except – that didn't make sense, either. He was holding the kissing cup in his hand, and the Alkahest heat hadn't got any hotter.

The devil in the cup was a deep sleeper. Its voice sounded like that too – like the whisper from putting your ear to a seashell.

Last time he'd heard it, it had told him to kiss Beth.

Beth.

Jack heard a ghost of a sigh – there, then cut off sharp, a mouse flashing into its hole – then nothing, not the slightest whisper.

'Hey . . . speak. What's happening?'

Jack stared at the cup with the devil-sight, and saw nothing. The imp flew down to look.

'See anything, Imp?' said Jack.

'Nix. All beflisted.'

Jack put the cup back in its box, and shut the lid softly.

'Next?' said the imp.

The next box held a dull, water-smoothed lump of glass. Jack could just make out ghost traces of the scowling face that had once been scratched into its surface. Just the kind of thing to house a devil. His hand was still throbbing, but it grew no hotter as he touched the glass. Again he looked with the sight. Again – nothing.

'All skrittert,' muttered the imp.

Jack shook his head.

He had an idea. He stepped across to the other set of shelves, the ones holding the bottles. The heat in his hand grew hotter. He touched a bottle, and it flamed up, burning hot.

'The Spiritus,' he said. 'That's what it was. Not the ones in the boxes . . .'

'Shuks and shuklets be dead?' said the imp. 'Satyr also?'

'They can't all be.' Jack started opening boxes, fast as he could.

He pawed through sawdust for small hard objects. Metal and stone – rings, brooches, lockets, old coins; jewels and ornaments and carved, polished amulets. All rumpskuttle. Never a stab of devil-heat from any of them.

'Quickens, master,' said the imp. 'Going time, soon – dangewrack to linger . . .'

Jack nodded, closed one lid and opened another. He was working fast, taking care to replace the boxes just as they lay – Beth would be proud – and he'd nearly reached the end now. He was beginning to hope he wouldn't find the little red bead. To find the satyr dead would be worse than not finding it at all.

'Master, going time . . .'

'Last few,' said Jack, groping along the final shelf, and finding – a dagger with the blade rusted away. A bronze dog the size of his thumb. A piece of stone bound up in wizened scraps of leather.

No Alkahest heat: all these devils were either dead, or lying so far dormant they might as well be.

No little red bead, either. But the satyr had come here, to this building: Kit was sure of it. Someone had dug it up and brought it here.

So where was it now? Who had it?

'Master,' said the imp.

'Aye, time to go,' said Jack.

He heard a door slam open, out in the infirmary. A loud, angry voice boomed out. 'Saints and sawdust! I leave you a single morning, and all Hell breaks loose!'

'But . . .'

Heavy footsteps sounded, coming rapidly towards Jack's cupboard.

'No excuses. Enough. I will deal with this.'

Right outside the door now. Jack's heart jumped into his mouth.

The door handle turned. There was nowhere to go.

'Hide, Imp!' hissed Jack.

The imp went dark, and flopped to the floor.

Darkness, and then a wash of light as the door opened slowly. Jack stood still, watching the light advance towards him. He knew he was caught.

He looked up.

'What's this?' said Tom.

And Jack saw the surprise in his face give way to something else.

'You!'

Chapter 22

Every morning at eleven o'clock, Artemisia Devine took a cup of coffee at Ambrosini's in Golden Square.

At a quarter to the hour by the golden clock on the mantle, Beth stood in front of her looking-glass while her maid put the finishing touches to her grey Brunswick dress.

'*Mamselle* is still out of sorts, I think,' Jeanette said.

'Not at all,' said Beth.

'*Mais non, c'est charmant*, this little colouring. I could never achieve with rouge alone. *Mamselle* should be out of sorts every morning.'

Beth tilted her chin, and made the blush go away. 'I *was* out of sorts, Jeanette, but now I am better. Fetch me my fur-trimmed cape and . . . the otter comforter. I am going out.'

Jack was gone. Lord Ravenscar would know of last night's scene by now. A tight little corner Jack had left her in: lying to Ravenscar was no simple thing. She must play Artemisia Devine to the hilt.

Artemisia never took her carriage unless the weather was foul. Today was sunny, and so Beth strolled out as if she didn't have a care in the world, turning right down Oxford Street towards Mayfair.

Her cares were just as plaguey, for all the face she put on them. Jack was gone, and as usual he'd left a bitter mess for her to tidy up.

The mess, though, she could compass. She'd wash clean. She always did.

Beth took a deep breath and held it for a moment.

Gone. For ever. It was hard to take in.

As was her custom, she paused outside Holland's print shop to look in at the window. The hack artists had wasted no time. Already there were three new offerings devoted to last night's events: *Death at Drury Lane*; *The Lady Libertine Reaps Her Grim Reward*; *The Devil's Mistresses, Old and New*. The last one featured Beth – no surprise there, they never lost a chance to draw Artemisia. As usual, the picture looked nothing like her.

Five different Ravenscars stared down at her from the window. Three of them had horns, and one had a long, hairy tail. Despite the additions, he still managed to look handsome, in his own particular way – brutish and exquisite at the same time.

Beth remembered last night, Jack's talk of devils and hellfire – Ravenscar killing Ada, had he really said that? Nonsense, of course. Jack was jealous – devil-sight or not, he could still be wrong, and he was wrong about Ravenscar . . .

'Contemplating the fine arts, Devine?'

As if she'd summoned him up, there was Ravenscar behind her, reflected in the shop window like an elegant ghost. He was leaning on his gold-topped cane, striking a pose.

She'd expected him at Ambrosini's. He must have waited here on purpose to surprise her.

She didn't give him the satisfaction of letting it show.

'Ravenscar, you pounce like a cat, I declare,' she said, turning to face him and holding out a lazy hand. He bent over it, brushing her glove with his lips.

'Ah! But you are no mouse, Devine.' He peered over her shoulder into the window. 'They never quite get your likeness, do they? Nor mine, of course,' he added, smiling. 'As for your brother – well . . .'

'My brother?'

'Up there.' Ravenscar nodded at a small, garish print, high in one corner. 'See: *Bedlam Inverted, or, the Poetical and Ironical Justice Wreaked upon Those who Mock at Madness.* Really! Who writes these titles?'

In the print, a crowd of fine ladies and gentlemen capered and howled while white-shifted lunatics whipped them on. A boy stood apart from the frenzy. His upraised hand was stained livid red. He looked far too cheerful to be Jack. They'd got poor Ada Seward quite neatly, though – standing up there beside him, wild-haired, clutching his other hand.

'I'd never have known him. My brother has never looked so noble,' said Beth, with just a trace of spite – no need to act this part at all. 'No matter what he *thinks* he's doing.'

'Oh?'

'He always was a damned mooncalf, ever since we were young. Doesn't surprise me he'd end up a Bedlam Tom, nor that he'd figure in that nonsense –' nodding up at the print – 'nor that he'd make trouble now. It's all quite usual.'

Beth scowled. There: the play was begun. Ravenscar raised an eyebrow, which was about as surprised as a super-fine wight like him would ever let himself look.

'My my,' said Ravenscar. 'So hot – and yet last night, Devine, you spoke up for him. In the most *remarkable* circumstances, too. Is this a change of heart?'

Beth laughed – a cold, false laugh such that Artemisia might give to cover hurt feelings.

'You are flustered, Devine,' said Ravenscar. 'I never thought I'd see it. Come, take my arm: a cup of coffee, to restore your spirits.'

Beth took his arm and allowed him to lead her up Oxford Street, before making the turn down towards Golden Square. 'Truth be told, Ravenscar, I am quite vexed. Such a scene he made, after we arrived at my house . . .'

No sign from Ravenscar that he knew all this already. He simply inclined his head, with his usual urbane expression.

'It seems he is jealous of my honour,' said Beth.

Ravenscar's face lit up with understanding. 'Jealous,' he said, 'but of course: who wouldn't be? Half the town is jealous of me already. If only they knew.' He shook his head.

'Quite,' said Beth. She sniffed, and looked pained. No need to act that part. Whore, Jack called her. But she'd never. She was Beth Sharkwell, and needn't stoop to such.

She smothered her anger in a laugh. 'You get little enough for your jewels, don't you Ravenscar? A poor return, some would say.'

'But they would be wrong,' said Ravenscar. 'I get the divine pleasure of your company, do I not? And . . . the thrill of the chase.'

Beth felt the muscles of his arm swell beneath his coat, squeezing her hand.

'And here's your mad brother, chasing after you to London, burning with jealousy; when all the while, you have been quite, quite – *chaste*. How delicious.'

She was almost sure he was mocking her. She allowed herself to colour, just a trifle.

'You wouldn't have said so if you'd heard him. Some of the things he said – unrepeatable things. I told him to get out of my sight. He is gone, back west for all I know. Good riddance.'

'The scoundrel!' Ravenscar's head was tilted to one side. He contemplated her, like an artist assessing a near-completed painting. 'But he followed you all the way here, from . . . where was it you said? No matter: a long, long way, at any rate.'

'No matter, as you say, since he is gone.'

'Is he, though?' said Ravenscar.

They had arrived at the coffee house, but Ravenscar did not go in. He reached into his waistcoat pocket and toyed with something inside.

'You see, I fancy I have something that concerns him. Perhaps it concerns you, too. It will, if you still choose to join my guests tonight.'

The hand came out, palm up, something resting on it.

A red stone bead, carved with the face of a laughing old man.

Beth recognized it at once. It set her atumble, mind racing down all the different corridors of what it might mean.

For her.

For Jack.

Ravenscar's eyes danced at her – mocking, unreadable, devilish.

'What is it?' she said. 'A jewel?'

'It is an ancient amulet, Devine: Egyptian, I am told. Would you believe, Tom dug it up just the other day, in the very place where your brother first . . . appeared?'

'I wonder, then,' she said, 'that you could suppose I know anything about it. You know I take no interest in your friends' grubbings.'

'Oh? I could have sworn you looked twice at this.'

Ravenscar tossed the bead from one hand to the other. Beth made herself look up, meet his eye. She was feeling an urge she hadn't felt in months – a scaly, thieving sort of urge.

'Never mind,' said Ravenscar. 'I had an idea that your brother and this stone were somehow related. A wild idea, I am sure. Forgive me.'

Even as he slipped the bead back in his pocket, Beth knew exactly what to do next. She was on the wing now, shaping things as they played out – a good feeling, one she'd missed all those times on the stage, reading other people's words.

'Forgive *me*, Ravenscar,' she said. 'I didn't mean to scoff at your amulet. I'm sure it's most fascinating. Perhaps . . .' Steady. No haste with the bait. 'Perhaps you will show it me again, tonight.'

'So you still intend to come.' Ravenscar smiled. 'How magnanimous. I had thought, with your brother gone west and my little club's dangerous reputation, you might try to wriggle out of our bargain.'

'I never wriggled in my life,' said Beth.

Ravenscar blinked. Off balance: good.

Now the hook.

'You think I'm afraid?' Beth let a single breath of laughter part her lips. 'It's you should be trembling.'

She leaned in, and whispered in his ear.

I'm a very dangerous girl.

She turned on her heel, and marched up the steps into the coffee house before he could reply.

'What are you doing here?' said Tom.

Jack wanted to ask the same thing himself.

'Well?' A little sharpness had crept into Tom's voice. Jack realized he'd been gaping like a slackwit.

'I can explain,' said Jack.

But how? He was caught cold. Icy-arsed, frozen cold.

'Can you?' said Tom. '*Idiot brother*, are you? Breaking into my workroom?' He took a step forward, his face darkening. 'I should hope you can explain it!'

Jack didn't dare break gaze with Tom. This was turning sour, fast. If Tom didn't believe in him; if he turned Jack over to Ravenscar now . . .

Jack snatched hold of the first thought that came to him.

'She said you were her friend.'

'Who?'

'Ada.'

'*What did she say to you?*' Tom came at him in two quick strides, took him by the shoulders and shook him hard. Jack's teeth jolted down on his tongue, drawing blood.

'Stop!' said Jack. 'I'll tell you!'

Darkness hooded Tom's eyes, but he held still.

'What did she tell you?' There was a desperate tremor in his deep voice, like someone on the edge of tears. Jack felt a mad, gambler's boldness take hold of him.

'It's why I came here,' Jack said. 'I thought you'd want to know.'

'Know? Know what?'

'Ada . . .' Jack hesitated.

'*What?*'

'Ada was murdered.'

Something bloomed in Tom's face. Horror, and grief – but something else, too; something that gave Jack hope.

A sort of recognition.

'Murdered . . .' said Tom. He let go of Jack, took a tottering step back. Behind him, Jack could see the doctors in the infirmary, moving from bed to bed.

'How?' said Tom. '*How?*' He glanced over his shoulder,

then turned back to Jack and lowered his voice. 'How do you know?'

'I couldn't tell it last night – not with him there.'

'Who?'

'Him, Ravenscar. But you, see, I wanted *you* to know it. For Ada.'

'Him . . . ? Tell what?' Tom stared at Jack, mouth hanging open. 'What do you mean?'

'I cured her, in Bedlam . . .' Jack pulled back a little and pushed his stained right hand up between them, showing the red mottling on his fingers. 'I did it with this. I can feel things, see? See things, too. I know what happened, at the theatre – to make her ill again. To make her jump.'

Tom stared down at him. All the colour had drained from his cheeks, as if he'd been leeched.

'Why should I believe you?' he said.

'Sir?'

Tom spun around. A worried face was looking in at the door.

'I am coming.' Tom said. 'Wait . . .'

'Let me come too,' said Jack. 'Let me show you.'

'What?' said Tom.

'Just watch.' Jack waggled his rust-coloured fingers. 'Then see if you believe me.'

Time dragged. Jack counted his own breathing – three long breaths – before Tom shook himself, and nodded.

'Show me, then, if you can.'

Jack picked up the imp and set it on his head. As they passed into the infirmary, the black spot on his finger throbbed cold. The instant he set foot in the room, the Bedlamites began to thrash and howl.

Three doctors dashed to the nearest bed, and grappled with the man in it. Tom offered no explanation for Jack's presence. The doctors didn't ask, either – too worried about their patient – and no wonder, thought Jack. It was the turnkey, and he was yelping like a broke-backed dog, his body strained against the straps that held him down. Two men forced his mouth open. The third held the tip of a long tube positioned just over his tongue.

The tube was connected to a forest of metal and glass pipework that hung above the bed. At the top of each pipe was a glass bottle, like the ones on the shelves in the next room. Thin drips of liquid flowed down the pipes, mingled together, and trickled down the tube into the patient's mouth.

Squinting with his weird eye, Jack could see that all the liquid in the pipes was Spiritus. The droplets glowed like dew in the sun.

'What're you doing to him?' said Jack.

'Administering medicine,' said Tom. 'Now: you said you had something to show me.'

Jack moved closer, and looked into the turnkey's face.

Just under the man's skin, invisible to everyone else, was a foul black grub. It was long and fat, with a big wet mouth at one end. Its tail coiled around one of the man's eyes.

A drop of Spiritus slid down the tube and into the turnkey's mouth. As soon as it dropped, the drop was sucked up by the hateful grub.

The grub got fatter. It opened its mouth. Three glistening black flies came crawling out. The turnkey's eyes rolled back into his skull.

'Well?' said Tom.

For a moment Jack was too aghast to speak. Medicine, he called it! Not for this man: not for this trouble. This was like giving a drowned man a drink of water.

'Stop that,' said Jack. 'Take out the tube.'

'Is this a joke?' said one of the doctors.

'Stop it – now,' said Jack. 'You're making it worse.'

There was a moment of shocked silence. Another drop fell, and was sucked up by the grub. It birthed out more flies, and something else, long and spindly with lots of legs. The turnkey gave a long, sobbing howl.

At last, Tom spoke. 'Do it. Do as he says.'

They removed the tube, and screwed stoppers into the feeder pipes. One of the doctors swung the whole apparatus aside, giving Jack space to work.

Jack stepped to the side of the bed and leaned forward. A pulse of cold, aching and bone deep, shot through his finger. The grub twitched. The man writhed. His neck was a rope of corded muscle. His face was lobster red. His eyes swivelled towards Jack, and he started screaming.

'Never! Never! Never! He comes!'

Jack raised his right hand. Cold-hot, freezing-scorching, making his fingers claw up. The black grub's tail coiled and tightened. The turnkey screamed himself raw.

'*He comes for* you!'

Jack lowered his hand onto the man's face.

He felt the things inside, crawling, shifting under the skin. He felt the grub. It bit like an adder. The heat was searing; the cold was worse.

Jack trapped the foul thing and held it tight until it burst.

When he finished, there was silence. He looked down at his hand. The black spot had spread a quarter inch down his finger.

The turnkey was lying so still that Jack was afraid he might have killed him. He watched his lips – waiting for a sign – for proof.

It should have worked. There was no more grub inside the turnkey now, no flies, no Swarm at all. He'd crushed it all out.

'*Come on,*' Jack whispered.

Slowly, carefully, the patient sat up, rubbing his head.

'Oo the bloody 'ell are you?' he said.

Jack watched Tom. He was very still, very pale. He gulped.

'It's . . . it's . . .'

All the men gathered about were goggling at Jack as if he'd just plucked a brace of doves out of thin air.

'It's remarkable!' said Tom. He turned to Jack. The wind had changed and fixed a new expression on his face. He looked thunderstruck.

''Markable?' said the turnkey. 'I'll give you 'markable, you lump!'

Chapter 23

J ack left the Upper Ward feeling more tired than he'd ever felt in his life.

His right hand trembled at his side. He knew this only by looking at it: all feeling was gone, the cold, the hot; and when he tried to move his fingers, nothing happened.

The blackness had spread every time he touched the Swarm. Now it covered half his palm, and veiny tendrils were reaching down towards his wrist.

All Tom's patients were cured. But now was not the time to count the cost: Tom was not done with him yet.

They walked together down the white-painted corridor, and up the stairs, to a room on the top floor – a room lined with books, fusty from the smouldering embers on the hearth. On either side of the fireplace were two comfortable chairs.

'Sit down,' said Tom.

Tom bent down to get the fire going. Jack scoped about him. It was a strange sort of room, this. Two desks in opposite corners. One, neat and tidy; the other as if a whirlwind had passed across it, whipping books, papers and piles of clutter out across the floor. The mess reached an invisible line about halfway across the room, and stopped dead. On the other side, order was instantly restored.

Jack flicked into the devil-sight. No satyr – or no living, visible satyr at any rate. Though if the little red stone was dead like the other devils, it could be hidden anywhere in the room.

'Smell anything?' whispered Jack to the imp.

'Nix.'

Tom was still wheezing away at the bellows, rousing up licks of flame from the embers. Above the fireplace hung an old map, faded brown-inked parchment with more recent markings done in red. Jack's glance passed over it, snagged, and returned again.

A shiver ran up his spine. Once again, he had the dizzying feeling of things sliding together.

The map was old, yes. Two hundred years old, to be exact, and he'd seen it before – in the house of Dr Dee.

It was Nicholas Webb's map, showing all the devils of London.

'Please, sir,' said Jack. 'What's that?'

'That? Tom glanced up at the map, then bent back down over the fire. 'It is an ancient map of London. It belonged to an ancestor of mine. Ada and I discovered it.'

Jack darted a glance at Tom, mind racing. An ancestor – Dr Dee's map; and as Tom turned to face him, Jack might have been looking into the eyes of the old doctor – dark brown eyes, a brown so dark it was almost black.

It was uncanny. Jack clenched his jaw to keep his astonishment from showing.

What had Ada said? *For a broken clock, or an unknown spider, or a question about the nature of light – Tom's your man.* That sounded enough like the old doctor. Though there was nothing of the lamb about old John Dee. And he would have exploded at the notion that devils weren't real.

Still, if he was anything like his ancestor, Jack could see why Ada had an affinity with this man. Her quickness, the way her mind leaped about: she'd have got on well with the old doctor.

Tom straightened up from the grate.

'This was our study, you know,' he said. He waved his arm over at the messy half of the room. 'She stopped coming here, but I left it all . . .' He half swallowed a sob. 'Murdered, you say. I must know who is responsible.'

'Please, sir,' said Jack, 'if I tell you, will you let me go free?'

'Free? I am not your gaoler,' Tom said. 'But I would like to know the truth.'

Jack looked up into those dark magician's eyes. Dr Dee's descendant. He had a strong sense now Tom would help him, so far as he could; and it was plain too that the man was in agony.

But truth was always a risk – and besides, what was there to tell, really? A sentence Ada hadn't had time to finish. A glimpse of Malpas's face in a crowded corridor.

'Please,' said Tom. 'Please. She was my dearest friend.'

Jack swallowed. She had been his friend too, and he had let her down. He couldn't do that again.

'Malpas killed her,' Jack said.

Tom breathed out, a long slow sigh, and sank down into his chair. For a long moment neither of them spoke – Tom sitting slumped, eyes darkening, turning inward.

Jack looked away, and saw Ada's empty chair standing before her scruffy old desk.

'Why do you say this?' said Tom.

Jack didn't know where to start. Beth would know what to say – the story would come out warm and savoury; but Beth wasn't here.

'He'd done something to Ada,' said Jack. 'Before. At the Hellfire Club: she told me. And when she was mad, she had hellfire inside her. Like what you call Spiritus, only . . .' Jack shook his head. Best not mention the Swarm. He was

294

stretching Tom's belief quite enough already. 'Thing is, I can . . . feel it, with my hand. You saw, back there with those people . . .'

'Yes, yes: go on.' Tom was sitting forward now, hunched and impatient.

'So, it was in her again at the theatre. And I think Malpas put it there. Made her sick again. Made her jump. To stop her telling.'

'My God.' Tom's face lit up with horror. He gave a single high-pitched sob. 'Oh my poor Ada. Oh, the villain . . .'

'So you believe me?' said Jack – but Tom wasn't listening. Something had happened to him – his eyes were full of horror and something else, the same recognition Jack had seen dawning when he first said the word 'murdered', only now it was there in full, high noon, blazing bright.

'How could I not see it?' said Tom. 'My God, I *helped* him! I am to blame!'

'No,' said Jack. 'You didn't know. You couldn't have stopped him.'

Tom shook his head. 'Not Malpas,' he said. 'Oh, you've seen them together, haven't you? Malpas is his creature, his pet! Whatever he did, Ravenscar began it. *His* Hellfire Club, *his* mistress – *his* danger if the truth came out. He's been corrupting her for months, using her up, right under my nose. And I helped him on. What you saw, what killed her: I made it. Oh, I made it for the best of purposes: but

I shared it with him, too. I have been his tool. So blind!'

Tom's words came feverish quick, and all the colour was gone from his face. 'She always told me he was harmless – frivolous, a pleasure-seeker. I wanted to believe it! I was caught up in my work, decocting the Spiritus, building this place up from nothing – oh, such an enterprise! Centuries of superstition – devils, indeed! – and I was bringing it into the light, discovering cures for the body, cures for the soul, for all mankind's ills. A beacon, a purifying flame. You should have seen us, Ada and I, in the early days. The power we'd discovered – the *light*!'

The way he said it, Jack could swear he believed it. But there on the wall behind him was his ancestor's map showing the devils of London. In the room they'd just left were boxes and boxes, filled with the objects where those devils had once dwelled.

Jack began to get a cold feeling. He remembered John Dee, the way he'd reacted when Jack dug up just one devil to use for his own purposes – his horror at the danger, the foolishness of it. And here was Tom, his descendant, doing exactly the same thing – except how many boxes had been in that room? Doing the same thing, a hundred times over, and not even knowing he was doing it.

'I turned a blind eye to Ravenscar's other activities,' said Tom. 'I needed his money, so that the work could continue. To think how I helped him on. The power I gave him. The most potent of my finds.' Tom squeezed his eyes shut. Fat tears oozed out and streamed down his cheeks. 'It is my fault, what happened to Ada. Corrupted, used up, cast into the gutter.'

Jack thought of Beth, of the heartless way she'd talked with Ravenscar. The rubies at her throat.

Corrupted.

Someday I will see you all in red, Devine.

A log crashed down in the fire, startling them both.

Tom wiped his cheeks on his coat sleeve. 'I – I thank you, Jack. I will not detain you any longer. I am truly grateful – I know you ran a grave risk, telling me all this. It is a deadly secret. Go far away. Avoid Lord Ravenscar.'

'What will you do?'

'What will I do?' Tom said. 'He stole my Ada. God knows what he did to her, that night. Something so unspeakable that he must kill her to keep it secret . . . and *I helped him on.*' Tom's face was tear-smudged, dazed. He blinked hard. 'And so. I must atone. For you, Ada.'

'Let me help,' Jack said.

Tom shook his head. He was drawing himself back together. Those eyes again: Jack remembered John Dee, the Queen's magician, girding himself up to fight a devil named Nicholas Webb – and hadn't he won?

Not without Jack. Not without the power in his hand. And this Dee knew less than the other.

'You have done your part,' said Tom. 'The guilt is mine. I must do this alone. I will – I will decide what is to be done. And then I will do it. I will avenge her.'

Tom drew himself up very straight, and nodded, once.

'I will prevail.'

Jack wished he could believe it.

Chapter 24

L ondon's devils might have vanished, but its appetites most certainly had not. The city was a maw that was endlessly hungry. Hungry for spices carried over the seas. Hungry for laughter, for money and scandal. Hungry for lives to chew up.

As Jack slipped south again, scurrying back towards the river, the city's mud-splattered streets throbbed with noise: the scraping of fiddles, the cry of a death hunter, the sing-song cries of traders.

'*Cats' and dogs' meat!*'

'*Bellows to mend!*'

'*Sweep for the soot-O!*'

'*Milk below!*'

On Snow Hill and Bread Street, on Paternoster Row and St Martin le Grand, there flowed the muted rush of clerks and lawyers, eager for home and mutton pie. Their twice-daily ebb and surge had never changed and never would – but this evening there was an edge to it. An odd rhythm; a dark whisper in their music.

Something was coming.

Something, yes, haven't you heard?

It happens tonight.

'*Show! Show! Show! Show!*'

Kit was leaning against one of the massive stone columns fronting St Paul's cathedral, eating oysters from a paper package. Jack felt a twist of annoyance. Dusk was falling. He'd been gone far longer than they'd agreed. The man might at least have looked worried.

At least Jack hadn't got lost this time. The head and shoulders of the new St Paul's were visible for miles. Up close, it *pounced* – the soaring columns, the acres of white stone steps, the looming, impossible dome. Far above, a second city of shrieking gulls wheeled and bickered amongst statues and buttresses.

Jack glanced down at his hand for the hundredth time. The skin around the black part tingled unpleasantly. The blackness itself was completely numb.

No satyr meant no door. And no door meant he couldn't get back to Dr Dee – the only man he knew who might be able to cure this new affliction.

Still spreading. What if it never stopped? And there was Kit, sucking on oysters, blithe as a lark.

Jack climbed the steps to meet him.

'Jack, Imp,' said Kit, nodding first at Jack and then at his wig. Jack felt one of the side-curls twitch a greeting.

'Well met. Something, ain't it, this place?' Kit gave the column a proud pat, as if it were his very own prize-winning pig. 'An improvement, *certes*.'

'What happened to the old one?'

'Ain't you heard? London burned, Jack – steeple to sewer. Last century, I'm told.' Kit smacked his lips. 'A disaster I plan to take full advantage of.'

'What?'

'*What* sweet boy? Ain't it obvious? We'll leap out your devil door in 1666, wheeling barrows full of gold: buy up all the prime sites while they're still smoking cinders.' Kit fished inside his oyster package. 'Buy cheap. Sell dear. Come to, Jack, expand your thought – think *vast*. No half measures. You won't win a queen like Beth with that. No. We are going to *possess* this city.'

Kit slurped up two oysters, chewed them to a pulp, swallowed, and grinned. Damn him. Kit always landed sweet, no matter how awkward he fell. Better than a cat.

'It ain't my devil door,' said Jack.

'How generous,' said Kit. 'Our devil door, then.'

'No, I mean it ain't . . . I didn't find the satyr.'

Kit nodded. 'I thought you might say that. Well, tell me what happened.'

Jack told him.

'Hm,' said Kit when he'd finished. 'I didn't know old Dr Dee had any children. Some sort of great-nephew, perhaps. Blood will out, I suppose. Perilous game he's playing, though. I hope he's not too close a friend . . .'

'Strumph!' said the imp. 'Spundlewit bear-brain.'

'Imp's taken 'gainst him,' said Jack.

'Jork-head speaks chuff,' said the imp. 'Sayeth: shuks and shuklets be stuff of superstition!'

'More fool him, Imp – more fool him,' said Kit. 'I'd love to say that we'll be long gone by the time he unleashes Hell, or whatever it is he's about . . .'

'He ain't like that,' said Jack. 'He's trying to make things better. Anyway, talk of games – this was all your idea, case you'd forgotten, lifting the satyr and all . . .'

'Granted.' Kit nodded. 'Did anyone ever tell you you'd make a good lawyer, Jack?'

The imp snickered. 'Lokmok makes funny of master.'

'Aye, well, looks like we ain't going anywhere,' said Jack. 'We're stuck, and Beth's lost, and all's—'

'All's well, Jack,' said Kit. 'At least, all is somewhat better than it was this morning.'

'How's that?' said Jack. 'All's *worse*, Kit, all's *lost*. Ravenscar's—'

'Hush.' Kit laid an oystery-smelling finger over Jack's lips, leaned in and whispered in his ear. *'I know where the satyr is.'*

Kit fished out his last oyster, slurped it down, then spread out the sodden, smelly wrapping paper with a flourish. The paper was thick with print, densely packed into narrow, dark columns.

'Know what this is, Jack?'

Jack grunted no.

'A newspaper. A Wonder of the Age: does all your intelligencing for you, writes down all the latest happenings. Wrap food in't . . . hang it in your privy . . . endless useful. Now where was it?' Kit squinted down at the paper. 'Ah, yes.' He cleared his throat. '*"The tragical death of Ada Seward . . ."* you know all about that . . . Here, though. *"The Courant urges that the most Severe Punishment be meted out against the Diabolical Lord Ravenscar. The Numberless Outrages of this Malevolent Fiend, whose continuous Debauch sullies the Shining Citadel of our Great and Glorious Nation, ought to be prosecuted to the Utmost Extent of the Law. The Courant now understands that his Notorious Hellfire Club will meet tonight, at that Den of Iniquity he is pleased to call his House."* There,' said Kit, looking up at Jack. 'Sure, the writer is jealous not to have been invited himself, but ignoring that: ain't it obvious now?'

'Tonight . . .' said Jack. Remembering what Tom had

said, how he'd given Ravenscar *the most potent of my finds*
. . . Kit was right, it was obvious, but that was nothing beside
tonight.

'Come, it's not that hard.' Kit was grinning like a dog
with a mouthful of sausages, answering his own question.
'The Hellfire Club meets tonight. What better devil for a
revel than the satyr? *Ravenscar's* got the satyr. So we'll just
have to take it off him.'

'No,' said Jack. 'I mean, yes, but: what about Beth?
They're meeting *tonight.*'

Things were sliding together again, words and meanings
falling into new and horrible shapes. Tonight: the Hellfire
Club: Ravenscar's invitation to Beth. *Take him, on one condition. I play host here, tomorrow night. You will grace me with
your presence.*

First Ada. Now Beth. She hadn't bought Jack's freedom
so cheap after all. She'd offered herself up to Hellfire. A
picture flashed into Jack's mind: Beth, chained up in
Bedlam, clots of living flies where her eyes should be.

Tonight.

'Stop moping, lad. If Beth's there, all the better!' Kit, still
with that grin, still not listening. 'We arrive, masked, and
present ourselves as guests. They all wear masks to these
things, it says here somewhere.' Kit rustled his paper. 'If I
can't talk my way into a night of revels, I've no more use
for life: throw me in the Thames, let eels eat my tongue.'

Jack shook his head. He couldn't believe he'd been so stupid.

'Beth didn't believe me,' he said.

'Believe what?' said Kit.

'About Ravenscar. She doesn't know . . .'

Christ, what if the door had worked last night, and he'd gone through it? Leaving Beth, like Ada . . .

'We'll get one of them chariots,' said Jack. He started off down the steps.

'Chariots?' said Kit. He hadn't moved.

'Carriages. Whatever they call 'em here. Get there quicker. Come on, we've got to stop her.'

Tonight: and already the dusk was gathering.

'Stop her from what?' said Kit, following now. Jack broke into a run, didn't waste breath on an answer.

It was full dark by the time they arrived at Beth's house. They walked the last stretch, Jack fretting that it was too late, that she would have gone already. Kit maintained that no one would arrive at something like the Hellfire Club much before midnight; but it wasn't till they turned the corner into Beth's street that Jack knew for sure.

At the corner of the street, a carriage was waiting. Jack recognized it immediately. She hadn't gone early. She was still home. But she was going, small doubt of that.

Black horses, golden harness; gleaming black body like a fat beetle: it was Ravenscar's carriage.

Luckily the night was dark. They passed the carriage on the far side of the street. Ravenscar's lackeys were sitting on the backboard, passing a bottle back and forth. The driver sat still on his box, a huddled shape under a cloak.

A minute later, Jack and Kit were hidden in a dark and shadowy porch, looking up at Beth's house opposite.

The ground floor windows were dark; but there was bright light on the first floor, and a candle glow on the second.

'Well I think you'll agree we can't just knock,' said Kit.

Jack nodded slowly.

There was some sort of creeping plant growing up the front wall of the house. Most of the strands were flimsy, dead; but a few living sinews knotted together at the centre. They looked tough. They might hold. One of Mr Smiles' couplets dropped into his head: *Vegetal is ripe to fall, so bring a grapple, darksmen all.*

Jack had no grapple. He had climbed only once since his Wallwork Trial, part of the testing to join the Sharkwell Family. Both times had ended badly.

'Have a look in that window, Imp.'

The imp flitted up, and returned.

'Lovey-dove therein,' it muttered. 'Raven glitterman also. Sitting close, chuckly natterchatter. Hellstuff sipping.'

Jack nodded. He couldn't trust himself to speak.

'Tsa,' said the imp. 'Dump-skull master, to speak chuff to sharklylove, and now see—'

'Quiet.'

The imp must have recognized this as a dire command: it went silent.

'Jack, I mislike this look of yours,' said Kit.

'Go speak to the carriage driver.'

'Jack, consider—'

'No. I'm doing this either way, so: do it or not.'

Kit looked at him for a moment, shook his head, and walked off down the pavement. After a moment he began to sing to himself, in a drunken sort of way. He was walking drunk too, now, weaving from one side of the road to the other – then he bumped into the near front wheel of the carriage and swore to the heavens.

Soon a nice little scene was afoot, Kit cursing the coachman and both lackeys. He was asking for a beating; but that wasn't Jack's concern. Their attention was distracted. Now was the moment.

Jack ran across the street, scrambled over the iron railings and threw himself at the front wall, his fingers gripping the vine, his feet scrabbling for purchase. The vine sagged, but Jack swung himself up fast, swarming for the window.

The vine creaked under his weight. Down the street, he heard a thud, and Kit swearing. Then running feet. He kept his eyes on the wall in front of him.

As he reached the first-floor window, Jack wrapped one foot in the best-rooted twist of vine he could find. He rested his weight on the window ledge, panting slightly.

There they were: and it wasn't so bad.

The room was all lit up like a stage. Beth sat with her back to Jack, her bare neck curved as she looked down at something in her hands. Empty bottles and the remains of a dinner were spread on the table before her. Ravenscar was lounging on a couch with his feet up. He'd slipped one shoe off. He had a bunch of grapes in his lap, and was eating them slowly, peeling each one before popping it into his mouth. Deep inside his eyes, visible by devil-sight, something glittered and danced.

Jack couldn't see Beth's face.

By cupping his ear to the glass, he could just make out what they were saying. A choice then: hear or see. For the moment he chose to hear.

'Not everything can be told, Devine. Some things must be lived to be known.'

'But there's plenty you could tell, and you're not. Don't say it isn't so.'

'The same is true of you too, my dear.'

'My brother, again? I've told you—'

'I know what you've told me,' he said mildly. 'I don't believe it, that's all.'

'You needn't worry about Jack, anyway. He's nothing to me. Not any more. Do you believe that?'

In his black anger, Jack's foot slipped. He nearly fell.

'Kra!' The imp quivered. 'See!'

When Jack looked up he saw Beth crossing the room. He saw her smile.

She had it too. Inside her. Very faint – less than Ada and Kitty that time – but there it was, glimmering like stars underwater.

Spiritus.

She stopped in front of Ravenscar. She stooped slowly and plucked a grape from his lap; ate it, looking down at him with solemn, sparkling, laughing eyes. This was worse than anything else; for she'd never looked at Jack that way.

Ravenscar made as if to rise, but Beth pushed him back down. He didn't resist.

Jack had an urgent desire to stab his own eyes out. Instead he turned his head and put his ear back to the window.

'. . . believe me now?'

Beth's voice.

Ravenscar laughed. 'With you, Devine, I never know what to believe. That is your charm.'

Jack heard a creak: Ravenscar, getting up off the couch. A pause stretched out. Jack turned to look, heart thudding in fear of what he might see.

Ravenscar was holding a box in his hand, holding it out for Beth to look. She was staring down into it, eyes agleam. By stretching up as high as possible, Jack could just see what was inside.

On a bed of black silk lay a red mask. A half mask, coming down to just above the mouth, with pure, expressionless features. It gleamed like fresh-spilt blood. Ravenscar tilted it, observing the play of candlelight across the lacquer. He began to speak. Jack cupped his ear to the glass.

'—for Ada, poor thing. Now you will wear it, if you choose.'

Beth murmured something, too low for Jack to hear.

'I think your brother would like to know it, too, no?' said Ravenscar, in that light, mocking way he had.

'Certainly not. I keep telling you, Ravenscar, he is the merest churl.'

'Wear the mask. No one passes through my doors tonight without a mask. I've a costume prepared – for Ada, so it will want some alteration. My carriage will take you . . .'

Footsteps, then, and Ravenscar's voice faded. Jack turned to look – and saw the two of them leaving the room, Ravenscar's hand resting on Beth's shoulder.

Jack heard footsteps on stairs, going down: going outside. He was plastered up here, nowhere to hide. One glance up, that was all it would take.

The front door opened. Ravenscar stood on the threshold, his back to the street, his head bent forward.

'Now remember,' he said, 'as we cannot arrive together – the watchword is *Speranza*. They won't let you in otherwise.'

'*Sperrrranza*,' said Beth, giving the 'r' its full, Italianated roll.

She sounded merry-drunk. Jack couldn't see her – and then Ravenscar tottered back, laughed, steadied himself with a gold-topped cane, and there she was in his embrace. Laughing too. Ravenscar whirled her around, and her head tilted up to meet his, and that was when she saw Jack.

He strained to put all his warnings into his eyes. *Don't trust Ravenscar. Don't go tonight. That place is deadly.*

'What is it?' said Ravenscar, looking down at her.

'Nothing, nothing.'

'No, but—'

'Come here.'

She pulled him down to her. They were clinched together for a long time. Jack heard little wet sounds of mouths moving together. When Beth's face came into view again, it was flushed, her lips swollen and red. She was looking straight at Jack. The Spiritus burned deep within her. Jack had never seen anything so fair.

'Walk me to the carriage,' said Beth. They walked over arm in arm. Lord Ravenscar handed her up, saying something to the coachman. A crack of the whip – and she was gone, into the night.

Ravenscar came walking back up the street, twirling his cane and whistling. He passed right beneath Jack, but he never looked up. Jack watched him out of sight. Ravenscar was a very good whistler. Jack could hear the notes echoing long after he had disappeared round the corner. It was a wild jig of a tune, a dance for Tartars.

Jack waited. His arms ached. The imp didn't say a word.

After what seemed like a very long time, he heard a *Psst* from across the street.

'Safe to come,' said Kit.

Jack slithered down the vine.

'I saw her leave,' said Kit. 'I take it we're going, then?'

'Costumes,' said Jack. He glared about: as if there might be some dressmaker's on this street, open in the middle of the night . . . 'Swive it, Kit, he said no one's getting in without a mask and a costume.'

Kit was staring up at Beth's house.

'Costumes, eh? *Tch-tch-tch* . . .' He tapped his teeth with his fingernail. 'Here we are, standing outside the house of the most celebrated actress in Town, with only a periwig that unlocks doors to help us.'

Kit grinned.

'How will we *possibly* find ourselves costumes?'

Chapter 25

The revels began at midnight, but the guests began to arrive much earlier.

From west of Regent Street came the great carriages, the coats-of-arms on their doors covered over to ward off scandal. Plainly dressed footmen handed down their masters and mistresses onto the icy pavement outside Ravenscar House. The lords and ladies all wore dark cowls over their costumes, but the blazing torches that lined the carriageway lit up the masks beneath – a curl of lion's mane, a flash of dragon's teeth, the tight savage curve of falcon's beak.

From Drury Lane and Covent Garden came shabby hackney cabs and sedan chairs and even some guests on foot. Actresses, all of them young, noted beauties; some in borrowed theatre costumes; some in satin dresses, gifts from rich admirers; all wearing their masks, for that was the rule. They greeted each other, and strode arm in arm along Oxford Street, little flocks of jewelled birds on their way to Lord Ravenscar's feast. Passers-by nudged one another and stared. The girls held their heads high. They knew what was said. They were not ashamed.

At eleven, the young Viscount Verney careened into Eden Gardens in his French-built racing phaeton, standing up like a Roman charioteer, cracking his whip over the panicked horses. He hadn't bothered to disguise his arms – the phaeton was in any case unique – and his arrival caused just the stir he'd intended. It didn't last as long as he'd hoped, however, because just as he leaped down onto the pavement, another carriage rolled into the square at a brisk trot. This one, too, was easy to recognize – black as midnight, its plumed black horses harnessed in gold.

All eyes turned from the viscount to the new arrival. Some of them had heard the rumours, but that wasn't the same as actually seeing it. Yet here she was, stepping down from Lord Ravenscar's own carriage – face hidden by a gleaming red mask, hurrying past the torch-lit steps to enter by a little side door.

The whispers spread and rippled through the crowd. Here she was – Artemisia Devine – pursued by many, caught by none.

Until tonight.

*

'*Speranza*,' tittered Kit – and they were in.

Wrapped in Beth's rustling silk, Jack and Kit swept through the marble hall and up the curving staircase. Footmen holding forked candelabras lined their path.

'Vertlick glintry,' said the imp. It was back in its beetle shell, glittering in the piled-up curls of the lady's wig balanced on Jack's head.

Jack paused at the head of the stairs, between two mirrors. A million Jacks and Kits slanted out and away to either side. The jewelled mask they'd found for Jack fit well enough, and matched the finery of his costume. Kit had called him Queen of Sheba, whoever that was. Jack thought he looked like a boy in a dress. The wig teetered over his head – ridiculous. He'd hung Lud's key around his neck, under the dress. It pressed against his chest, a cold reminder of home.

'Courage, Jack,' said Kit, taking his gloved hand. 'You make a very pretty girl. I've always thought it.'

Kit did not make a pretty girl. He hadn't found a mask to fit, so he wore a silk cushion cover with holes cut out for his eyes. His hairy chest was bursting out of his tight-laced, yellow bodice.

They walked on, following the lines of candlelight. The silk of their skirts whispered across the floor. Up ahead, brighter light shone through open doors. Jack could hear the soft rustling sounds of people waiting, expectant.

Through the doors, and they were at the head of another grand staircase. In the great hall below them, the Hellfire Club was assembled in all its glory.

There were at least two hundred guests. Rich old men; wild young bloods; women and girls, young and comely and dressed to make the eyes start from your head. Every last one of them was masked. There were masks crusted with jewels, masks made of gold, monks' cowls and silken veils and tatty lepers' bandages. There were eagles, dragons, sea-devils brandishing tridents; teeth and tusks and fat slobbering lips. At this moment, as Jack and Kit paused at the top of the stairs, every eye in the great hall was on them.

Jack felt a wave of heat pass across his skin.

'*Ware*, master,' said the imp. 'Vast kittling of hellstuff.'

At the foot of the stairs, on a raised dais, stood a huge silver urn. The imp was right, it did look like a kettle. Jack's hand was numb all over now, not even the faintest twitch of feeling; but when he looked with the devil sight he saw what was in the urn.

Spiritus. Lots of it.

Most of the crowd were keeping half an eye on the urn – and Jack didn't like the way they did it. Even though he couldn't see their faces, he could smell it.

The room was waiting. Holding its breath, like there was a surprise about to happen, and they all knew about it, and he didn't.

A hungry sort of look.

Jack didn't like surprises.

'Look at that! A million in money, if you could clean 'em out,' said Kit, taking Jack's arm and starting down the stairs. 'Keep your head, nipper.'

Kit was right: if Jack had been on the nipping lay tonight, the low-hanging fruit alone would be sufficient to retire contented. So rich. So foul: it was enough to make him long for some good, honest London muck – a mound of nightsoil, say, or a month-dead dog.

They pushed into the crowd. Someone pinched Jack's arse. He whipped round, remembering just in time to smile.

'*Bonsoir*, my pretty,' a fox-headed man smirked back. 'A pretty *boy*, if I'm not mistaken.'

'I'm Jacqueline,' said Jack, trying to put some simper into it.

'And I'm Kitty, milord,' said Kit, holding out his hand to be kissed.

As the fox man recoiled, all conversation stopped.

Jack looked up to see Lord Ravenscar at the head of the staircase.

Ravenscar nodded to the assembled company. He wore a golden mask with smooth, blank features. The girl beside him was masked as well, a half mask that stopped just above her straight set mouth. Jack felt a bittersweet swelling in his throat.

The mask was red, gleaming red. The dress was red too, floating about her like a mist of blood. Jewels glittered. Hair tumbled in artful disarray. None of it mattered half so much as the way Beth carried herself.

The jaw of the gauzy-robed nymph standing just in front of Jack dropped open, and stayed that way. Her fat male companion – his head encased in a bristling boar mask – wobbled and groaned.

The silence lasted just a breath, and when it lifted everything was rearranged.

"Pon my soul! Is that Devine?' whispered the girl.

'Bless you, Sally, it ain't the Seward chit. Hah!' Boarface jiggled at his own wit.

Jack could imagine Ada standing in that very spot. In that very dress.

Beth made no sign that she knew – let alone cared – that every eye in the chamber was fixed on her. Just the set of her chin told them all that they were far beneath her notice.

Ravenscar raised his hands.

'Welcome, my friends.' He smiled at Beth. 'Welcome to the Inferno.'

Deep silence fell. Jack felt the tension around him again, the expectation: something was about to happen.

Ravenscar looked towards the shadows at the back of the ballroom, and beckoned.

Two servants came forward, and the crowd parted before them. They were wheeling a table filled with an odd assortment of objects. A little way behind them was Tom. He wasn't wearing a mask. Jack watched him walk, sloped and hunched, down the full length of the ballroom.

He looked neither left nor right, as if the devil masks, the jewels and silks and wobbling flesh of the Hellfire Club were not even there.

Ravenscar descended the stairs and waited beside the giant silver urn. The servants wheeled the table to a halt in front of him. It was covered with complicated glassware and strangely shaped implements; several candles, lit; and a rack of bottles made from thick, whorled glass.

The crowd closed in. Tom hung back on the edge of things. Jack saw him look up at Beth – standing there above them all in Ada's red dress.

I will avenge her. Would it be now? Bring down all the Hellfire revellers, along with their lord?

Jack knew what it was to be a revenger.

Tom might do anything.

Servants in black and gold livery began to flit about the ballroom, extinguishing the candles. The space dimmed until the only light was coming from the table. It was very dark now.

'My good fellow denizens of Hellfire.' Lit up in the candlelight, Ravenscar's masked face floated in the darkness.

'Tonight, we play host to a pair of neophytes. The first, you all know of.'

A few faces turned up to look at Beth, standing at the head of the stairs. No more whispers and tittering now, though: not with Ravenscar's eyes on them.

His head turned slowly, light sliding off the polished surfaces of his mask, until he faced Tom.

'The other – the learned Mr Dee – is the author of our most diabolic pleasures. He has penetrated the outward show of Nature, and laid out her deepest secrets for our delectation.'

Everyone turned to stare at Tom. He was sweating, face frozen in a ghastly death's-head smile.

'Your friend looks apt to bolt,' Kit whispered. 'What's his game, do you think?'

'Tom,' said Ravenscar. 'With your permission?'

Tom blinked, looked wildly from side to side, as if hoping someone else would answer for him – and then nodded, very fast.

With a showman's flourish, Ravenscar dropped a small object from his sleeve into his hand. A wooden box.

He opened it carefully and drew out a tiny red bead. His movements were slow and precise.

Kit nudged him, but Jack didn't need telling.

'Satyr-shuk,' said the imp.

A quiver of impatience stirred in the crowd, but Ravenscar checked it with a glance.

'Soon, my dears.'

Jack glanced quick with devil-sight. The urn still blazed with Spiritus, but there was no sign of life inside the bead. But then, he thought with a new yawning dread, maybe the satyr had good reason to hide.

Hadn't the satyr hidden from Jack, when he came to steal it?

And what then?

Something bad was going to happen.

'As always,' said Ravenscar, 'this urn has been filled with Spiritus, of my own private mixture.' He glanced up at Beth. 'But for tonight, I felt something . . . extraordinary was called for.'

Ravenscar gave a low weird laugh and bared his teeth. He reached for a casket in the middle of the table that Jack hadn't noticed before. With elaborate caution, he opened the lid.

The inside of the casket gave off a faint glow – a dapple of crimson light that lit up his face from below.

'O Zdeck!' said the imp. 'Most mecktik hellstuff! Fell fly! Fell fly!'

'Quiet,' whispered Jack, with a calm he didn't feel.

The imp fell silent. Jack could feel it quivering in his wig.

The old, familiar hot-metal smell raked his nostrils. His cursed eye burned, and even his numb hand tingled.

Somewhere beneath the black, something of the Alkahest remained; and now it sang out, like to like.

'Is that what I think?' said Kit.

'He doesn't know, does he?' said Jack. 'He can't know . . .'

'Tonight,' said Ravenscar, 'we will all witness the unlocking. The coming of the Spiritus. The key to heart's desire. For what else is it that man seeks in life but the fulfilment of his inmost, secret self?'

For once, the usual lazy drawl was gone. It was clear that Ravenscar's task intoxicated him. Behind the mask, his eyes glittered and danced.

Jack glanced at Tom. His attention was fixed intently on his enemy. He did not know he was observed; and his hatred was horrible to see.

'The Alkahest unlocks the Spiritus,' continued Ravenscar. 'The Spiritus unlocks us all.'

But how had they got their hands on the Alkahest?

Jack struck quick on the answer: the same way Tom got his hands on the map. His ancestor's things, hidden away these past two hundred years. Found again, now that the knowledge of their danger was lost.

Something bad was going to happen.

'What wonders shall we witness tonight? What wonders shall we become? What devils raised to Paradise, what stars thrown down in flames?'

With a pair of tweezers, Ravenscar teased out a single

grain of Alkahest. The crowd was deathly silent, as if his absolute concentration compelled them to be still.

Jack glanced once more at Tom. His face was calmer now, and tilted up. What was he planning?

In the darkness it was hard to tell; but Jack had the strongest feeling that it was Beth he was gazing at.

Why Beth?

And then, on the heels of that question, came another strange thought.

He doesn't know you're watching him.

Ravenscar dropped the grain into a bowl of water, and gave a satisfied grunt. There was a hissing, fizzing noise. Red sparks leaped from the water.

Everyone in the room craned in to get a better look.

Jack's mouth was dry. The hot metal stink of magic was getting stronger as Ravenscar blew out the last two candles on the table.

The sparks stopped jumping – the hissing died down. A dull red glow rose up from the bowl, lighting up Ravenscar's face as he picked up the satyr's bead and dropped it into the water.

'Behold.' Out of the darkness, he spoke. 'The Alkahest unlocks the Spirit.'

A puff of pale mist climbed into the air. Moving fast, Ravenscar clapped a heavy glass dome over the bowl, trapping the mist inside.

The crowd gasped.

Jack's hand and eye were itching like fury. Beneath the dome, tiny glowing lights sparked into life. Little dots trailing fox-fire tails – red, green, blue-black. They soared and swooped like kites on a strong wind.

Spiritus.

They were beautiful.

Cries of wonder and amazement were spilling from the audience. Jack realized that they must be able to see all this as well: he wasn't using the devil-sight.

The imp was shaking uncontrollably. Jack reached up to steady it.

'Spy! *Scoppen*, master!'

Jack blinked into devil-sight.

Beneath the dome, something small and misshapen was thrashing in torment. Jack saw a mouth stretched wide in silent screams; a pair of eyes wild with panic; hooves drumming against the glass, horns melting away like wax in boiling water . . .

Jack realized he was looking at the satyr – melting as the Spiritus burned off it, melting away to a nub of twitching flesh.

It's a devil, Jack told himself. It's not your friend, it's done you nothing but harm. It's a *devil*.

Beneath the glass, the satyr was dying. And everyone was smiling as they looked at the pretty lights.

'That's our way home,' said Kit.

'Make it stop,' said Jack.

'*Balkutt YAYN!*' screamed the imp. It shot from Jack's head, knocking his wig off, blazing white with rage.

The dome exploded. Glass sprayed into the air. The imp curved up through a mist of Alkahest. It rose higher, now glowing red, covered in tiny droplets.

Uproar all around. Shouts of anger, moans of fear, Ravenscar calling for lights to be brought.

'Eeeeeeeeeeeeeeeeee! *Gishgishgishgishgish!*' The imp was in agony. The scream cut above all the other sounds.

Jack threw himself forward, slipping low through the chaos. Someone was hurrying down the stairs with a lantern. The imp was a faint red glow bobbing through the air. It was trying to reach a window. It was sinking.

Jack writhed and leaped, reached for the imp – and missed. An elbow smashed into his chest. He staggered sideways, and fell.

The lights behind him were getting brighter. Dazzling. Jack could no longer see the imp. He scrambled to his feet.

It was only then he realized that he'd lost his mask.

There was a moment of stillness. Lights shining on Jack's naked face. He looked up into a circle of masked figures all around him. Teeth and tusks and long sharp beaks; eyes, glittering points behind the holes; all of them looking at him.

325

Nowhere to run.

'Seize him!'

Hands grabbed Jack, pinning his arms to his side. Voices were rippling out across the crowd, outrage spreading fast.

'What is it? An intruder?'

'A God-damned Jacobin!'

'Let's gut the sprat!'

'Your brother returns, Devine!'

Lord Ravenscar sounded delighted.

Beth was looking down at Jack. The eyes behind the gleaming red mask were unreadable. Ravenscar stepped forward, standing straight and tall, proud as Lucifer.

'A spy in our midst,' he said. 'Let us show him what he came to see. We may have lost our fresh extraction; but my private mixture should prove more than sufficient.' He turned, and bowed to Beth with a flourish. 'And rest easy my friends: I will deal with our spy in good time.'

He clapped his hands, and servants busied themselves around the urn, tapping off Spiritus into crystal tumblers. Tom had not moved. He stood surrounded by broken glass, staring at Jack like a man who'd seen his own ghost.

A large circle had formed around Jack. He was still wearing his ridiculous costume. Everyone was staring at him – some of them laughing, some still suggesting ways to kill him.

The trays went around. Eager hands snatched up the

tumblers. No one drank yet. The liquid in the tumblers was dark amber, sparkling inside with a rainbow of devilish light that only Jack could see.

Spiritus: and now he knew what it was – the raw stuff of magic, drained out of devils like blood from a twitching pig.

A servant appeared at Ravenscar's side. He carried two tall, slim glasses. Ravenscar carried them up the stairs to Beth himself.

'Drink.' Ravenscar raised his glass to the assembled company. 'We all must drink. It is the one rule of this gathering. Drink, or go home.'

Down below, everyone raised their tumblers. Up above, beside Ravenscar, Beth lifted her glass.

Jack watched her, and his heart filled with despair.

'Go to it, then,' said Ravenscar, and a broad grin stretched out beneath the white mask. 'Go to it, Hellfire fiends – and devil take the lot of us!'

Ravenscar drained his glass in a single draught. Artemisia Devine tossed hers back, then smashed the crystal on the floor.

She did not look at Jack as he was led away.

Chapter 26

Ravenscar House had many hidden corners. Some were intended for the doing of forbidden things. Of these, many were in use on the night of the Hellfire Club, and they were often to be found surprisingly close by the main rooms of the house.

Others were deep underground, in the traditional manner of dungeons and oubliettes: for although the house was modern, Lord Ravenscar had certain needs that were as old as the most medieval of strongholds – the need to keep secrets safe, for instance. Jack was no secret, but Lord Ravenscar was certainly keeping him safe – in a locked room, in the deepest, furthest recess of his cellars.

Time stretched. In the dark and the silence, there was no way of marking minutes and seconds.

Then, at last, came a measure of sorts – the sound

of drumming from above. A tripping off-beat, apt for dancing.

The Hellfire revels had begun. Beth was up there. Whatever was going to happen to her, would now happen – and there was nothing Jack could do about it.

He paced the room, hand trailing against the walls. No way out, of course. The door was very solid – oak, from the feel of the grain – Mr Smiles had taught him that, back in Southwark, a lifetime ago. *A darksman must see with his fingers – oak from ash, gold from brass, trout from good red herring – feel again,* tocca-tocca, *my pretty raggattso!*

Kit. Kit might save her. Now that the revels had begun, perhaps he'd be able to slip her away. Maybe he'd even find the imp, too – though the imp had looked bad, burned by Alkahest. The imp would be too weak to help much.

It would be a comfort to have it here to talk to, at least. Anything was better than being alone in the dark, and imagining what they were doing to Beth up there, and waiting, and waiting, and—

Jack heard the footsteps late – drowned out by the drum-beat till the last minute. He stepped smartly away from the door, listening hard.

The footsteps slid slow and quiet, coming on the sly. Too heavy for Beth: definitely a man. Could it be Kit? Or . . .

Jack stared at the darkness – fear rising strong now. Ravenscar wouldn't come sneaking; but the other revellers, the ones who'd wanted him dead – or Malpas: yes, Malpas, creeping up to finish him off . . .

There was a soft tap on the door.

'Jack?' A large voice, booming even when it whispered. 'Are you there?'

It was Tom. Jack breathed out a hiss of relief.

'Jack?'

'Yes!' said Jack. 'I'm here. Get me out!'

'I can't,' said Tom. 'Not yet. I don't have the key.'

Jack's heart was still pounding.

'What happened there Jack? What did you do?'

'Nothing. I don't know. Listen, Tom, she's up there, B—' He caught himself. 'My sister's *up there with him*.' Jack heard the panic in his voice, fought to control it. 'Can you bring her out? See her safe?'

'You think she'll listen to *me*?' said Tom. 'She's dancing with Ravenscar. I don't know how . . .'

'I don't care how: just get her out!' said Jack. 'Before they do . . . like with Ada . . .'

'I'll do my best.' Tom hesitated. 'But Jack, *you* must escape too. They'll kill you else.'

'Her first,' said Jack. 'And listen: there's someone up there who can help. She knows him. He's called Kit. Dressed as a woman. Yellow gown.'

'I'll do my best,' repeated Tom. 'I'll try to find him. Has he some experience in this type of affair?'

330

'He's good.' In fact Jack couldn't think of anyone better: cross-dressing, terrible danger, oceans of drink. Kit could do this. 'What are you planning?'

'You said that Malpas killed Ada, but he is nothing but a damned puppet. Ravenscar murdered Ada. So I will take away what he holds most precious. I will destroy him.'

Tom sounded not like himself at all. He cleared his throat, and Jack could picture him shaking himself, drawing himself together. 'In all candour, your actions have complicated matters. I must see you safe before—'

'No,' said Jack. 'Her first. Right now.'

'Before she's undone. I understand. And I commend it, Jack. If only I'd been as vigilant, with Ada . . .' Tom stopped, caught his breath. 'I must make sure this time. If I can't find this Kit – how can I convince her to come? She's never taken to me, you see.'

Tom sounded forlorn – as if Beth not liking him was as much a tragedy as the rest. Jack clenched his mouth to stop from screaming with frustration. Every moment mattered now.

'Here,' he said. 'I've an idea.'

And now a dread worse than all the rest rose up. He had an idea, sure, but would she come, even if she knew the word was from him?

'Jack?' said Tom. 'Please, quickly now: I cannot stay here . . .'

'Tell her I sent you,' said Jack. 'And call her by her real name. Call her Beth. Beth Sharkwell.'

'Good,' said Tom. 'Very good. Wait, then, and do not fear. It should not be long before I bring you both to safety.'

Forced bravado: Jack could picture the sweat running down Tom's ruddy face. The tremor in his hands. The doubt in his eye.

'Be quick. Get Beth first,' said Jack. 'Remember? *Beth Sharkwell.*'

'Beth first,' Tom agreed. 'Very good, Jack. I will return for you once she's safe.'

The footsteps faded away as soft as they had come, leaving Jack alone in the darkness once more.

He crouched down on the floor to wait. He tried to tell himself he'd done all he could. Tom's heart might be honest enough, and Jack was sure he'd meant what he said – but he was not the man for such a deadly game.

The imp hadn't come. He could forgive that: the imp was half dead, and would do well to lie low for the night.

But the imp wasn't the only friend – or supposed friend – that Jack had here tonight. Say what you like about Kit Morely – and Jack would be first in line to damn his crooked tongue – but he had a knack for washing clean, even from the murkiest, most awkward spots.

Well this was the murkiest, most awkward spot that Jack had ever known. It was time for Kit to repay his debt.

*

Kit was very surprised at the way the evening had turned out.

It had always been a point of pride with Kit that no drink on Earth could best him. Make him merry, sure; but till this night he'd always kept hold of the reins, even after days of firewater and stingo.

Whatever had been in that tumbler – which he'd had to drink or be thrown out – well . . .

Whatever had been in that tumbler had bested him. The reins were lost. The horse had bolted, bucked, and flung him headlong into . . .

What?

Kit had no idea.

There were two Kits now: one was his old body, a rump-skuttle thing, a puppet made of sticks and wires – but how drab it was! Like looking through muddy water.

The second was made of night, dark and airy – billowing from shape to shape. He was floating in darkness; dancing without moving; treading in space. Faces, bodies whirled before him, devils of the mind's making, from daydreams and nightmares and feverish fancies.

Like a dream within a dream he saw the Red Queen, leading the Dance with her King beside her. Darkness coiled about them like billowing smoke. Everyone watched as they twined together, leading the revels. Kit felt their joy swelling sweet and dangerous in his chest. The drums pounded, the fiddles shrieked and called.

The King and Queen put their heads together. He whispered in her ear, and took her hand, and led her away. As was his right. They entered a green door – like a mossy cave.

It shut behind them.

Kit knew that there was something terribly important about that.

But then a tiger came, and spun him into the wild dance. He sprang and snarled, and forgot.

Chapter 27

Wild music tiptoed down the stairs. Gusts of wicked laughter scampered along the corridors. A distant, regular throb – the beating of demons' drums, in Jack's imagination – shivered the floorboards.

Try as he might, Jack could not ignore the sounds – nor stop the fevered thoughts they conjured up.

There was still no sign of Tom. Time passed slowly, waiting alone in the dark. Where was the man? Why this bowel-shriving delay?

The drum pounded on, muffled by distance, and then—

A scratching, much closer to hand.

Scratching at the door.

Jack crawled over. There was something poking through the crack beneath the door. It glowed, a feeble pale yellow.

'Imp?' Jack leaned in close.

'Magic-boy!' The imp's feelers and forelegs flickered like a dying candle.

'You crusty cuffin! You came! Open the door, come on, let's get out of here.'

The imp gave another flash, then its light wavered and almost went out.

'Ferdammit,' it said. 'Shuklet too weak for bindings, and this chink be strecklick small . . .'

'You can't get me out?'

'Dolorous nix, master. But . . . hitherly ist . . . str'*crax* . . .'

The imp retreated. More scratching – a harder sound now, of stone on stone – and something small and round came edging in under the door. It gave off a dim red light, and a dangerous sharp reek of hot metal.

'Is that . . . ?'

'Satyr-shuk,' said the imp. 'Haply to helply. Swab and swash it, master: off with poison Alkahest.'

Using his left hand – the other was jangling too hard – Jack gingerly picked up the bead in the hem of his skirt. He rubbed it against the silk very slowly – knowing that one slip meant agonizing pain or worse.

Bit by bit the red came, and soon it was the skirt, not the bead that was glowing.

Jack cursed himself for a fool. Why hadn't he torn away a strip of silk first?

He put down the bead and reached for the laces behind. Getting out of a dress like this without help was hard, it turned out. Getting out of a dress that was stained with poison was even harder,

At last he managed to rip the skirts safely away from the rest. He tossed them into a corner. He didn't think he'd got any of the stuff on himself: judging by the only other time he'd touched Alkahest, he'd know if he had. He'd be doubled up with agony.

Jack looked down at himself. Silken bodice on his top half, breeches beneath, with the ragged remains of the skirt hanging over them. No stranger than many of the costumes he'd seen upstairs . . .

He heard a soft, high-pitched humming behind him.

'Imp?'

'Nix I,' whispered the imp from behind the door. 'What ist?'

Jack turned around and peered into the darkness. The humming continued. There was nothing to be seen but the faint glow from the torn-off skirt.

Jack turned again, looked with the devil-sight – and choked with fright.

There right in front of him, hovering over the bead on the floor, an ill-formed slug of naked skin twitched and danced. It was no bigger than a finger – but it was growing as he watched.

'Satyr be harmlost,' said the imp.

It was the satyr – what was left of it. It had no legs, no arms, no real head. There were withered, twitching lumps in the right places. A few grey hairs.

It was twitching in time to the music from upstairs. It had no mouth, but somehow it was humming all the same.

Jack scrambled away from it, backing into the corner. The humming was getting louder, deeper – getting ferocious, getting to sound like a devil.

'What's going on, Imp?'

The imp shivered.

'I kennit nix, master. Fearly nearly dead, poor skrittered satyr-shuk . . .'

'Well . . .' said Jack. 'It's not dead, it's growing.'

The humming was getting louder and louder. The lump of skin was twitching faster – and already it had doubled in size.

'Z'pooks!' said the imp.

Upstairs, the drum throbbed. Down on the floor, the nub of skin stretched and creased with it. Two hairy legs budded out, complete with hooves – already stamping in time to the beat. Arms sprouted, fingers unfurled. With a sound like tearing linen, the face grew teeth and covered them with new lips. Last of all, two little horns sprouted from its forehead.

It all happened in three heartbeats. The humming never

stopped. Suddenly there was a tiny, wrinkled half-man lying on the floor before Jack. The satyr's goat legs were covered in mangy, patchy hair. Its ribs stuck out in pauper's wings.

One eye opened, and stared craftily at Jack for a moment. Drifting down, it fixed on Jack's right hand and flashed yellow.

It was still growing – growing fast, pulsing taller and fatter in time to the music from above.

'Ho! It's the boy!' Sargastes the Satyr sprang to his feet, fully grown. His voice sounded like he had swallowed one barrel of gravel and another of ragwater and left them to steep together for a thousand years.

'Beneezens,' murmured the imp, poking a foreleg under the door and waving.

The yellow eye swivelled. 'Ah, little scratling. I know you.' The satyr chuckled. His eye returned to Jack. 'And I knows the red boy too. Har*ghoooooooh*!'

The howl shook the room. Jack's back was pressed against the wall. He couldn't retreat any further; and there was no pentagram trapping the satyr now, no Dr Dee to bargain with it.

He held up his right hand, palm outward, warding it off.

The satyr frowned. 'Red no more, eh-hey? Red to black, is it? Been playing posies with the Swarm? What is it boy: you addicted to peril?'

'Please,' said Jack. 'I – never meant you no harm . . .'

'Please, is't?' The satyr clapped a hand to his forehead, and rolled his yellow eyes. 'Gizz a drink then, sniveller.'

'I ain't got one,' said Jack.

'Hrngh. Wasn't you the landlord, betimes? Lovely cellar full*abooze* you had . . .' The satyr sat up straight, and sniffed the air, then pointed up at the ceiling, dancing a jig in the air with his fingers. 'Above, then. Revel and rave, my beauties. Cos I be waking! I feels *fiesta*! Feels it close and clear. Feels its strength rising in my bonies, and my squelching, melching *gut*. Where's my toping hat?'

The satyr began plucking a succession of hats out of thin air. He tried them on, then flung them away: a red one with a picture of a yellow bird on it; a fancy, feathered chapeau; a horned helmet that crashed to the floor before vanishing as instantly as it had come.

Finally he settled on a small black cap, pulling it down tight over his ears.

'Zakatakawaka-oooooooOURGH!' He turned to Jack and grinned. His teeth gleamed gold. 'I do like a nice *beret*. Reminds me of a famous night in . . .' He frowned and looked thoughtful. 'Antioch? Was it . . . ?'

The satyr punched himself hard in the face, and leaped high, kicking his heels together.

'Ah, thass better.'

Strange piping and fevered cries fluted louder from above. Deep inside Jack's numb right hand, something was

340

stirring – an itch, a prickly burn like fading nettlerash.

'Back! Oh Lord, like he's never been away!' The satyr smacked his lips. The music swelled up livelier with every stomp and twist, as if the satyr's caperings were feeding it in turn.

'Wait. Listen.' Jack pulled out Lud's key and held it up for the satyr to see.

'You made this work. You can make it work again, can't you?'

Ignoring Jack completely, the satyr shimmied across to the door, reached *through* it and picked up the imp. He stroked its shell with a long yellow fingernail.

'Now then. You saved me from the furnace, little freshling. And I pays my debts.'

There was a flash of light. Every one of the imp's legs stood out rigid and glowed a different colour.

'Aiiiiiiiiiiiii!' screeched the imp. It flew up in the air and gave a jaunty wriggle, then swooped down like a swallow.

The satyr chuckled. 'Better? Good. Come with me, and we'll go a-melching, oh yes indeed: the sap – will flow!'

'Great honour, grand sire.' Stopping in mid-air, the imp bowed low. 'But I bide with master.'

'Noeeeeeeee! Can't you hear? The sap *flows*.'

The imp didn't move.

'Last chance, little scrat.' The satyr bent in close.

'I bide,' said the imp.

The satyr's face wrinkled into a mask of despair. 'Tragic! A grand and gruesome pity.' Then he was grinning again, rolling his eyes, clown-like. 'Well. Tarala, then.'

'Wait,' said Jack. 'No. Where're you going?'

'I've a revel to unravel!' The satyr turned to Jack, and bowed. 'As I said: the sap rises. Toodle-oo . . .'

He began to spin on the spot. The music from above rose and rose, wrapping round the devil as he whirled.

'No!' Jack dived forward and grabbed him by one goaty ankle. The satyr stopped. Beneath Jack's fingers the hair was smooth, the bone beneath it hard and cold as iron.

The imp darted down and tugged at Jack's sleeve.

'Caretake, master!' it cried.

'Do you desire death?' Looming down at Jack, the satyr seemed to swell out and grow even taller. 'Lucky you are: lucky you didn't grab me with your other hand, my chummer. The black and red one. Cos I'd have crushed your pretty head like a melon.'

The satyr bent like a crouching heron, his face inches from Jack's.

Still, Jack clung on.

'I was there for the very first *Shoom*,' continued the satyr in a quiet, conversational voice. 'I was there when Rome burned, and Emperor Nero capered to *my* tune. I danced the *tango di muerte* with the snake-hipped Marquez *hermanas* – and tonight's a revel to stand with the best of 'em. I've a belting masquerade to unhinge – so unhand me, varlet.'

The satyr pulled a little red horn out of the air and parped it in Jack's face.

'And come along yourselves, it'll be quite the entertainment, I promise! I've brought candles.'

'No,' said Jack.

'Magic-boy!' hissed the imp. 'Be wareful granden satyr-shuk.'

Jack gritted his teeth and gripped harder. The satyr crouched down. He looked puzzled.

'Truly no? You confuse me, Voltaire.'

'No,' said Jack. 'You said you pay your debts. Well, Imp here saved you. And I helped. Even though it's all your fault.'

'How's that?'

'You dragged Beth here. You dragged me here. You have to tell us how to leave.' Jack brandished the key, bold with anger. 'Tell me! How do I work this?'

'Work it? Why, you've done it once already! And I never *drag*!' The satyr gave a sudden bark of laughter.

'Tell me about the girl,' he said. 'Sharp little birdie, as I recall.' He pulled a red flower out of the air, and sniffed it, eyes fluttering. 'Does your heart *swell* when you think on her pretty nose?'

'Aye,' said Jack, without hesitating. 'And you took her away. Don't tell me you don't remember it!'

343

'Away ... away ... no, I think not,' said the satyr. 'There's no away for me, you see – only waking and dreaming. And when I'm awake – why, it's all *one*, don't you see?'

'No.'

'No?'

'Please,' said Jack. 'Speak plain. You brought me here, and since then I've not seen a single devil, and this here's not even *twitched*.' He waved the key again. 'How do I get home? It was you made it work before, weren't it?'

The satyr stroked his chin.

'How to make simple things clear to a dunder-head bassoon? Hear this, little black-hand. Listen most attentive. Haply you just discovered the moon, eh? See?'

'No,' said Jack.

'What am I now?'

The satyr stared fixedly at Jack, as if sighting down a pistol barrel. His hairy belly sucked in and out.

'You're ... a devil?' said Jack.

'True! But most of all I'm *awake*. I'm *visible*.' The satyr winked. 'Couldn't see me before, could you? Seen none of my kind of late, you said?'

Jack nodded.

'Well, little red-hand, I hid the first time you came, recall it? And all us devils have had good cause to hide, this recent while. Very good cause indeed. Got better at it, too.'

'Aye, that's what I thought,' said Jack. 'Hiding from Tom Dee.'

'Hiding from *him*?' The satyr cackled. 'Why, where's the use in that? He's got his cheaty map to lead him to us . . . no, no, no.' The satyr paused, and leaned down to whisper in Jack's ear. 'There's something worse coming than any Alkahest bath, boy. Swarm lord's looking for a way, and we all know he'll find it. He's come close already. Won't be long now.'

'The Swarm lord . . .' said Jack, feeling something lurch open inside him – seeing Ada at Bedlam, the darkness within her, crawling like flies. The same thing happening to Beth: happening right now, for all he knew.

'Open the door for me,' said Jack. 'Make it work now.'

'Door, pshaw! It's all one for me when I get my fire lit. This revel, that revel.' The satyr's eyes wobbled this way and that. 'This time, that place – all one.' He turned to the imp. 'This poor fellow is very slow, you know it? Sure you want to throw in with such a clummox?'

The imp snorted.

'Master, with key is not to reach lovey-dove. With key, only to elsewhile, fartimes . . .'

'Pox on't,' said Jack.

'But shuklet ist restored, all mecktick strengths: *shuklet* can ope doors.'

'Slow, slow, snail-witted boy,' said the satyr. 'Listen to

your shuklet-slave, and as for yonder key – try it and see. Enjoy *my* revels, whenever you be!'

The satyr jumped away, kicking free of Jack's grip. It landed neatly in mid-air, hopped once, whirled like a spinning top, and vanished.

'Flacktet!' The imp jumped straight up to the ceiling, and stuck there, glowing bright lime green.

Music was playing in the corridor outside. Not the music from upstairs: this was right outside the door, there out of nowhere, a wild reel of skirling pipes.

The key in Jack's hand quivered into life, jerking like a fish on a line. Jack clapped hold of it. It thrummed – such as it hadn't done, not once, since he'd left his own time.

The key settled into a new shape – long, thick, forged from plain black iron. Jack could feel the power in it thrumming in his fingers, like a warhorse ready to charge.

'It's happening again,' he said. His right hand was waking from its numbness, crawling with invisible fire – devil magic, strong as he'd ever felt.

The key squirmed in his grip, changing shape, and the music outside changed with it – much, much louder, with bright lights flashing through the keyhole and the crack under the door.

'Satyr wakes,' said the imp.

'The key – d'ye reckon . . . ?'

'Satyr wakes.' The imp shrugged. 'Alltimes are opened.

346

Now all is to find lovey-dove and lokmock, and then – away.'

'A-aye,' said Jack – not wanting to jinx it by eagerness. 'So: let's go find Beth and Kit.'

'Nix to delay,' said the imp. 'Shuklet enacts.'

It flitted over to the door and settled on the handle. The light in its shell went out. In the same instant, the music from beyond the door was gone, and Lud's key settled cold and still in Jack's hand.

Inside the door, a bolt slid back. The hinges groaned as the door swung open. 'Thiisss way, maaster.'

Jack waited for the imp to bind back into the beetle. It rose up and settled on his shoulder – and he walked through the door.

The corridor beyond was dark and empty. Jack could see the staircase beyond, leading up to the grand rooms above.

He made himself breathe deeper, slower.

He was free. He had the key. He was in one piece.

Now for the Hellfire.

Chapter 28

Ravenscar House had seen many a wild night – but tonight was something different. Those who lived to recall it would tell their tales in whispers, and only to each other: no one else would believe them.

From the start, there was an edge of excitement to the revels. A spy at the Hellfire Club! What punishment must await him? Lord Ravenscar's guests speculated, and laughed; and then, as the Spiritus took hold, abandoned themselves to whatever pleasures their fancies conjured up. This was what they had come for, and the gilded halls of Ravenscar House echoed with sighs and laughter.

And then, as the evening progressed, something different arose. Something unlooked for, unwished for. Something that drove the revellers on to excesses beyond their wildest, darkest dreams.

Sargastes the Satyr was awake.

*

With every step, Jack drew closer to Hell.

He could smell it. The air was hot and close, and filled with wild, unsettling cries – more animal than human. Somewhere in the distance, the satyr's music pulsed deep, like a giant's heart.

Swarm-lord's coming.

The door into the grand entrance hall stood slightly ajar. Holding his breath, Jack peeked through the gap at what was become of Lord Ravenscar's Hellfire Club.

The candles had melted down to puddles of wax. The faint light from the few that still burned glinted off crystal glasses, the marble floor, the mirrors on the walls – and the revellers.

They wore masks, and little else.

Was Beth among them? The thought was too foul. But Jack had to look – and as he looked, he felt the Spiritus misting off them, whispering in, planting stranger's footprints in his mind.

Spiritus – a pretty lie now he knew what it really was: the lifeblood of devils.

He remembered old Dr Dee standing over a chalk star spattered with mouse blood. Telling him how the sacrifice must fit the devil: mouse blood would summon something small and squeaky, cat's blood something more . . . toothy.

What manner of thing did you summon with devil's blood?

Swarm lord's coming.

In the gloom, he seemed to glimpse long, unnatural limbs; questing snouts; tails that coiled like whips – all tangled together in a bed of flickering flame.

The shadows writhed on the wall.

'Dread not, master,' whispered the imp. 'Ist only a dreaming.'

'Are you sure?'

Jack closed his eyes and pressed hard against them with the heels of his hands. When he opened them, the flames had vanished and the bodies on the floor were human again.

Jack stepped through the door and walked out into the room. Though he was terrified, he forced himself to look at every face, praying he wouldn't see Beth.

The imp hissed like a kettle.

These weren't devils. This wasn't really Hell. Just a pack of gilded lechers, with a pox-pussed notion of pleasure.

No Ravenscar. No Beth.

It was no comfort at all. They would be somewhere deeper. They would be somewhere worse.

Just on the edge of sight, strange shapes writhed.

Steady, Jack.

Jack crossed himself, and mounted the stairs. In the next room, a great feast lay smashed to pieces, like a city pillaged by a rampaging army. Crushed fruit, bones and scraps of meat had been flung against the walls. Wine puddled on the floor. Fat grunting forms crawled about, rooting in the ruins, squealing in triumph over every morsel.

They shrank away as Jack hurried past.

Again – no Ravenscar, no Beth.

Through the next archway came a throbbing of drums and a savage skirl of pipes and fiddles.

It was very dark.

Jack breathed. The dream was strong here, overwhelming: it felt like he was deep underground, like the wall at his back was made of hard-packed black earth. A stream of dancers spun through the dimness, moving too fast to follow. A frenzy of motion, blurred limbs; black shapes thrashing and twirling, too fast to be human. There was no sign of any musicians.

Steady, Jack.

Beth could be here; it was impossible to tell. The dance was a blur, and Jack could not imagine it ever stopping.

He hugged the wall, feeling his way into a corner. He tried to pick out Beth's red mask, Ravenscar's white one – but the masks didn't look like masks any more. Jack saw beast faces, devil faces. None of them looked anything like Beth.

The music stopped.

Everything stopped, and a light flared up.

As one, as if each of them knew exactly what to do, the revellers turned towards the centre of the room, and the light. There, puffed and proud, stood Sargastes the Satyr, holding a single candle aloft. The room was silent as death.

Beasts and green-skinned maidens; feathered, scaled, and furred; nameless, horrible things – all waiting on their king. Jack searched their faces – but he couldn't find Beth.

The satyr was standing beside a slim, blond-haired youth, a couple of years older than Jack. The youth was masked as a cherub, lips curved into a sweet smile.

Watched in breathless silence by the throng of devil figures, the satyr looked amongst them, over them, sought out Jack's eyes – and winked.

Then he turned, and set the candle to the boy's hair. The flames quickened well, as if to dry tinder. They wrapped over the mask, crackled down his body, up his arms.

Jack swallowed a scream of horror.

The youth smiled. The flames roared up around him.

The fiddle began to scratch again, and the burning boy began to dance. His foot tapped. The masked crowd moved with him. Fingers. Feet. Twitching and stirring.

Now came the drums and the pipes.

The flames sheeted higher and higher. The youth spun slowly on the spot, arms raised. The satyr capered about him. The crowd began to step in time. The music rose up with a clattering, jerking tumble.

The boy burned. All at once the dance was in full swing. The drumbeats twined and curled and called for Jack to move with them. The dream dance: it would be so easy to join it. Forget everything . . .

Steady.

Jack stared at the faces as they flashed by, lit up in the hellish firelight. Every creature under the sun, every devil. Every shape you could imagine.

But no Beth.

No Ravenscar.

The burning boy was laughing now. The flames raced high, but they did not consume him. He danced. The music shrieked. The devils tripped by, faster and faster. The satyr led from the front, leaping highest of all.

The floor of the cavern fell away. Jack was floating over a black and fathomless deep. A million stars glittered as the dancers spun in space, ringing the fire. Their dance old as time, filled with fierce joy. It sang in Jack's blood.

It took every ounce of his strength to keep from joining in.

He pushed the dream away, and the line of dancers rippled back from him, as if he'd dropped a stone into a pond. But they did not stop. The dance and the dream were far too strong for that.

Then, out of the corner of his eye, Jack glimpsed something familiar – something he knew. A flash of yellow, spinning past.

He followed the colour with his eye, as it passed quickly around the circle and came spinning back towards him.

A beautiful lady with golden wings, twirling a fan made of peacock feathers as she danced. Jack screwed his eyes up hard, fighting the dream, and saw – a hairy man in an ill-fitting dress, with a cushion cover over his head.

Kit.

Jack pounced, grabbing hold of Kit's arm, and pulled him from the line. Kit struggled. Jack swept his legs away and knocked him to the floor.

The dancers whirled on, regardless.

Jack pulled off the cushion cover. Kit's eyes spun bright and feverish with devil-blood.

'Unhand me! The Sky Dance! The curse of a thousand thorns on you.' A foreign lilt to the voice, but it was Kit's own.

Jack couldn't believe it: Kit, dancing, not a care in the world.

'What were you thinking!' Jack said. 'Where's Beth?'

Kit shuddered. 'Dancing! I was – watching.' He sounded worse than drunk.

'Watching her? Beth?'

Kit flapped his arms like wings, and seemed surprised when nothing happened.

'Lokmok! Listet!' The imp flew down and bit him on the nose.

'Leggo, fiend!' Kit plucked weakly at the imp. 'I was twirling with a tiger.'

Behind Jack, the dance roared on. He cursed under his breath. How to rouse the fool?

'Listen,' he said. 'Kit. The satyr's woken.'

'Satyr? Yes . . . saw him. Goat-legs, burning the boy, ha!'

'I know,' said Jack. 'He's here. But listen: the key's working! We can make our fortunes. Merchant princes, Kit! Remember?'

Kit's tongue appeared, and licked slowly across his lips.

'Bathing in rubies, all that,' Jack said. 'We can do it now!'

Kit reached up and pulled weakly at his moustache.

'Jack?' he said. His eyes were still clouded with devil-blood, Jack saw. 'Bravissimo, lad. Told you we could work it. Ships, that's the thing – buy up the whompers.'

'We're not going without Beth,' said Jack. 'Where is she, did you see her?'

'She was dancing. By God it was fine.' Kit blinked, shook his head. 'Aye, more than fine – you know, Jack, you were quite wrong about this place – most glorious rumpus I ever saw . . .'

'And where is she now?'

Kit bit his lip, and squinted.

'She stopped. Dancing.'

'Please, Kit, when? You have to remember.'

At least he was trying now; but looking into his eyes,

355

Jack could see the thoughts tumbling about like snow-flakes.

'She's with Ravenscar, isn't she? Try and remember where they went.'

'Well . . .' A dirty-minded grin split Kit's face. 'Ain't it obvious?'

'*Where?*' Jack leaned forward and grabbed Kit by his shirtfront. His head lolled loose. Jack put his hand against Kit's face. He closed his eyes and concentrated.

Alkahest banished devils. It had even worked against the Swarm, the biggest devil of all. Jack hoped it did the same to Spiritus. He hoped his hand still worked.

Kit moaned.

Deep inside Jack's hand, the Alkahest burned. Jack felt the devil-blood misting away, streaming from his touch.

'Stop, wretch!' Kit howled. 'What are you doing?'

With grim patience, Jack held on until he'd burned off every last speck of the stuff.

Kit moaned. 'I feel . . . unwell.'

'Never mind it. I sobered you. Think now: where'd she go?'

Kit sat up and rubbed his head. His eyes were clearing.

'The mossy cave,' said Kit.

'The what?'

'The green door . . . I remember.' He pointed. 'It's over there.'

Jack jumped to his feet.

'Can you run?'

Kit frowned, considering. 'I think so.'

'Good.'

Jack would never have found the door if Kit hadn't shown him. For one thing it wasn't green. It looked just like an ordinary door. Innocent.

Was that strange?

Jack had seen magic and riot, devilish doings; yet even with the satyr spurring them on, what were they? Gilded wasters playing at wickedness.

No. If there was a terrible secret to the Hellfire Club, it lay here.

Before he opened the door Jack sank into the devil-sight and gazed through it, bracing himself for horror.

Nothing.

That was stranger: if Ravenscar was summoning the Swarm . . .

Jack smothered the thought.

'Ready, Kit? We find Beth. Then we leave.'

Kit was leaning against the wall, looking gaunt and sickly.

'Are you ready?'

Kit grimaced. 'As a plague-pit.'

Jack opened the door and stepped through, into a long

dark corridor with a red carpet running down the middle of it like a tongue.

The corridor was empty. Heavy wooden doors leading off it. Walls covered in paintings of naked men and women.

Kit examined the nearest painting. 'Is this a cat-house, Jack?'

It certainly wasn't what Jack had been expecting.

'Shuklet make scoutings, haply?'

The imp flew ahead, giving out a soft glow to light the way.

Jack padded forward, listening at the doors. At each one, Lud's key leaped into a new shape, and Jack heard the frenzied sound of a different revel in a different time.

There was no way of telling what was going on behind those doors here and now.

'What's this madness, Jack?' said Kit, brushing a door with his fingers.

'Far times. The Satyr's magic. It's how the key works.'

'Far times?' Kit frowned.

'We open a door with the key, and we're somewhere . . . oh.' Jack stopped dead, struck by the neatness of it.

'What?'

'We can leave through *any* of them. Soon as we find Beth, nearest door: we're gone. Different time. No following us.'

'Grand. So let's find her.' Kit pushed open a door and stepped through.

The room was small, with a bed in one corner. In the bed were two masked women. They screamed and covered themselves with the sheet. Neither of them were Beth.

'Sorry to intrude,' said Kit with a grin.

The next door yielded an old man in a baby's bonnet crouching on the floor, and a stout lady standing over him. She spun round and threw a hairbrush at Jack's face.

In the next room they found a familiar face.

Malpas looked sadly reduced. He was standing in front of a mirror, holding an empty wine bottle, weaving from side to side and mouthing silent words as he gazed at his reflection. He'd taken off his mask, and his face was a mess of smeared rouge and clotted powder. His clothes – and his sword – were lying on the floor.

Was this the man who'd defeated Kit in single combat? The killing gentleman who'd murdered Ada on the spur of the moment? But then, thought Jack, that had been Ravenscar's doing really. Lord Ravenscar's pet, Tom had called Malpas. He looked like a very sick dog.

'He's mine, Jack.' Kit moved forward.

Malpas was either very drunk or out of his mind on devil's blood, because he didn't seem to mind that Kit was coming towards him.

It helped that the room was dark.

'Who's that?' he snapped. 'I'm busy.'

'*Mon cher,*' said Kit. He giggled and swayed towards him,

fluttering his fan in front of his face. 'I have been wanting to do this for some time.'

'You 'ave?' Malpas looked thoughtful, then shrugged. '*Eh bien*, the trio most always beats the duet.'

He reached out to fondle Kit, drawing him close.

Kit did not resist; instead, with a blow of terrifying force and precision, he drove his knee straight into the Frenchman's cods.

Jack almost felt sorry for the wretch.

Malpas turned pale, and fell to the floor like a dead man.

'Remember me?' said Kit, lowering his fan.

'Y'you!' Malpas's eyes widened with surprise.

'Yes.'

'I . . . killed you.' Malpas moaned through gritted teeth. 'I kill you again!'

Swift as a viper, Kit had the man's own sword at his throat.

'I think not. No tricky pistols this time, eh? Where's Ravenscar hiding: tell me, quick!' Kit clicked his tongue, and grinned. 'Don't gulp so, or you'll set me off: it is my dearest wish to gut you like a carp.'

Malpas pointed away down the other end of the corridor.

'Th-that way,' he croaked. 'Four doors.'

Chapter 29

Devil's blood raced in Lord Ravenscar's brain.

He closed his eyes, and felt the loosening of time.

Thirty centuries unravelled in a moment. A dizzying stream of dreams and memories flashed past. He saw pharaohs, knights and magi; sailors, cunning-men and courtesans. Every manner of person in every time and place since each devil was summoned and bound. The devils shaped all who touched them, and were shaped in return. And now . . .

A thousand shards. A flood of lives, shattered and mingled together.

Lord Ravenscar breathed slow, and rose above the flood. Then, like a hunting swallow, he dipped, sifted, and sipped.

It had taken some practice, to tell the different strains apart.

Screams of dying bulls; the smell of blood; pagan kings beheaded on stone altars. Hackle Hex, the Sanguinary Fiend of Hockley in the Hole. Ravenscar bared his teeth and snarled like a wolf.

Snatches of music – a single child's voice, a harp, a mighty orchestra – swelling in heartbreak harmony. Ravenscar knew this one as the Bard. Its real name could only be sung, in a language taught to nightingales by the druids of Dumnonia, long before the coming of the legions. Ravenscar sighed. A single tear trickled down his cheek.

Next came a bloom of bracing agony from the thing beneath St Helen's Church. Ravenscar laughed and screamed – body lashing up and down, pain and pleasure merging into one.

Tom Dee had wanted no part in that particular strain of Spiritus. Tom Dee saw what he wanted to see – a Great Spirit to wash mankind clean. Ravenscar cared nothing for all that. He was a connoisseur, nothing more. He knew the truth of what he tasted.

Persons – loose from time, dark with secrets, bled dry for his pleasure. For a moment it was too much, the knowledge crackling in his bones like golden lightning. Life took hold, and surged up within him. The lightning gathered into a howling, cackling fireball.

Lord Ravenscar seized the fire and shaped it into something that was *him* – a dark angel – a man with devil's blood.

He thought of Artemisia Devine, who was dark too; whose mysteries he would dearly love to unravel. He thought of her so-called brother. *Loose from time.* Yes . . .

He smiled, and opened his eyes.

'Jack!'

No answer.

'Pox on you, Jack. Pox and plague and blisters . . .'

Beth moved on to the next door. At least this part of the house was quiet. He could be anywhere, that was the trouble . . .

Only that wasn't the half of it.

Beth had been in the deepest trouble ever since Ravenscar showed her that infernal bead. Knowing that he had it, and that Jack could not have left – knowing she might see him again: she'd never felt such relief.

Pox on him, to come and ruin all, just when she was sitting pretty. Pox on herself, for letting him do it. Even if he hadn't turned up tonight, the ruin would still be. She'd come here intending to steal the satyr for him – and then he'd have left, and she'd have gone too. Hand in hand to a fresh crock of trouble: Jack drew it like flies to a dungheap.

She couldn't stay here now, anyway. Not after the lies she'd told Ravenscar. Not after stealing his prisoner, gulling him in his own house. He'd be murderous angry at that . . .

Beth smiled, thinking that actually he'd probably make

a joke of it. She smiled again, thinking of the ways he might do it.

Jack was wrong about him.

Jack was jealous.

Here: another locked door. She stooped to the keyhole, and whispered through it.

'Jack?' No reply. '*You limp-head dullard,*' she added under her breath.

'He's not in there,' said a voice behind her.

She turned. Tom Dee stood there looking down at her with an odd secret smile on his face. He held out his hand.

'Beth Sharkwell, I believe.'

'How d'you—'

'Jack told me. Jack sent me to find you, to bring you both to safety.' He held out his hand. 'Come – I'll take you to him.'

Jack ran along the corridor, ignoring the blasts of far-times revelry coming from behind the doors. Lud's key twitched and danced around his neck.

The fourth door was shaking on its hinges. Wild witch-lights flashed around the edges.

What if it's happened already?

No. Those lights and music were the satyr's magic. *Far times.* That wasn't the Swarm, that was somewhere else.

There was still time. There had to be.

The imp buzzed down to settle on the door handle.

Jack felt Kit's hand on his shoulder.

'Nix locked,' said the imp.

Kit was reaching for the handle. Jack had time to think that it didn't make sense, the door should be locked, they'd murdered Ada to keep this secret . . . and then the door was open, the far-times racket stopped dead, and Jack was looking straight into the eyes of Lord Ravenscar.

The eyes of a devil, was Jack's first thought. This was not the drunkenness of the Hellfire revellers. It was not the madness of the Swarm he'd seen in Ada, either. It was more like looking into the face of the satyr, or Black Dog, the devil hound of Newgate. Eyes like embers, smouldering with veiled power. A smile that was old and pitiless as the sea. Heat pulsed through Jack's hand, the devil-heat slow and deep.

The devil that was Ravenscar lay on a heap of cushions in the corner of the room. Other than the cushions, and a richly patterned carpet, the room was completely bare. There was nowhere he could be hiding Beth. Nowhere for any of the terrible secrets Jack had imagined might be concealed here.

The devil blinked, slow and lazy like a cat in the sun, and Jack realized that whatever it was, lying there on those cushions, it was still Ravenscar – because it recognized him.

'Hello, brother Jack,' said Ravenscar. 'I've been waiting.'

'What?'

'Where's Artemisia?'

Exactly what Jack had been about to ask. This was making less and less sense.

'Well?' said Ravenscar.

'That's not her name,' said Jack.

'I know,' said Ravenscar. 'I made it up for her.' He chuckled. The sound was dark and sweet, like drips of black treacle. 'You're a funny toy, I declare.'

Kit strode up to the bed, raised Malpas's sword and pointed it at Ravenscar's throat.

'What did you call him?' said Kit.

'A Jack-in-the-box,' said Ravenscar. 'Always popping up.' He turned his head to look up at Kit. 'How astonishing. I thought Malpas killed you.'

He didn't sound astonished, or scared either, Jack thought.

'Malpas thought the same,' said Kit. 'Jack, I don't know what you expected to find in here, but Not This would be a fair guess, I fancy.'

Jack shook his head, trying to think. Beth had left with Ravenscar. Ravenscar had brought her . . . here?

Then what?

'Why don't I just put the sword *here*,' said Kit, placing the point under Ravenscar's chin, 'and you can ask your question again.'

Ravenscar laughed again. Jack couldn't believe it. The man, or devil, or whatever in Hell or on Earth you might call him, was enjoying himself.

How did you scare a man so full of devil's blood that he was half devil himself? How did you shame him, or compel him, or reach him in any way at all?

'No jest, my lord,' he said. 'Tell me what you've done with her, or it's your life. I swear I'll do it.'

'What I've *done* with . . . but she went to look for you.' Ravenscar frowned, as if trying to remember something that had happened a long time ago. 'She spun me some kind of story, but – no, it was quite clear to me. I thought I'd see what happened. But she didn't find you . . .'

'What did you do to her?'

'Do to her?' Ravenscar shrugged.

'Don't mock me, you bloody murderer!' said Jack. 'I know all about you, see? What you did to Ada, you and Malpas – and then killing her to keep it quiet, and . . .'

'*What?*' said Ravenscar.

Jack looked at him. He couldn't quite go on speaking.

He'd reached him this time. The lazy, sweet-voiced devil was gone: this was a man; and if ever Jack had seen a man completely taken aback, it was Ravenscar, now.

'Why . . .' Ravenscar shook his head, as if trying to clear it. 'What the devil do you take me for? *Killed* her? Why would I do such a thing? I loved her!'

'You did it . . .' Jack struggled against a swirl of panic. If he was wrong about Ravenscar, then—

He'd been gulled, and—

No. Impossible. Ravenscar was the one gulling him. Who else, after all?

Jack searched for a flicker of recognition, a sliver of guilt. All he saw was bewilderment.

'Who told you all this?' said Ravenscar. 'Ada?'

'No. I mean, some of it . . .'

'Who else?'

Jack shook his head. 'I ain't telling *you*.'

Ravenscar narrowed his eyes. Something rippled across his face, hot and wolfish. That devil part again – only now, it was anything but lazy. It was a hunting devil now. An *angry* devil.

'You've been played for a fool, my boy,' he said. 'So it wasn't you, at the theatre, was it?'

'Wasn't me what?'

'That killed Ada.'

'Course it wasn't, it was you—'

Ravenscar closed his eyes, ignoring Jack; and Jack didn't blame him, either. Even as he spoke the accusation, it felt false.

'Not you. Not I . . . Who, then?'

Jack was asking the same question. Thinking: if not Ravenscar, then who?

Who had gulled him?

There was an answer: he felt its touch, like cold cobwebs.

Ravenscar opened his eyes. A little bead of blood was running down his throat, where Kit's sword point pressed against it. He didn't seem to notice it. He looked relaxed, and although the devil part still burned hot within him his eyes were very clear.

'The little – jilted – festering – toad,' he said.

Jack shook his head. It couldn't be.

He remembered the moment at the theatre, Ada saying *'It's him'* – meaning Malpas, or so Jack had thought.

But Malpas hadn't been the only person there.

Ravenscar rose to his feet. There was no question of Kit stopping him. There was no question of anything stopping him, Jack thought: the shadows of a hundred devils rose with him, like dark wings billowing, like water flowing uphill.

'It was Tom Dee, wasn't it?' said Ravenscar. 'Tom Dee put this whole story in your head.'

Jack tried to speak, but his throat had gone so dry that no sound would come.

He nodded.

Chapter 30

Darkness.

For a long moment, she didn't know where she was, or how she came to be there.

'Now to prime the flow,' said a voice.

A clang, like something heavy turning over. Footsteps.

She knew the voice.

Her heartbeat quickened.

She tried to stay calm. Back, back, trace back. *Ninth Law or Eighth?* Which was it? Cold sand in her head. She remembered searching for Jack. She remembered meeting Tom Dee. She remembered . . .

'Beth Sharkwell,' said the voice.

Her name. He knew her name. Jack had told it him. Tom Dee was taking her to Jack. He'd brought her to his infirmary across the square. He'd given her a drink of water.

And then . . . darkness.

Beth realized she wasn't breathing. With the knowledge came the need to gulp down air – but it wouldn't come, her nose was pinched shut, something soft and heavy was filling her mouth.

She tried to scream. She hardly made a sound. Her teeth struck hard against metal.

A metal tube in her mouth. Packed in with a cloth gag.

'Beth? Or do you prefer Artemisia?'

There was something heavy gripping her cheeks and nose and forehead. Bands of metal: tight. They held the gag in place. Her arms and legs were bound, too. She could not move her head.

'I know you're awake.'

She could breathe through the tube, but only a little. She must slow down, not panic. Slow.

She was Beth Sharkwell. She did not lose her head.

Slow.

There.

She opened her eyes.

'At last. Good girl.'

Tom Dee was leaning over her. Dark ceiling behind him. A pair of green-tinted spectacles covered his eyes. The glass was thick and oily.

Floating in the lenses as if seen underwater, Beth saw a pale, terrified face, clamped and gagged till it hardly looked human.

That's me, she thought. She tried to shout again. Her throat rasped. Her teeth ground against metal.

'Do not be afraid,' said Tom Dee. 'There is nothing for you to fear here. No harm.' He smiled. 'Only the most glorious transformation.'

He was adjusting something by her head, tapping with a jeweller's hammer.

'There. Now we can begin.'

They were still in the infirmary. Lines of empty beds. White linen. Very neat.

No one else here.

No one who knew where she was.

No way out.

Trapped: she knew it animal deep, real and rancid as bad meat.

Beth pushed her head forward, straining hard. The metal bands didn't budge. Looking down, she could see the leather straps binding her tight against the bed.

'I promise this will be quick.'

Tom Dee came into view. He was trundling something on wheels. It looked like an alchemist's nightmare of a tree – a short copper tube for the trunk, glass pipes branching up and out and instead of blossoms, each branch was topped by a bottle of thick, whorled glass. The whole apparatus was hoisted up on a metal frame, so that the base of the copper tube was level with Beth's face.

Tom Dee wheeled it over until it was poised right above her. Bending down, he fitted the copper tube to the one in her mouth, screwing it tightly in place. The metal braces held her head rigid.

She watched as he fiddled with something overhead. It was hard to see with the confusion of glass pipes, but she heard a squeaking – as of a tap being opened.

'I was wrong about Ada, you know.'

More twisting sounds, and now Beth could see dribbles of liquid running down the pipes.

'When we first discovered the Spiritus ... I always thought, she would be the one.'

Tom Dee's motions were precise and careful. He moved above her, opening taps one by one.

'I was to be, what would you say? A messenger. A helper. Baptist to her Christ.'

Tom Dee chuckled, low and indulgent.

'My poor ancestor was deluded – speaking to devils?' He chuckled again. 'If only he knew: not darkness, but Light! Light, and Reason, and Truth, there for the taking. And yes, it speaks. I've heard it. The voice of *Spiritus Mundi*.'

Beth felt a rising tightness in the air. The liquid trickled down through the pipes overhead, each drop leaving an oily trail behind it.

Tom Dee gazed down at her. 'It wants to join us so badly. I thought – Ada. This was what she wanted, before *he* took her away. Win her back, I thought: join her to the Light . . .'

Beth saw tears welling up behind the oily dark lenses, and on his face a look of great gentleness, more nightmarish than anything yet.

Here was one thing Jack had been right about: something was done to Ada. And now it was being done to Beth.

This *cannot* be, Beth wanted to shout. You can't. I *won't*.

Tom Dee pushed up his goggles, tugged a handkerchief from his sleeve and wiped his eyes.

'I was wrong, of course. *He* had tainted her. What was needed was a pure beginning. A blank page.' He cocked his head to one side, eyeing her with satisfaction. 'She must be chaste, too, of course. Chaste, but flexible.' He leaned forward and tapped a finger upon her nose. '*You.*'

Beth cursed the gag. If Tom Dee thought she was anyone's pure beginning, she could think of a few ripe words to show him otherwise. She, Beth Sharkwell, a blank page? The man must be mad.

Not that a Bedlam bellstaff wouldn't fit him quite well already.

He stroked her cheek. 'You will redeem us all, my dear. The Spiritus told me so.'

Beth bit down on the tube in her mouth. She mustn't panic. If she could speak to him . . . but she couldn't. She tried to think of some other way to save herself, and then she gave up on that and tried to think of ways she might be saved.

No one else here.

No one who knew where she was.

No way out.

The trails of liquid reached all the way to the bottom of the pipes now, all the way to the copper tube. Beth tried to stop it up with her tongue.

That was when she tasted it.

The taste was old spices, burnt sugar, a prickling that sifted and tingled inside her. At once, she felt the need rise up.

Spiritus – but stronger and faster than any she'd tasted before.

She moved her tongue. Not stopping now, but sucking. A warm sensation cradled her neck, and rose up her legs. Warm but shivery. Beth shivered. Tom Dee saw it.

'See: no need to be afraid. Is it not pleasant?'

The sensation was spreading slowly, pulsing in time with her heartbeat. Beth felt as if she was slowly sinking into a warm bath.

She wasn't afraid any more.

She didn't want it to stop.

Pulsing gold bands wrapped around the backs of her knees, the nape of her neck. She could feel her heart slowing, chiming with the heartbeat that cradled her.

There had been a part of her missing, all her life. She had never known it till now.

Tom Dee stared into her face.

'I've watched you, on the stage. You do not *act* like the others, do you? You *become* the role. The perfect vessel.' He was leaning in close now, his voice rising urgent. 'This is the same. You are a vessel, you are empty, you must *become* the Spiritus Mundi . . .'

Beth could hardly hear him. The Spiritus rose and rose, a tide in her head. The bliss of it was so strong, there was no turning from it. It went all the way through her. It made her bones glow.

'You will be the first. Such radiance, when you emerge.'

The Spiritus flowed. Beth welcomed it. With her new eyes she could see it rushing down through the pipes, falling into her, a wondrous ocean of light.

And somehow, from somewhere, she saw Jack, eyes darting, chary under his scrunty shock of hair. Always watching, always careful. Her Jack.

She smiled to herself. If only he could feel this too. Dancing motes of light wriggled into her. She wanted more, and it came. More and more and more.

Tom Dee stood up straight. He had a wooden box in his hand.

'This next part is strange,' he said. 'But, on reflection, only natural. Of course there must be a sacrifice. A price.'

Somewhere beyond the ocean stream of light, Beth saw him lift a necklace out of the box. It was a rumpskuttle thing, cheap little blue glass beads on a rusted chain.

Beth gazed at it, still filled with the glory of the fire, the glory that was filling her. To her amazement she realized she could see a shape inside it. A devil. The devil looked like a Saracen woman with raven hair and black-rimmed eyes. A snake coiled around her shoulders.

This was what Jack saw. Lucky Jack.

Dee reached up into the tree of pipes and dropped the necklace into a deep glass jar full of water. The Saracen woman danced and thrashed, but she could not escape.

Tom Dee took no notice.

'I cannot tell you how long it took me to understand. So many failed experiments – but the Spiritus showed me the way.' His voice was an echo, leaping from wall to wall.

Beth smelled it first. Hot metal and brimstone, a sting that went right through her skull. Now Tom Dee had a spoon in his hand. It was filled to the brim with a glowing red powder.

Alkahest.

'No,' she tried to say.

He tipped the powder in with the necklace, and then clapped a stopper over the jar, sealing it.

Trapped inside the glass, Beth watched the devil die. It melted like wax in a fire, shrieking and writhing. The water in the jar went dark. It was red, the thick dark red of vein-blood.

'You are so brave, my dear,' said Tom Dee. 'So strong.'

And Beth remembered another Dr Dee, scattering rooster's blood over a chalk circle – the white light stretched out flat . . .

A Summoning. That was what this was: a Summoning.

She heard the squeak of a tap being turned.

A tiny trickle of devil's blood began oozing down one of the pipes. When it reached the bottom, it didn't drop at once, but beaded up against the lip, slowly gathering.

Dee tapped the pipe. The drop dropped.

She had the briefest moment of horror before it hit her.

It was a shrivelling inside her. It spread, over and into her, as if every point of light inside her were being hunted down, and changed to black.

She would have gasped, but there was no air.

'The Spiritus Mundi,' whispered Dee. 'A beacon for the world. Do you feel it coming? Do you feel yourself, *becoming?*'

Beth whimpered. Her arms and legs were taut as bowstrings. She shut her eyes. It made no difference

'The light,' said Tom Dee. 'See as it comes!'

Her eyes swivelled down in their sockets, and she saw it. Flat white light. She was trapped in the light, and now it began to tremble, and open up, and become not flat but *deep*.

Something was coming.

Chapter 31

London shivered in its sleep.

The animals knew it first. As if warning of an earthquake, the cocks rose early to crow into the night. A herd of pigs whipped down for slaughter burst from their hurdles and thundered, shrieking, through Clerkenwell. A great flock of winter geese rose from the river and fled into the darkness.

In the bright warm places, where drink flowed and music played, they felt a bump in the world, a wash of disquiet, a squirt of terror – and the tune turned flat, and the beer turned sour.

In the dark cold places, where the devils of London had hidden themselves away, they knew it too – and worse, they knew what was to come.

The bells of St Giles Cripplegate tolled once and fell silent.

Daubed on a brick wall near Change Alley – river side, heading north – words appeared in fresh red blood.

HE WILL DRAW OUT THE BONES.

And at St Paul's, a black raven came awake, rustled its feathers, and dropped from its perch.

It circled over the frost flowers on the rooftops, over noble houses and pestilential rookeries, restless as a general watching the enemy approach.

The war was older than the city itself. The fight now beginning had been two hundred years in the making. The battle lines were drawn. Now, all that remained was to watch.

Jack was running across the square when the Swarm came.

He felt it as a jolt of ice up his spine. In the black rot in his hand, tiny shapes came alive. They wriggled and writhed. Burning cold took his breath away.

He knew what it meant.

Swarm lord's coming.

'Fretlick, fretlick!' muttered the imp, close in his ear.

Lord Ravenscar threw himself against the front door of the Infirmary. It was locked fast. He stepped back, and Jack saw devil-wings rise up about him, flickering black. Next moment, the door was splintered in two; and then they were through, Jack in the lead. He didn't wait for Ravenscar or Kit.

He knew where to go. The terrifying cold in his hand pulled him up the stairs surer than a compass. He burst into the ward at full tilt.

There was Beth, lying down with a mess of pipes coming out of her face. A circle of lamps stood all around her on the floor, throwing crazy shadows about the room. Where the bed should be was a hole made of light.

Tom Dee stood over her. He looked up at Jack, eyes flaring wide. Something appeared in his hand, something bright and small.

A scalpel. He put it to Beth's throat.

'One step more . . .' he warned.

Kit and Ravenscar skidded to a stop, just behind Jack. Kit held Malpas's rapier low at his side.

'So,' said Ravenscar. 'This is what you did to Ada.' His eyes glimmered with Spiritus light, and shadows bunched around his shoulders. His voice was half human, half devil – soft, calm, and filled with cold black fury.

Tom's eyes flickered down at Beth, then back at Ravenscar. 'It was you,' he said. 'Your fault. You ruined her. But you can't stop it this time. See – the Light . . .'

Jack edged forward a step. Immediately the scalpel was hard against Beth's naked throat, Tom's knuckles white about the handle.

'Stop!' Jack shouted.

A golden streak whirled over Jack's shoulder. Jack barely

marked it before it smashed into Tom's wrist with a crack of breaking bone, and the scalpel went flying.

'*Balkutt Yayn!*' the imp shrieked in triumph. 'For Samaz! For shuks and shuklets of Lud!'

Kit sprinted forward and hammered his sword hilt into Tom's chin, knocking him out cold. Something tumbled from his pocket as he fell. A wooden box. It cracked open on the ground and a dusting of red powder spilled out.

Jack felt a dangerous pulse of Alkahest heat as he stepped over it.

No time to worry about that. He blinked into devil-sight.

The Swarm was all around Beth. Flies and locusts, grubs and centipedes, a million nameless things in between. They boiled over her limbs, crawled under her clothes, coiled through her mouth and nostrils.

As Jack drew closer, the icy pain in his hand redoubled. The black skin strained and bulged. Something was wriggling inside there – trying to break through, trying to join the rest.

Beth was still alive. She was fighting, fists clenching in and out, throat moving up and down – the only parts she could move with her head braced tight and the straps across her body. Jack couldn't see where they ended: the Swarm was too thick.

A fat drop of dark liquid beaded in the pipe above her

lips. Jack knocked the whole apparatus away in a shower of shattering glass. He reached forward to unbind her, gritting his teeth.

The instant he touched her, the Swarm roared through him like a frost wind. The cold black rot seethed up his arm. He could feel its freezing hatred, tearing at his bones.

He'd never known pain could be like this. The heat of the Alkahest, the cold of the Swarm, wrenched his mind out of his skull and sent it tumbling loose.

'Bleeding Christ!' Kit's voice. So far away. Everything was fading – everything but the cold, and the pain, and the hatred of the Swarm.

Mustering up the last shreds of his sanity, Jack grabbed Beth by the hand. Her fingers were colder than ice. He couldn't tell if she was alive or dead.

Black frost flies filled his eyes and ears. Long, many-legged things burrowed icy pathways through his veins. The Swarm sucked him down into its frozen, hating heart.

Old. Old and patient, filled with malice, with a will and a purpose beyond fathoming.

A thousand voices rustled like dry wings in his skull. He didn't understand their words, but he could feel their hatred.

He heard another voice too, so tiny it was almost lost in the relentless buzzing.

Beth Sharkwell, it said. *Beth Sharkwell of Southwark, Beth Sharkwell Beth Sharkwell Beth Sharkwell, Beth Beth Beth catches coneys plucks gulls lives in Southwark . . . Beth Beth Beth Beth . . .*

Through the Swarm Jack glimpsed a flicker of pale fire, a flash of grey eyes, bright and terrified – there and then gone.

Beth. Freezing to death in here too.

Her voice was getting quieter. She was fighting, but in the end fighting would only make it worse.

Somewhere in another life, he was standing over her bed. Kit was shouting. The imp keening with panic. His hand, holding Beth's.

Jack was hardly aware of it. It was another life. Everything he'd thought was real was as thin as paper lanterns. There was only the Swarm, and its icy hate. He was the Swarm, and the Swarm was him. He felt what it felt: he knew what it knew.

Still – one last thing.

Goodbye, Beth. He squeezed her hand tight. It felt good: a good last thing, before the end.

Beth squeezed back. She knew it was him: she recognized him, he could tell. It wasn't a hard squeeze, but it was fierce and warm and it was *her.*

Jack, she said. *Poison Jack Patch, with the red right hand.*

She squeezed harder.

Goodbye, Jack.

Freezing black cold enfolded them both for ever.

I love you.

Jack felt the truth of it, blazing hot as molten steel. *This* was real: Beth's hand in his, clutching hard, the fire between them. Deep inside, where the Swarm was feeding, he felt something falter.

He felt what it felt: the Swarm was surprised.

He knew what it knew: and the Swarm knew nothing of love.

Now, he thought. *Together.*

He felt Beth answer.

Together.

The Swarm screamed. Jack knew its agony and their triumph and a tearing, a *taking* – and then nothing more.

Jack came to his senses slowly. His right hand still ached. Better than before, though, because he could feel his fingers. And he could feel something cool and soft pressing against them.

He opened his eyes. Beth was crouched over him. Ravenscar and Kit stood behind her, looking down at him. The imp hovered above Kit's head, trembling in every limb.

'Beth.' Jack didn't recognize his own voice.

'Beth, is it?' said Ravenscar. 'I'd often wondered . . .'

'Boymaster?' said the imp. ''Tis you? Veritlick?'

'Beth,' he said. 'How . . . ?'

She kneaded his hand between hers.

'Careful,' said Jack – but when he looked at his hand, held between her slim fingers, he saw a miracle.

The black rot was gone. So was the red of the Alkahest stain. The skin of his hand was quite ordinary, the work-roughened hand of a Judicious Nipper from Southwark.

'Jack,' Beth murmured. 'Jack, Jack, Jack.'

'How'd we get out?' said Jack.

'You pulled her out,' said Kit. 'Bravest thing I ever saw, with that hellhole pouring out its damned uncanny light . . .'

'It's still there?' said Jack.

'No,' said Beth. 'You beat it.'

'No,' said Jack. 'No. *We* beat it. Together.'

He tried to turn over to see. None of his muscles seemed to work.

'Beth,' he said, 'help me.'

She lifted his head and shoulders, shuffled him round, and now Jack could see down the infirmary, to the bed.

There was no white light. No Swarm.

It looked like an ordinary bed, with the sheets somewhat rumpled. The nest of glass tubes and bottles lay to one side, where Jack had pushed it. Dark liquid fell in drips from the broken glass pipes.

'We killed it,' said Jack again, not quite believing.

'Killed! Nix! Blazing beskewering!' The imp flashed

purple, as it turning little loops in the air. 'Master van-
quered! Lovey-doves be champion!'

'Lovey-doves?' said Kit.

Jack was delighted to see that Beth was blushing.

'But where's Tom?' he said.

'Over there,' said Ravenscar, pointing to the shadows
beyond the bed where Beth had lain. 'At least, he *was* . . .'

They heard a groan, and the sound of something
dragging on the ground. A hand, covered in blood, reached
up from behind the bed.

'Enough remains,' said Tom, hauling himself up. 'Quite
enough. I. *I* shall be the vessel.'

He clamped his teeth to the broken glass, where the
dark blood of devils still dripped – and sucked.

'Oh for goodness' sake,' Ravenscar said.

Beth had fought it. Jack had fought it. Tom Dee
welcomed the King of Swarms like a long-lost lover – and so
its coming was very quick indeed. The flat white light
opened up. The black cloud streamed out of it, bunched and
drew together, becoming solid, becoming man-shaped. It
rose to its feet like a puppet dragged up by clumsy hands.
It shrieked. Its face was a flat white hole cut out from the
world.

Then came the darkness, welling up like blood from a
wound.

Chapter 32

Jack wanted to move but he couldn't. Perhaps ten paces separated him from the shape that had been Tom Dee. He wanted more than anything to increase that distance as fast as possible – but he couldn't.

The shape shambled forward. It moved jerkily, like something learning how to walk with every step. It stumbled against a lamp and knocked it flying. The lamp shattered, spilling burning oil across the floor.

The shape was Tom Dee's – but it was not nearly human. Beneath its rotten skin, wriggling shapes seethed and roiled. Its tongue was made of worms. Its eyes wept flies like tears.

The imp was muttering its name, over and over, in a trance of terror.

'*Blzlb'b. Blzlb'b. Blzlb'b.*'

The Lord of Swarms was come.

Come to eat up all.

The thing stopped, flexed itself, and looked straight at Jack. Beneath its skin a thousand creatures squirmed into a new shape.

'S-sassah-ah.' The awful fly-blown eyes darkened with terrible amusement.

Jack felt his stomach turn over. Suddenly he was looking at himself – at his own face on the monster's body.

'*Mine*,' it said.

'Get up.' Beth was tugging on Jack's hand, trying to pull him up. But his legs were frozen, filled with ice.

'Come on, come *on*,' said Beth.

The thing started forward again, its skin swelling and unknotting as it lurched slowly towards them. Behind it, flames from the shattered lamp were licking up around the bed. It did not take its eyes from Jack.

The cold gripped hard, pinning him down.

Beth was still trying to drag him backwards. The imp was moaning in his ear. But Jack couldn't move. He knew he should get up and run, but he couldn't.

'Go,' he said to Beth. 'Can't 'scape it. You go.'

'*No!*'

Beth heaved, dragging him across the floor. It was no good. Those ice-cold eyes held him fast: he couldn't turn, couldn't tear his gaze away. The power in his hand was gone. No Alkahest stain to drive it back.

It was going to get them.

And then Ravenscar stepped forward.

'Tom Dee, I believe you've done yourself a mischief.'

The voice was cold black velvet – the voice of Newgate dungeon, of dusty bricked-up temples, of all the dark forgotten places beneath the city. All the devils who had bled for his pleasure, all the power that Lord Ravenscar had consumed: rising strong now, rising to the surface.

Still those eyes didn't move from Jack. Still he couldn't turn – just watch, helpless, as the demon lord advanced upon the Swarm. Slowly, his sword trailing idle at his side. Pacing out his steps like a formal dance.

'Ordinarily I would not kill an injured man, but – well, a mad dog must be put down, ain't it so? And you killed Ada.'

Devil shades flowed all about him – dark wings billowing, water flowing uphill. There on the floor at his feet, Jack saw the wooden box that had fallen from Tom's pocket. He saw Ravenscar flinch from it, the devil-stuff within him shrinking from the Alkahest. He saw him bend down and scoop it up all the same. Ravenscar went rigid, staggered, gave a single low croak of agony – and then the monster sprang, and Ravenscar's sword point whipped up so fast that the thing drove itself onto it, full tilt, running itself straight through the heart.

Impalement didn't stop it. The Swarm didn't make a

sound. It flowed up over the sword hilt, over Ravenscar's hand, clothing his arm in a crawling mass of horror.

Ravenscar grunted, twisting the sword in its chest, tearing and slashing at the hole he'd made. Flies churned up to fill the gaps. The Swarm reached his shoulder and swirled about his throat, eating him alive. The Swarm was laughing. Its face was rearranging itself again, all its features sucking inward until the whole head was nothing but one big mouth. It threw its arms out, and now there was nothing of the human left about it at all – only a pulsing, buzzing cloud, enveloping Ravenscar, and that great black mouth drawing back to strike.

Ravenscar threw out his left arm. The wooden box was in his hand. Open. Dappled red light against the gaping dark.

Alkahest.

He thrust it into the Swarm's mouth. Everything went white. The Swarm and Lord Ravenscar were a blinding flat white shape cut out from the world. Two screams went up – gut-wrenching deep, ear-stabbing shrill, every possible note in between, louder and louder until Jack thought it must kill him – and then cut off sharp, leaving a ringing silence.

As the dazzle faded, Jack saw two men locked together, lit up by flames – the bed behind them, burning merrily. Tom's arms were thrown around Ravenscar. Ravenscar's sword point was sticking out of Tom's back, dripping blood. For a moment they stood there, held up by their rigid embrace – then they tottered sideways and collapsed to the floor.

Limp. Dead.

Beth was saying something. Jack could see her lips move, but the ringing in his ears drowned out the words. His head slumped forward onto his chest.

It was done. The Swarm was gone. Back to Hell, and Ravenscar gone with it.

Kit stepped forward. Jack's hearing was coming back now. Kit was saying something about fire. Snatching up a blanket, advancing towards the burning bed – where Tom's apparatus was still dripping with devil-blood, the flames rising higher . . .

Jack's eyes widened. A flurry of fire licked up over the sheets – bloomed and blossomed – a *whumph*, and then the whole room was burning, wall to wall, and Kit was somehow lying on his back next to Jack, face blackened, both mustachios burned clean off.

The next moment, Kit was on his feet, dragging Jack upright. Jack's legs buckled under him. He felt Beth's shoulder in his armpit, Kit pulling his elbow, the imp tugging at his hair; and he was staying up, somehow they were stumbling away from the terrible heat, turning their back on the flames, running for the door.

There was something wrong about the door, but Jack

didn't have time to think what it was until they were through, and it slammed shut behind him, cutting off the scorching heat at his back.

By the light of imp-glow, Jack recognized Tom Dee's medicine cabinet. The rows of Spiritus bottles. The shelves of empty devils.

He turned and fumbled at the door. As soon as it opened he had to slam it shut again: it was like opening the door to a furnace.

There was no other way out.

Beth was backing away from the door, past the shelves. Jack stumbled up to her and took her hand. Her face was very pale, in spite of the heat they'd passed through.

No way out.

They were going to die here.

'Well, this is a little hot for my liking,' said Kit. He slid to the floor, back against the door, and sighed. 'They do say the smoke kills you first. I hope they're right.'

Beth smiled, and shook her head. Jack felt her hand squeeze his, just for a moment.

'I never liked goodbyes,' said Kit, 'but I suppose now's the time. Here's mine – goodbye – ach, so quickly over! You two will do it better, I'm sure.'

'Bye-bye, lokmok,' said the imp.

'Ha! Easy for you to say, you little villain: you're pretty well proof against fire, I suppose?'

'But without boymaster . . .' The imp made a small scratchy sound, and said no more.

'G'bye, Imp. Kit,' said Jack. He turned again to Beth, and found he didn't know what to say. Her eyes gleamed wet. Her throat moved, swallowing. She reached out and took Jack's other hand.

And then she frowned, as if she was trying to hear a very faint noise.

kissherkisshernow . . .

'Beth,' said Jack. 'I—'

Beth looked up at Jack, a strange expression on her face.

kissherkissherkissherkiss . . .

The voice was right inside his head, a whisper like the ghost of surf inside a seashell.

Jack saw the imp flash past him, blurring fast. One of the boxes crashed from its shelf and burst open on the floor.

Inside it was a large silver cup with two handles.

The devil bound inside the kissing cup was very old.

The sorceress who first bound the devil into the cup had been dead thousands of years before it found its way to London. She wrought the cup out of love for a prince of Old Ur, by the Euphrates delta. She was well versed in the ways and names of devils (though they were not called devils, then); her Summoning was sound. She sought a spirit to bring about True Love's First Kiss – and she got it, and she bound it into the kissing cup with powerful spells.

But the cup did not work for her, and she cursed her luck and threw it away and pined the rest of her days for the prince, who never favoured her with so much as a kind look, let alone a kiss.

The reason the cup did not work was simple: the sorceress might have known the names and ways of devils, but she did not know what True Love was.

The devil knew.

It was very simple.

A kiss is only True Love's First Kiss if both parties know, at the time of kissing, and without any doubt whatsoever, that they would each die for the other.

In all the years it was bound, the devil in the cup only had the chance to bring about four such kisses. Four moments when it woke and knew its power. The rest of the time it slept, and dreamed; and those who came near it felt a sweet pang that was really regret, for something they would never know.

But those four kisses were like a necklace of bright burning stars. By human reckoning, they were centuries apart; but time works differently for devils – for the devil in the cup, they were all one blazing moment with no past and no future.

In human terms, though, one of the four was about to occur, in the city of London, in the year of our Lord, 1792.

*

kissherkissherkisshernow . . .

Jack was starting to feel very strange indeed. Something was happening inside him, right inside his heart.

They were going to die.

There was nothing he could do to save them.

And here was the strange part: Jack looked into Beth's clear grey eyes, and he was not afraid. They were together. There was nothing to fear. All he had to do was kiss her: that was what the thing growing in his heart wanted, and it was all that mattered.

'Do it,' she said.

Jack didn't know how long it lasted. The key ended it, but even the shock of it leaping against his chest was hardly enough. His head felt light as he pulled back. Beth's eyes were still closed. She was smiling – a small, secret smile. He'd never seen her smile like that before.

All the noise from beyond the door had stopped.

The imp flopped to the floor. Kit yelped with amazement.

Beth opened her eyes.

'What happened?'

'We woke the devil,' said Jack. He looked down at the key in his hand. It was silver now, smaller than before – just the right size and shape for what it had to do.

How long would it last?

Long enough, the devil in the cup answered.

Jack took Beth by the hand and led her to the door. He took the key from around his neck.

'Quick now,' he said.

He fitted the key to the keyhole – and the world turned over like an old, reluctant lock. Jack reeled, but they held him steady, Beth on one arm, Kit on the other, the imp urging them along.

The door swung outwards. No flames: no burning infirmary.

Outside.

Morning.

As Jack stepped through, he felt something cool and soft against his face.

There was a bit of a mist rising.

The fire burned itself out in two days. When the embers were sifted, the bones of Lord Ravenscar and Tom Dee were found jumbled together around the puddled remains of a sword. Artemisia Devine had disappeared, and was presumed to have died in the inferno. For two weeks London talked of little else; but then the French put their king on trial, an act so scandalous that the drama and tragedy of that night was quickly forgotten.

The Hellfire Club would never meet again: Lord Ravenscar had died childless, and his vast fortune passed to a distant cousin, a curate in Gloucestershire. Ravenscar House was closed up and sold off, and its notoriety faded quickly. As the years passed, Lord Ravenscar's memory lingered only as a glint in the eye of ageing roués and fading beauties, as they toasted – half-disbelieving – the indiscretions of their youth.

Tom Dee took the secret of the Spiritus Mundi to his grave; but some secrets are harder to silence. When workmen cleared the ruins of his infirmary, they found a cache of ancient artefacts had miraculously survived the blaze. Many of these items – a Viking brooch, a kissing cup, an Etruscan helmet in ragged bronze – found their way down the road to the galleries of the British Museum.

Other treasures found their way into workmen's pockets, and from there they spread out across London. These little thefts had consequences both big and small. In Deptford, a strange cult sprang up worshipping a fox-faced goddess. In a Seven Dials soup kitchen, a cook devised a recipe for mullet chowder that has never been bettered. In Southwark, a man had a run of luck at the dicing tables so extraordinary that he never had to work again. His son would go on to be Mayor of London. His great-great-great-grandson would walk on the moon.

As for the others, the ones that had stayed buried – the days after the fire brought a slow awakening. Ravens flew out over the city. They dug for worms in churchyards, and perched in the branches of ancient trees; they sipped at forgotten wells, and gathered in parliament amongst the sad-eyed statues of St Paul's. That winter the ravens' yellow eyes, and their croaking, triumphant call, were everywhere.

And deep down, beneath ancient trash and buried stone, the devils heard their King. They turned their faces to the sun, and slowly – for haste and time have little meaning to the ageless – they stretched themselves out along familiar, well-worn grooves.

There is no one left to see them. There is no one left who even knows they exist. But deep beneath the streets, in the city's silent stony heart, the devils of London whisper out their magic to this day.

THE BOOKS OF PANDEMONIUM: BOOK 1

BLACK ARTS

ANDREW PRENTICE AND JONATHAN WEIL

'A SPARKLING AND INTELLIGENT DEBUT'
GUARDIAN

London is a teeming warren of thieves and
cutthroats. Young Jack fits right in. But when he picks
the wrong pocket, he finds himself in a London far more
dangerous than he ever imagined. A metropolis of spies
and dark magic. A city that will change him.

A CITY WHERE DEVILS ARE REAL.